THE ENIGMA

DRC PUBLISHING

3 Parliament Street
St. John's, Newfoundland and Labrador
A1A 2Y6
Telephone: (709) 726-0960
E-mail: info@drcpublishingnl.com

Library and Archives Canada Cataloguing in Publication

Badcock, T. C. (Thomas C.)
    The enigma / T.C. Badcock.

ISBN 978-0-9809369-9-5

I. Title.

PS8553.A285E53 2009   **C813'.54**   **C2009-901490-4**

Interior Design: Becky Pendergast
Cover Design: Becky Pendergast

Published 2009
Printed in Canada

We acknowledge the financial assistance of the Government of Newfoundland and Labrador, Department of Tourism, Culture and Recreation.

For Mary Sullivan from Three Rock Harbour.

AUTHOR'S NOTE

On October 14, 1942, the passenger ferry *SS Caribou* was sunk just off the coast of Port aux Basques, Newfoundland, by U-69, a German U-Boat commanded by Captain Ulrich Graf.

This is a story about that U-Boat, its captain and crew and one young girl from Three Rock Harbour who kept this story a secret for sixty-three years.

On January 16, 2005, a seventy-nine-year old woman who called herself Mary Sullivan summoned me to her hospital bed. She said she had an incredible story and she wanted me to tell it. For two days she told me her story. When I went back to the hospital five days later her bed was occupied by an elderly man, and there was no record of a Mary Sullivan being admitted or discharged.

Everything she told me I was able to confirm except for the presence of the U-Boat in her community. Maybe someday that information will be released. But I doubt it.

I have taken some degree of literary license with this tale only to fill in the parts of her story about which Mary had no direct knowledge. I have not changed any of the names. They remain Mary's names, not mine. I have added some characters to the story only to fill in the blanks from Mary's failing memory.

Before I received my commission in the Canadian Forces, I was a cryptographer and stationed at Fort Pepperell, or Pleasantville as it had been re-named. The equipment I used and continued to use throughout my career functioned nearly exactly like the German Enigma Machine.

At the outbreak of World War Two, the German Enigma Cipher Machine was considered to be the best and safest mechanical cipher machine available to any country. A machine about the size of a portable typewriter, the Enigma used variable electrical connections to perform enciphering and deciphering operations. It was used by the German

Wehrmacht (Army), Luftwaffe (Air Force) and Kriegsmarine (Navy) to encrypt messages sent by radio. Kriegsmarine procedures on sending messages with the Enigma were the most complex and elaborate of all the forces, as prior to encryption the message was encoded using the Kurzsignalheft codebook.

CHAPTER ONE

September 1942

Captain Ulrich Graf stood on the deck of *U-69* as she sailed out of St. Nazaire harbour, into the mouth of the River Loire and the Atlantic Ocean. His boat was the first German Type V11C submarine of the Kriegsmarine.

It was a cool, calm evening and the sun had set a few hours earlier. Graf stood on the deck with a half or dozen or so of the crew and watched the smoke from the factory stacks wisp up to the moonlit sky. The powerful engines moved the boat silently out of the harbour and as he rested his hand on the cold grey-blue of the conning tower, he knew that he was in command of one of the finest submarine in the German U-Boat service.

Graf was 28, married without children, and his wife lived in Kiel. He spoke excellent English having spent two years in the United States studying marine engineering. In 1937 he graduated from the Naval School at Wesermunde and did tours of duty on various surface ships. When the Second World War broke out in 1939, he joined the U-Boat service and served on two boats before being given command of *U-69* in March 1942. The Korvelten Kapitan, Herbert Sohler, had personally signed Graf's current orders and there were fewer than ten people in the entire German Navy who had knowledge of his orders.

Graf looked back at the U-Boat pens built from thousands of tons of concrete and his sister boats relatively safe from Allied attacks. He remained on the deck of *U69*, now renamed *Sea Shark*, as he and his crew sailed out of St. Nazaire harbour into the mouth of the River Loire and the Atlantic Ocean. His mission would last until mid-November and he would keep his communications to the absolute minimum. He would rigidly enforce the concept of short signalling. He would not have to report his position daily like every other U-Boat nor would he have to report kills. He was given a location where he could replenish his torpedoes and provisions and determine the end of his mission himself. He had Enigma codes to last him until the end of December. He needed the codes to monitor communications from other U-Boats in his area and to communicate with the German Admiralty when necessary.

U-69, aka *Sea Shark*, was a single hull design meaning that its pressure hull was also its outer watertight hull. Around all of this was another thin structure which streamlined the U-Boat and contained the ballast tanks. Along the top of it ran a flat-topped deck-casing which allowed the crew to stand and work. Space between it and the hull was used to store extra torpedoes and ammunition.

Equipped with eleven torpedoes, an 88-mm deck gun and a flak gun, the boat could travel further and faster than any of her predecessors. She was finished at the Germaniawerft in Kiel in 1940 and ready for service in November that same year.

In the centre of the boat was the multi-layered structure containing the watertight conning tower that gave the crew access to the boat. Surrounding it was a watertight structure that provided a protected area for the four lookouts that manned it at all times.

The bow of *U-69* was given over to the forward torpedo room. The four-torpedo room projected four meters into this room with two on each side of the boat. Behind each of them were the two-metre long compressed air cylinders used to launch them from their tubes. As the boat widened, two rows of three-crew bunks were laid out on either side of the compartment. They were folded away when working on the torpedoes. There were removable deck plates with storage beneath for additional torpedoes.

Aft of the forward torpedo room was crew accommodation, a forward head on the port side and a small food storage locker on the starboard side. Next aft was a small space to accommodate the four chief petty officers. A thin bulkhead and hatch separated the chief petty officers from the officers. The captain had a private compartment on the port side separated by a heavy curtain. Directly across from the captain was the radio and sound room. Just aft, and separated by a watertight bulkhead, was the control room.

Shafts for the two periscopes dominated the centre of the room. On the starboard side of the control room were the two planesmen's positions that controlled the vertical movement of the boat. The navigator's chart table was just behind. The auxiliary bilge pump took up the aft end of the starboard side of the room. The port side was filled completely with machinery that controlled the periscopes, the flooding or venting of the ballast tanks, and the main bilge pump.

Between the two periscopes was a watertight hatch and a ladder giving access to the conning tower, site of the equipment needed to aim the boat's torpedoes. The smaller of the two periscopes was the attack periscope. It had a much smaller head than the sky periscope, making it less visible to the enemy, and included a stadimetric ranging system that used split optics to determine the range to the target. The sky periscope was used primarily to check for enemy aircraft before surfacing.

Aft of the control room and separated by a watertight bulk head were storage lockers and accommodation for the petty officers. Aft of this was the tiny galley where meals were prepared. The cook had a small range, two small ovens and a boiling pot. An after head was usually filled with food and used for storage. Below the decking was a battery compartment.

Finally there was the engine room. Two large 6-cylinder, 4-stroke diesels powered the boat when on the surface. They were very lightweight and located side by side. Aft of them were the two electric motors and the single aft torpedo tube. The boat was powered by the two diesel engines and could maintain a speed of 17 knots. Air for the engines was channelled through a pipe down through the conning tower. That allowed the boat to remain very low in the water while still getting air to the engines.

U-Boats spent nearly all of their time at sea on the surface. On the surface the boat had the agility and speed to overtake convoys, but submerged it was blind and helpless. Once an order to dive had been given, the engines were shut down and power came from the batteries. While submerged, the boat could maintain a speed of seven knots but only for one hour. However, at two knots it could stay submerged for up to 36 hours. After that it had to surface for air and to charge the batteries.

All U-Boat recruits started their training as infantryman, learning basic combat and survival skills. Basic naval training aboard sail training ships and cruisers followed that, and then submarine school where they underwent special training and, based upon their training and exam scores, were appointed ratings as officers, radio men, mechanics, etc. Training lasted nearly five years before they reported for their first tour of duty on a U-Boat. The normal crew complement was 45. There were three other officers besides the captain. The first watch officer or executive officer was second in command. He shadowed the captain very closely so that he could take command if the captain fell ill or was killed in battle.

He was also responsible for the boat's weapons systems and conducting torpedo aiming during surface attacks.

The second watch officer was responsible for the watch crew on deck, the flak gun, the deck gun, and the radio men. The engineer was responsible for the boat's engines, motors, batteries and other mechanical systems, including setting the demolition charges if the boat had to be scuttled.

There were four chief petty officers. The navigator looked after navigation and provisions. The chief bosun was responsible for crew discipline. The diesel officer, who was subordinate to the engineer, was responsible for the diesel engines. The motor officer, also subordinate to the engineer, was responsible for the electric motors and batteries.

There were ten petty officers: two responsible for steering, two torpedo men, two motormen, two radio men and two bosuns. Duties for the rest of the crew included watch duty, manning the guns, loading the torpedoes, and cooking the meals.

On February 13, 1941 – after another captain and crew had put *U-69* through her paces in the Baltic Sea and delivered her to St. Nazaire – Kapitan Leutnant Jost Metzler was in charge as the boat headed for service in the Atlantic Ocean, specifically to the Faroe Islands off the coast of Northern Europe.

Metzler had a reputation throughout the U-Boat service as a tough but fair officer. At 24, he was one of the youngest captains in the submarine service. He had proven himself on his last boat as the oberleutnant zur see, the executive officer, and was now in command. This was his first command and he had something to prove both to his superiors and to himself.

Metzler had practically memorized the U-Boat manual. That single document contained practically everything a commander needed to attack and defend himself against enemy shipping. It was printed using the same ink as the codebooks. In the case of an emergency it simply was dropped into water and all of the ink would disintegrate. The codebook contained particularly sensitive materiel such as how and where a retreat should be made when under attack. It also contained information on how best to attack enemy shipping and where to go and hide after making an attack.

Six days out of port and southwest of the Faroes, *U-69* encountered *MV Siamese Prince* in the early morning hours. The sea was calm and the moon was shrouded in cloud. In a textbook attack, Metzler sailed to within 500 metres of the British cargo ship that was enroute to Liverpool and hit her midships with a single torpedo. The following morning, the first kill was recorded on the conning tower. It was tradition to paint the outline of a ship on the conning tower to indicate a kill.

Two days later, just before daylight, *U-69* met *SS Empire Blanda*. She was out of Halifax with a load of steel and explosives. A single torpedo sent her to the bottom. In two days, *U-69* had sunk two ships and been responsible for the deaths of 97 sailors.

On February 24, five days after the sinking of the *Blanda,* the U-Boat met and sank the *SS Temple Moat*, a merchant steamer enroute Buenos Aires. There were no survivors among the crew of 42. Metzler felt good about his successes and crew morale was high.

U-69 returned to her pen at St. Nazaire on March 1 and remained there until March 18, when she left for the coast of West Africa to perform mine laying duties off Lago and Takoradi. Shortly after arrival, she encountered *SS Robin Moor,* a commercial cargo ship with a crew of 45. The *Moor* was out of New York enroute Mozambique via South Africa. She was flying the flag of the neutral United States and as a result was without a convoy. She was stopped by *U-69* 750 miles west of Freetown, Sierra Leone. Captain Metzler ordered the crew into four lifeboats and then fired a single torpedo to sink the ship. Afterwards, he gave the captain some meagre supplies and explained the ship had been sunk because she was carrying supplies to Germany's enemy.

Nearly two weeks passed before the *Moor's* crew was rescued. When U.S. President Roosevelt was informed of the situation he branded Germany an international outlaw and ordered the closing of all German consulates. In October of that year, an American citizen, Leo Waalen, was convicted of espionage for radioing Germany with the sailing date of the *Moor*.

U-69 returned to her pen in July of 1941 after sinking six more ships, but the sinking of the *Moor* was like a curse upon her. In August, Metzler was replaced by Captain Jugen Aufferman. He proved such a failure he was replaced the same month by Captain Willhelm Zahn, who was captain until March of 1942 but never sank a single enemy boat.

Ever since the sinking of the *Moor,* *U-69* had been plagued with sickness among the crew, low morale, and mechanical problems. The U-Boat had gone on seven missions with two captains and not sunk a single enemy ship.

On March 17, 1942 Zahn was replaced by Captain Ulrich Graf, a career naval officer who was determined to eliminate the curse that had become widespread knowledge amongst his fellow captains at St. Nazaire. With crew morale at an all time low, Graf had been handpicked to command *U-69* and restore her earlier successes.

Graf was ordered to the Eastern Seaboard of the United States. Now that the United States had entered the war because of the attack on Pearl Harbour, there was an almost steady stream of merchant ships across the Atlantic to England.

Graf used the time crossing the Atlantic to drill his crew and hone their skills. He wanted them ready for combat and the best they could possibly be. Before the end of March, they had sunk the *James E. Newson* and another three ships. Morale was high and *U-69* held her bow high.

U-69 was recalled to St. Nazaire in early April and Graf was called to the Admiralty Office and congratulated on his success. He was told he was being groomed for a very special mission and his crew would be changed. Graf objected, saying his crew was the best he had ever sailed with and his success in America was a direct result.

He was told that he would understand later why this was happening. It was further explained that his entire crew would be English speaking. The working language of the boat would be English and communication with the German Admiralty would be in English.

Graf was told he and his new crew would first go to the Caribbean Sea where they would stay until August, when they would return and be sent on their new mission in early September.

Graf spent a few days with his wife in Kiel before returning to St. Nazaire and *U*-69. He was pleased to find that five men, including the executive officer, were members of his former crew. The crew spent two days provisioning before setting sail for the Caribbean.

U-69 engaged and sank two ships while in the Caribbean. Graf trained his crew hard, but before returning to St. Nazaire his navigator found an island and he gave his men a week of shore leave. Three weeks later, they reported back to St. Nazaire and were soon on their way back across the Atlantic.

Graf was given five new crewmembers. His two torpedo men were replaced because they were needed on other missions. The bosum was replaced because he was ill. And two extra radio men were for onshore duty at their final destination: Three Rock Harbour, Newfoundland.

CHAPTER TWO

Three Rock Harbour, Newfoundland. March 1936

Midwife Mary Church asked Bill if he would help with the birthing. It was unusual for a man to be present when his child was born but Mary expected problems so she asked for his help. When he was in position she lifted Janet's skirt and saw that the birth opening was almost dilated. "It won't be very long now, deary," she said. This was Janet's fifth child. The last one had been a problem. Janet had bled a lot and Mary thought she would lose both mother and child.

There was another contraction and Janet cringed and drew her legs up. Bill held her shoulders. "It's okay, you'll be fine," he said.

"It will be soon now, maid," Mary said.

Janet tensed and beads of sweat appeared on her forehead as her face assumed a look Bill had never seen before. Mary looked underneath her skirt again. The birth opening widened and she could see by the light of the kerosene lamp the reddish round head trying to push out. Janet began to pant in short breaths as the contraction returned and she drew her legs closer to her chest. The birth opening stretched wider and Janet gave a howl of pain.

Slowly the baby came out through the practiced canal, its eyes closed and its body covered with blood and the fluids of the womb. One shoulder followed by the other, then the hands, and finally the rest in a splash of birth. Almost immediately the birth opening closed.

"He's out," Mary said as she held the baby between Janet's legs.

She then set to work dealing with the umbilical cord.

"How are you feeling, sweetheart," Bill asked his wife.

Janet smiled. Bill had only called her sweetheart five times in her life. Each time it was after the birth of a child.

"Fine," she answered.

"Pass me the twine," Mary said to Bill.

He passed her the roll of twine.

"I'll need a knife," she said, and Bill pulled the one from the scabbard on his side. He wiped it on his trousers and passed it to Mary.

She cut off two short pieces of twine. Bill looked down and could see that the blue cord attached to the baby had stopped pulsing. Mary took the pieces of twine, looped them around the cord in two places, and cut it in two pieces, using Bill's knife.

"It's over," she said to Bill. "It looks like you have someone else to go out on the water with you. Now, go get me a bowl of water so I can wash this little bugger."

Bill looked at the baby as he was leaving the room. He had another son. The baby was christened George Hedley Sullivan on May 10, 1936, exactly two months after his birth. His mother passed him to Father Hartley who dipped his hand in holy water, made the sign of the cross on the baby's forehead and, while he screeched bloody hell, gave him his name. Despite the ceremony, the official Roman Catholic Church document duly signed and recorded, the marks of his parents, and the signature of the priest, and the protestations of Janet every time she heard it, the baby became known as Shoot.

The day after his birth, Mary came by to perform the circumcision ritual and when she grabbed hold of his package he gave it to her right square in the face with the force of the 'blowhole at Deadman's Rock,' according to his father. It did nothing more than slow the process a little but his father, who did not particularly like Mary Church, laughed so hard that he nearly burst a vein in his forehead and kept repeating, "Look at that thing shoot, look at that thing shoot." And so he became known as Shoot.

Shoot, of course, doesn't remember the momentous occasion. His memory began sometime around age four with the death of his grandfather.

He and his grandfather were the best of friends and went everywhere together. One of their favourite games involved Pop hiding large pennies, or coppers as he called them, and getting Shoot to look for them. He would hide them in the cuffs of his pants, under the elastic straps that shortened the sleeves of his shirts, in his pockets or any of a dozen places. In all cases they were hidden somewhere on his person.

Pop was too old to go out fishing anymore so he stayed home and usually he was the one who helped Shoot get dressed in the mornings. He had been sick around the time Shoot's memory started and when he got up that morning and there was no Pop, he went looking for him. His mother was outside hanging clothes on the line. Shoot found Pop asleep on the couch in the front room. He was lying on the couch and right in plain view were two coppers, one on each eye. Shoot ran to Pop, jumped up on his belly, and snatched the two coppers from his eyes. While he sat there enjoying his success, his mother came into the room let out a scream and fainted. Shoot didn't know that Pop had died the night before and the coppers had been put there to keep his eyes closed.

Home was Three Rock Harbour, a community that got its name from the three huge rocks in the harbour. Shoot was six in the summer of 1942 and starting school that year. He looked forward to it. There were one hundred and sixteen residents in the community, according to the Register in the church, and the only people who were not fishermen or the families of fishermen were the priest who came once a month, Paul Arns and his family, who owned the general store, and the schoolteacher who stayed until June, but usually did not come back in September and was replaced by another. There were 93 headstones in the cemetery, but many more graves without headstones because family members simply could not afford them or they had fallen down or rotted in the two hundred plus years since the community was first settled. There was a church badly in need of repair with a basement for socials and a one-room school also badly in need of repair. There was a public wharf for the coastal boat to tie up and a dozen other privately owned wharves. There was no electricity, no telephones, no roads other than footpaths and no indoor plumbing. Every household had a well, an outhouse, a clothesline to dry clothes and a root cellar for vegetables. There was a short-wave radio in the general store and every household owned at least one boat. Shoot's father was a fisherman. He knew that when he grew up he would be a fisherman too.

The community was located on the south coast of Newfoundland and accessible only by boat. It existed because of the cod fishery and when and if there was no cod to catch the community would die. But no one could imagine that ever happening.

Three Rock Harbour was sheltered on three sides by high hills and the narrow entrance to the deep harbour made it a natural place to wait out a storm. Early fishermen sailed into the harbour looking for shelter and quickly realized that it had everything needed for them to spend more than just a few days. And even though the bay might fill with ice it rarely came into Three Rock Harbour.

One of the most unique features about the community was the hole in the cliffs at the southern part of the harbour. The waves crashing on the cliffs for millions of years had created a huge cave extending several hundred feet high and wide.

North Harbour River ran down from the hills providing lots of fresh water from a pond named Gull Pond because of the huge cliffs at the far end of it where the gulls nested. Many people in Three Rock Harbour had hunting shacks up there that they used in the summer for fishing and the winter for hunting. There was a plateau of sorts that gently sloped towards the ocean and the glaciers had dropped sufficient topsoil to make the land perfect for growing the staple vegetables: potatoes, turnips, carrots and cabbages. About a mile from the shore, huge stands of spruce and fir trees climbed up the sides of the hills and provided all the necessary building material to construct homes and firewood for their stoves. There was lots of grass to sustain the livestock during the spring and summer months and enough for hay for winter-feed.

Their houses were constructed in the "salt box style." Two-story houses with flat roofs covered with spruce clapboard. Whitewash kept them white when the sun was out and a dingy grey colour when it was raining. Heat came from a wood stove in the kitchen and water came from a well sometimes dug before the house was built and then enclosed by the porch. Water was drawn up with a bucket and a rope when needed and stored in the porch. People did their business by visiting an outhouse a hundred feet or so from the house or by using the bucket under the bed on those occasions when weather prevented them from getting to the outhouse.

August 19, 1942 began just like every other day. It was 7:30 a.m. and Shoot opened his eyes to see that, as usual, he was the last one to get out of bed. He was the youngest of five. His brothers Ray, 13, and John, 11, were likely out in the boat with their father. His sister Mary, 16, was helping Mom clean up after breakfast. His brother Bob, 9, was downstairs in the kitchen, whining because he was not allowed to go out on the water with the others.

Shoot got out from under the heavy quilts covering the bed he shared with his brothers and walked down the creaky narrow stairs to the kitchen. His mother, Janet, was sitting at the table when he pushed open the door. His sister, Mary, was sitting beside her, peeling potatoes.

"Finally decided to get out of the bunk," his mother said as she got up, shoved another piece of wood into the stove and lifted the damper back to cover the hole as a wisp of smoke wafted up to the ceiling. Shoot walked without speaking across the canvas-covered floor and sat on the bench by the oilcloth-covered table. From a large cast iron skillet on the stovetop, his mother forked a touton onto a plate and slid it up the table towards him. He reached for it and the molasses.

His mother had made bread before sunup that morning and the left over dough was put in the skillet with butter and fried like pancakes. Covered with molasses and washed down with sweet tea and milk, toutons were a treat Shoot enjoyed every time his mother made bread. He didn't like porridge and that was what they had when his mother didn't bake bread. Fortunately, every second day his mother had to bake bread and there was always enough dough left over to make toutons.

"They're on the way in the harbour. I see them with my own eyes," Bob suddenly shouted as he jumped up from the daybed. "Looks like they got a good haul this morning. Come over here, Shoot, and have a look. See how low the boat's in the water."

"Stay where you are and finish eating your breakfast," his mother ordered Shoot. "If you want to go down on the wharf you had better get dressed," she said to Bob.

Bob jumped from the daybed and his feet barely touched the floor as he raced through the kitchen and upstairs to find his clothes. Shoot crammed the last of the touton in his mouth as Mary started dressing him. He could hear Bob mumbling upstairs as he rummaged through his drawer looking for his clothes.

Janet pulled down the door to the warmer oven above the Enterprise stove. There was a bread pan there filled with rising dough. Putting the pan on the table, she went to the water tank on the side of the stove, filled the kettle, and put it on to boil. At the same time, she moved the frying pan beside the kettle and added butter to it.

"Hurry up dressing him," she said to Mary. "Your father and brothers will be up here in a few minutes and you know how they act when they have to wait for their breakfast."

Mary finished dressing Shoot and pointed and pushed him towards the daybed where he stood up and looked out the window just as his father was tying up the boat.

"They're tying up now, Mom," he said proudly.

Janet took a handful of dough from the bread pan and rolled it in her hands like a baseball pitcher who had been given a new ball. Satisfied that it had been kneaded properly she threw it onto a wooden board and cut it into several smaller pieces. She picked up each piece of dough, flattened it with her hands and threw it into the frying pan where it sizzled as it hit the hot butter. As Janet prepared the toutons, Mary set the table. Just as the toutons were finished cooking, John pushed open the door to the porch. Shoot and Bob ran to greet him.

"How did you make out this morning?" Bob asked.

John filled a pan with water from a jug on the table in the porch and reached for a cake of yellow Sunlight soap before answering.

"We had a good haul," he said as he washed his hands and cupped them to scoop up handfuls of water to wash the saltwater spray from his face. He bent over the pan and did it several times until he held out his hand and Mary passed him a towel. As John was drying his face, Bill and Ray walked in through the open porch door. Shoot ran towards his father.

"Can I go out on the water this afternoon?" he asked.

"No, it's too rough out there for you today, Shoot. Maybe tomorrow," said Bill.

Once everyone had finished washing, they sat at the table to plates filled with hot fried dough and cups filled with steaming tea.

"How did this morning go?" Janet asked as she sat down next to Bill. No matter how busy Janet was she always sat to the table when Bill was eating, and she stayed there until he was finished, never eating anything herself. The one exception when Janet ate with her husband was for Sunday dinner.

Bill paused now to pour tea from his cup into the saucer to cool.

"We hauled the two traps and I'd say we got three or four hundred quintals," he said, as he raised the saucer to his mouth and sucked loudly until it was drained.

"There's a couple of salmon mixed up with them. We can have them for our dinner," said Ray.

"And that's what we won't," Janet corrected him. "They're going to the smoke house. You'll be glad of that when January comes."

Everyone in the family knew better than to argue with Janet. She had the final say on everything to do with the running of the household. She decided when a hen that had not been laying regularly would lose her head and be served for Sunday dinner. She decided which pig would die, when it would die, and what parts of it would be smoked and what parts of it would be eaten fresh. She decided when the vegetables would be put in the cellar and how high they should be piled in the bins so that they wouldn't rot. She told everyone where to hang the dried fish, where the hams and bacons should go, where the preserves should be stacked and everything to do with the winter food supply. They ate well. When the meat supply ran low, Bill went hunting and returned with a moose or a caribou. The quarters were always shared with family and friends and they never were without meat. They might have been poor but they ate like kings.

Once breakfast was over, and Bill had smoked his pipe, and the dishes were cleaned up, everyone went down to the wharf to clean up the fish. It was like an awakening as the families all left their houses around the same times and made their way down the incline to their boats and wharves. People were all headed in the same direction. No one was speaking, everyone was looking straight ahead with one thing on their minds: getting to the fish.

Bill fished with his brother Walt. Before their father died, Walt had fished with him. Bill and Walt were the only ones in the family because their mother had died giving birth to Walt. Uncle Walt was married but as yet he had no children. His wife, Aunt Ursula, joined them on the wharf a few minutes after they arrived.

Ray got there first and climbed down the ladder to the boat. It was high tide and he could have almost jumped into the boat instead of taking the few rungs nailed to the side of the wharf. It was his job to prong the fish from the hole of the boat up to the wharf, being careful to prong the head and not the body. Prong marks in the body of fish turned black and unsightly when the fish were salted.

As Ray readied to prong the fish to the wharf, other family members arrived and prepared to clean the fish and get it salted. Uncle Zeb had given up fishing longer ago than most people could remember, but there were few in Three Rock Harbour who could split a fish as quickly and as effectively as him. The table he used was made of rough wooden boards; its legs were criss-crossed pieces of spruce nailed to the top from underneath so that there were no nails sticking out on top to dull the knives. As the fish were thrown to the wharf John pronged them into a big wooden box at the end of the table, where Janet stood dressed in her rubber apron. She took the first fish from the box by grabbing it through its mouth and holding onto its lower jaw. She used her knife to cut the fish's throat and open the belly. The fish was slid up the table to Uncle Walt who removed the stomach or gullet and liver. The gullet was discarded but livers were thrown into a barrel, which would be filled and loaded aboard the merchant's ship when it arrived. The headless fish was then slid towards Bill and Uncle Zeb, the splitters, who removed the sound bone (backbone) and dropped the fish into a big vat of seawater.

Aunt Ursula scooped the fish into a wheelbarrow that John had pushed near the vat. The fish were moved to a tub where the children waited with rags in their hands to scrub them clean and throw them into another wheelbarrow. When it was full, Bill or Uncle Walt would push it to a stage or hut at the shore end of the wharf where the fish were dumped on the floor, ready for salting.

The sole purpose of the stage was to provide a place for the salted fish to cure, and to store fishing gear. Inside was a huge bin filled with coarse salt. Around the walls were several piles of salted fish. When Bill finished splitting, he went to the stage and was joined by the others as they finished their jobs. Bill began by throwing several shovels full of salt on the floor. Then he started picking up the fish and placing them stomach-side up on top of the salt. When he had covered an area approximately four feet square with fish, he shoveled more salt on top. He kept repeating the process until all the fish were salted. After twenty-one days the fish would not absorb any more salt, but it would stay in salt until the end of the season when it was taken out, washed, and put outdoors on the flakes to dry in the sun and wind.

By noon, the fish had been salted and the boat cleaned and readied for the afternoon trip. Before leaving the wharf, Janet took one of the cod and filleted it for the noon meal. It would be fried in fat pork and served with boiled potatoes.

That was the daily routine during the fishing season and it was repeated every morning and afternoon except Sunday, a day of rest. The only other time off during the fishing season were those days when the wind was high and it was unsafe to go out on the water. Those days were spent doing repairs to the gear and anything else that needed fixing. Sundays, however, were truly days of rest, interrupted only by emergencies. Sudden storms bringing heavy seas that would jeopardize the safety of boats or wharves were all that disturbed the Sunday routine. It was church in the morning, and then time spent reminiscing about the past week and contemplating what the next week would bring. Bill did this while sitting on the veranda at the front of the house looking out over the harbour. He usually did this with his eyes closed, his feet up on a stool, and his chin resting on his chest.

The summer of 1942 was a good one. Bill got lots of fish, there wasn't too much rain, and the vegetables grew very well. One day, Janet caught a moose eating her cabbages and ran and got her gun. The fresh moose meat was an unexpected treat.

John celebrated his twelfth birthday on September 3, 1942 and there was a party with handmade gifts. Shoot was sometimes envious of his mom and Mary because they could knit and sew and their gifts were sweaters and mitts, which were always appreciated. Shoot couldn't knit nor could his brothers so they had to make gifts that might not have been appreciated as much but were certainly imaginative. This year, with Janet's help and a piece of sealskin, Shoot had made John a scabbard for his knife that he could hang on his belt.

Birthdays were special because that's when the Sullivans had "How Many Cookies." The name had nothing to do with how many cookies they ate; it was about what was inside the cookies. Janet baked a cookie for every member of the family and filled each one with dogberry seeds in preparation for the family game. Shoot sat next to Mary and was the first person to ask his question.

"Mary," Shoot asked, "when you get married how many youngsters are you going to have?"

Mary had always said she didn't want to get married and have children so it was no surprise to anyone that she took a very small bite of her cookie. Then she spit it into her hand and everyone looked as she counted the seeds. There were howls of laughter as she counted five.

"There's no way I'm having five youngsters," she said, and they laughed even harder.

Then it was Mary's turn to ask Ray her question. "Okay," she began, "how many girls have you kissed?"

Ray was flabbergasted. "That's not a fair question. I'm not answering that," he shouted as he tried to get up from the table.

"You don't have to answer," Janet said, "but you know the rules. If you don't answer, you don't get to ask a question. If you tell a lie, everyone makes up your punishment."

Ray sat down and hung his head. He looked at his cookie and tried to take the smallest bite he could take. Despite it all, there were still two seeds in the bite and everyone wanted to know who were the two girls he had kissed.

The game continued until everyone had taken a bite from their cookies and answered a question. Despite the objections to answering questions, they all loved the game more than any other they played as a family.

After the game, they had supper and then Bill went to his usual place on the veranda. Janet sat beside him in her rocker, knitting socks. It had been a beautiful day and there was barely a breeze coming onshore from the ocean. The door was open and Shoot was inside on the kitchen floor playing fiddlesticks when suddenly there was a loud swooshing sound followed by waves crashing on the shore. Shoot ran to the open door. His parents had stood up and were looking towards the harbour. He manoeuvred between them to get a look.

His jaw dropped and his mouth opened because he couldn't believe what he was seeing. Something had appeared like magic from the ocean bottom causing the waves to crash on the shore and making all the fishing boats strain at their moorings. Within seconds of its appearance, the community came alive and everyone stood staring in a near state of shock. It seemed that aliens had come to Three Rock Harbour.

CHAPTER THREE

Three Rock Harbour. September 3, 1942

"My blessed Saviour," Janet whispered. "What is it, Bill?"

Bill continued to stare at the harbour. "I'll be dammed if I know," he managed.

"Shush," Janet said. "Remember it's the Lord's Day."

"Lord's Day or not, it's the biggest goddamn boat I've ever set my eyes on."

Shoot continued to stare. He was sure every other person in Three Rock Harbour was staring too. No one knew what it was they were looking at. It had to be a boat because it was in the water and it was floating. But where had it come from and how did it get here? It was like no other boat they had ever seen before. There were no sails to be seen and no oars sticking out of the side. They couldn't see an engine and there were no people unless they were hiding inside. It looked like a giant black pea pod floating in the harbour. It was about a hundred feet long and twenty feet wide with five feet or so of it sticking out of the water. There was a funny looking wheelhouse on the top but there weren't any windows. Suddenly the top of the wheelhouse popped up and a loud 'oooohhhh' could be heard echoing around the cove.

To everyone's amazement a man appeared at the top of the wheelhouse. He was wearing a hat like a policeman. He had on a blue jacket with three rings around the bottom of each sleeve. The top ring on each sleeve had a curl in it. He looked around and waved. People looked at each other before cautiously returning the wave.

Huge bubbles began to appear around the thing as one end of it started to turn in the direction of the cave in the cliff. Slowly, the thing lined up with the cave and began to move forward. Everyone watched as it slowly made its way to the cave and stopped in the middle. The man with the hat stayed at the top of the wheelhouse the entire time. Once the thing was inside the cave, the man climbed out of the wheelhouse, came down a little ladder and stepped onto the top of the pod. A few seconds later he was joined by two other men wearing white shirts and blue pants and funny little hats like piss pots without the handles.

"They look like they're sailors," Bill managed.

Everyone continued to watch as the sailors untied a little boat from the top of the pod and threw it into the water. As one of them held it, the one with the policeman's cap stepped into it. The others joined him and they began to row towards the government wharf.

"They're coming for us," Shoot said to no one in particular.

"Don't be silly Shoot," Janet said.

No one made a move towards the wharf as the boat edged nearer.

"I'd better go down and see what they want," Bill said as he headed for the wharf. Shoot raced after him.

"Come back here, Shoot," Janet yelled. "You come back here with us."

Shoot stopped dead in his tracks. "I want to go with Dad," he said.

"You go back with your mother," Bill said, as he continued towards the wharf.

The walk to the wharf was the longest Bill Sullivan had ever taken. Other fishermen were slowly beginning to drift down, but Bill realized that no matter how long he prolonged it, he would be the first to arrive on the wharf. As the small rowboat approached, Bill stopped for a moment to clear his throat.

"Good evening," said the obvious leader of the group from the strange boat as he climbed out of the rowboat and walked to meet Bill in the centre of the wharf. He stretched out his hand in greeting. Bill took it and they shook hands.

"My name is Tony Stewart, Commander Tony Stewart, and it looks as if my crew and I have caused quite a stir here in your little village."

"Yes, you have," Bill said. As the other fishermen joined them, Stewart greeted each of them with a handshake and an introduction to his fellow sailors, Karl and Peter.

Five minutes later everyone had been introduced and shook hands.

"I know," Stewart began, "that you all want to know who we are, what we're doing here and how long we intend staying. So, if you'll bear with me for a few moments I'll try and explain everything to you and answer any questions you may have after that."

"I've already told you that my name is Commander Tony Stewart. I am a naval officer of the British Royal Navy Submarine Service. My boat is

HMS Sea Shark. I have been ordered to this location because of increased attacks on Allied shipping by German U-Boats. My mission is to find a safe haven and to patrol the waters off the coast of Newfoundland in order to protect local and Allied ships. Our mission is top secret, and because of the ever-present threat of spies, I have to ensure that as few people as possible know of our location. That's why your village was chosen."

"That cave in the cliff over there will provide us with the necessary cover to allow us to recharge our batteries. We won't have to stay submerged all day and my crew will be able to see that the sun actually exists."

Stewart chuckled and then continued.

"It is critical that no one, other than my superiors and the residents of this village, know of our existence. Am I making myself clear?"

The fishermen looked at each other and then nodded.

"We will set up a temporary base of operations here. We will be leaving on patrols as well as responding when we are directed to do so by my superiors in Halifax. Because we are unable to receive messages when we are fully submerged, we will be setting up a communications detachment somewhere on shore. We will of course need to rent space. We will also need people to assist us with various monitoring activities and will be paying for that as well. I can't overemphasize the importance, at the risk of repeating myself, of ensuring that no one outside of this village becomes aware of our presence here. That is vital to our operation."

Stewart paused to wait for questions. There were none.

"I have a crew of 45 on my boat. Everyone will remain aboard with the exception of me and two radio men. Karl and Peter here are both radio men as are Max and Paul, two other members of our crew. I will be your liaison. Now, I'd like to meet with your mayor, or whoever is the head of your village."

People looked around. They didn't have a mayor nor was there any one person who spoke for everyone. The schoolteacher had not arrived. The priest was not expected to be there until the fall so there was really no one to speak for the entire community.

"How about you, Bill?" one of the fishermen shouted. "You've got a sensible head on your shoulders. Why don't you talk to him?"

"I'm not so sure about that," said Bill. "I'm a fisherman like the rest of you."

"Mr. Sullivan," Stewart said as he moved closer to Bill, "I'm sure that you are more than capable of speaking for the people in your village. If there is anything I am asking for that you feel you need to consult with the others then I'm sure that you'll handle it."

Several of the fishermen echoed their support.

"Okay then," Bill said reluctantly.

"Great," Stewart said. "Why don't you give me a tour of your village and we can talk as we do our walkabout?"

People parted as they made their way along the wharf and into the community.

"So, tell me a little about yourself, Bill," Stewart asked.

"Well, you know that I'm a fisherman. I've been fishing ever since I was 12 so I don't have much education. I have a wife. We've been married for 17 years and we have five youngsters. That's my place up there," he said, pointing at his house and his family out on the veranda.

"They're a fine looking family," Stewart said. He waved and the Sullivans waved back. "I'm not as fortunate as you, Bill. The call of the sea and military service has not given me the opportunity or the time to seek out female companionship. I envy you in that regard. But I do have my crew and my boat and they're my family until this damn war is over."

"And a fine looking boat she is," Bill said, as he paused to turn and look at the boat. "What kind of a boat did you say she was?"

"A submarine," Stewart answered proudly.

"Maybe you'll give me the chance to have a look at her sometime," Bill said, smiling.

"We'll see," Stewart answered. "Now, we're going to need a place for a couple of my men to set up a radio station. I'd like it to be as high a place as is possible for the antenna, if you know what I mean?"

"The highest place would be where the church and the school are located. The school is in the basement of the church. The school won't be used for another month or so, and we haven't had a priest here since last year. Bob Sooley has been holding services, but I don't think he would mind, especially if you say you're going to pay to use the place."

"Yes, of course we will pay. We don't want something for nothing. May we go have a look ?"

St. Anne's Church was located at the high point in the community, about a five-minute walk away. It was surrounded by a low picket fence with the cemetery at the rear. Karl and Peter were silent as they walked along behind Bill and Stewart, who continued to chat until they reached the gate. Bill untied the rope securing the gate and they went inside the churchyard. Huge flat stones had been placed on the walkway up to the church. Years of walking on them had caused them to sink below ground level. There were a few steps leading up to the main door of the church. When they reached the door, Bill lifted up the lever and they went inside.

For the next twenty minutes, Stewart and his men walked through the building until they finally settled on a little room just below the bell tower. Karl and Peter seemed quite pleased because they would be able to put their antenna up one side of the church steeple, making it difficult to detect. A cable could then be run straight down to the radio set. It was perfect.

"Now it's just a matter of the rent," Stewart said. "How does ten pounds a month sound?"

"You won't get any arguments from us," Bill said excitedly. "I'm sure that Bob doesn't get that much in the collection plates for a whole year."

"Okay then, it's a deal," Stewart said. He reached into his pocket and took out his wallet. He removed a $20 bill and gave it to Bill. Bill took it and examined it.

"It's been a while since I've seen any paper money," he laughed.

"You'll see a lot more of it if we can find the things we need," Stewart grinned. "You'll have to keep it under wraps, so to speak, until we're about to leave. If suddenly a lot of money starts showing up where there never used to be any, then people on the outside will begin to ask questions. Understand?"

"Yes, I suppose I do," Bill said.

"Now, how about we let my men get set up here and we go meet that family of yours. But first," he continued, "is there a radio transmitter in the village?"

"No, not really. We used to have one in Arns' shop, but last month it stopped working and no one has been able to fix it. It happens all the time, and we have to wait for the repair feller who comes in on the coastal boat. A few people have radios, but no one has a transmitter. We have a radio in our house, but my girl Mary is the only one who listens to it."

"Good, now let's go meet your family."

"Yes, I think that's a good idea. My youngest, Shoot, seems to think that you and your crew are aliens so I'm sure he can't wait to meet you."

The men chatted as they made their way down the hill to Bill's house where everyone was waiting on the veranda. Shoot was standing behind his mother peering out from behind her skirt.

"Mother," Bill began, this is Commander Tony Stewart."

"I'm very pleased to meet you, Mrs. Sullivan," Stewart said, as he removed his cap and extended his hand.

"It's Janet," she said, as she shook his hand and smiled shyly.

"And these are my youngsters," Bill continued. "There's Ray, John, Mary, Bob and Shoot hiding behind his mother's skirt."

"Hello boys, and you too young lady," Stewart said as he greeted them all. He paused at Shoot. "So you think I'm an alien, do you, young man?" he asked, as he reached behind Janet to shake Shoot's hand. "That's a very unusual name, Shoot."

"Don't ask," Janet said. "Now Shoot, don't go making out that you're shy. Shake the man's hand and stop the nonsense."

Shoot reached out and took Stewart's hand. "That's a fine grip you have there," Stewart said, laughing.

Shoot pulled back his hand. "You've got woman's hands," he said.

Stewart looked at his hands. "I suppose you're right," he laughed. "Compared to your father and your brothers, I suppose my hands do feel kind of soft."

"How about a cup of tea?" Janet asked, as she pulled Shoot out from behind her and pushed him away.

"Yes, I would love a cup of tea," Stewart answered. "In fact, there's nothing I would like more at this moment."

"Sit down here," Bill said, pointing to one of the benches near the table. "The rest of you go outside and play and leave us to our tea." Reluctantly, all but Shoot went outside. He sat on the daybed by the stove, not wanting to miss a word.

Janet moved the kettle to the centre of the woodstove. She scooped three heaping spoonfuls of loose black tea into the teapot and added boiling water from the kettle.

"How has the fishing been?" Stewart asked.

"Not too bad," Bill answered. "They're a bit small now but once the fall comes and they move off shore, they'll get bigger."

"What kind of fish are you catching?"

"They're cod, bye," Shoot said. "Don't you know anything about fishing?"

Before Bill could chastise his son, Stewart held up his hand. "No I suppose I don't," he said. "But I'd like it if you could teach me."

A huge smile appeared on Shoot's face. "Well if I'm not too busy," he answered.

Stewart laughed as Bill and Janet looked at each other and rolled their eyes.

"But I'm not doing it for nothing," Shoot continued.

"I wouldn't expect you to." Stewart reached into his pocket and came out with his hand closed. He reached towards Shoot who held out his hand as Stewart dropped a coin into it.

Shoot rolled the coin over a couple of times. "Five cents," he said, smiling.

"Can we call that a down payment?" Stewart asked.

"Yes sir," Shoot replied.

Janet put cups and saucers on the table, followed by a couple of small plates. She took the tea strainer from the warmer and held it over each cup as she poured in steaming tea. She put a sugar bowl and a jug of milk beside the cups. The men helped themselves, as Janet went to the pantry and returned with a pie. She cut two pieces and served the men.

Bill poured half of his tea in his saucer and drank from it, sipping very noisily.

"What kind of pie is this?" Stewart asked. "It looks delicious."

"Partridgeberry," Shoot answered. "You sure don't know much about things, do you?"

"That will be enough from you, young man," Janet said, pointing at the open door to the veranda. Shoot got down from the daybed and went outside.

"That's okay, Mrs. Sullivan. He's just a young boy," Stewart said.

"A young boy with very bad manners," she answered. "It's just that we don't get very many visitors here."

"Don't give it a second thought. I rather enjoy his frank comments. As a Royal Navy officer, I rarely have anyone being that frank with me so it's a welcome change. This pie is incredible," he continued, changing the subject. "I am going to have to get my cook to spend some time with you to learn how to cook pies like this. What are these partridge berries?"

Janet laughed. "I don't know what to say," she smiled. "The berries grow on the hills on low bushes and we pick them in the fall and make jam. It takes a lot of sugar to make jam because the berries are really bitter. I could give you a bottle," she offered. "In another month, they'll be ripe again and I have lots to carry me through till then."

"I couldn't impose on you like that," he said.

"It's nothing," Janet said, as she went to the pantry and returned with a bottle of the red jam and put it on the table beside him. She sat at the table beside her husband.

"You have a lovely home and a wonderful family," Stewart said. "I am very envious of you. But as I told your husband, my life is my boat and crew."

He finished the last of his pie. "I intend leaving my radio crew at the church when we go to sea. I wonder, do you have frequent visitors to the village?"

"No," Bill said. "We're about two hours away from Ship Cove and people there never have any reason to come here. The coastal boat comes in October month with our winter supplies. We expected a schoolteacher to be here the first week of September, but I heard there was trouble getting one to come here again this year, so I don't know if we'll have one or not. The priest comes by once a month, but that can change like the weather. Before everything freezes up, the fish buyer comes here and gives us credit for our fish. We use the credit notes he gives us to buy our winter supplies in Arns' shop."

"I'm asking you these questions, Bill, because we have to keep our presence here a secret, as I said to all of you when I was on the wharf. We don't want a lot people coming and going and talking. I'm sure you've heard the saying, 'Loose lips sink ships.'"

"No, I can't say that I've heard that," Bill answered, "but I understand your meaning."

"Thank you. And now let me tell you a piece of good news. My superiors have spoken with the government department responsible for sending you a schoolteacher. People there have been briefed on this mission and told that there will be no need to send you a teacher this year. I have your teacher on board my boat. I also have a priest. He will stay here with you. You'll be able to have a church service every Sunday."

"Oh my, that is nice," Janet said. "It means we won't have to listen to boring old Bob Sooley again."

"That will be a welcome relief," Bill said. "We should dig a few graves too, just in case. You see, Tony, we can't bury our dead in the winter because the ground is frozen solid and because we've never had a priest available to say a few words over the dearly departed. Now that we're going to have a full-time priest, we'll dig the holes and hope that we don't have to use them."

"Fine," Stewart said, "and yes, let's hope that we don't have to use them. By the way, how far offshore do you travel when you go out fishing?"

"We're all inshore fishermen hereabouts. The farthest off we go is Sandy Grounds and that's about a half an hour from here. So that would make it about three or four miles."

"Do you ever meet any other fishermen when you're out there?"

"Other than the fellers from here, no. Every so often we might see a boat off in the distance but they never stop."

"I'm asking these questions and I suppose you've figured out why," Stewart said.

"I suppose it has to do with you not wanting us making contact with other people and letting them know about you being here," Bill said.

"Yes, that's exactly it. Now, what about mail?"

"All the mail comes and goes on the coastal boat. The priest or the teacher reads and writes letters for anyone who can't read or write. And Paul Arns, who runs the general store, has the Eaton's catalogue so he writes up the orders for us and keeps track of our credit notes.

"We will have to make sure no one here writes to a family member who is away and tells them about us. We'll need a way to check the outgoing mail. We'll have to get a message to everyone that the priest will have a look at all the letters before they're sent. I know this is going to be a big inconvenience for everyone but it has to be done."

"I think everyone will understand," Janet said.

"We don't expect everyone to agree to everything we ask and I'm sure there will be some who will object," said Stewart. "But I'd like you to get a message to everyone. In return for their cooperation, we will give the head of every family in the village credit at the general store equal to the credit that they received last year."

"Would you say that again?" Bill asked.

"Let me use you as an example. Whatever you earned last year for the sale of your fish was given to you as a credit in the general store. Is that right?"

"Yes, that's right, " Bill answered.

"And at the end of the season did you still owe a little more than your credit could cover?"

"Yes, that's always the way it is. We always end the year owing a little. But we hope that the next year will be a better one and we'll have a little left over."

"Well, now you won't have to worry. Whatever the amount of the credit you received last year we will match it. Tomorrow, I will meet with Mr. Arns and ask to look at his books. He can show me how much you received from the sale of your fish last season. I will then give him that amount in dollars. Whatever debt you have with him will be immediately wiped out, and you will have a credit balance. I will do that for the head of every family in this village."

Bill and Janet looked at each other. "You mean that we won't owe Paul Arns a red cent?" Janet asked.

"No, Ma'am. Unless, of course, you owe him more than a year's sales."

"Oh, no. We don't owe him that much. Not nearly that much," Janet said with her eyes all-aglow.

"And for you, Bill, as my liaison with the village, when we leave there will be something very special for you."

Husband and wife looked at each other, not believing their good fortune. They couldn't wait to get a look at the Eaton's catalogue. This Christmas would be an especially good one. New boots and warm jackets for everyone. A couple of new pots to replace the old ones. The list was endless. Bill would have to break the news to Janet that she couldn't spend any of their good fortune until after the boat was gone. The credit would be recorded and they could access it after the submarine had left.

"How long are you planning on staying here with us?" Janet asked.

Stewart paused a few seconds. "I suspect we will be gone before Christmas," he replied. "But we will ensure you keep your teacher and priest." He got up from the table. "Thank you very much for your very warm hospitality, Mrs. Sullivan. I especially enjoyed pie. And I will treasure this bottle of jam."

"You're very welcome, Captain Stewart," Janet answered. "Come by any time."

"Yes," Bill said, as he got up and shook Stewart's hand. "Drop by any time."

"Thank you," Stewart said. "Now I had better get back to my boat. My radio men will remain onshore. I know you have an early day tomorrow so I'll take my leave. We will talk again tomorrow."

The Sullivan children waved goodbye to Stewart and watched as he got in the tiny rowboat and made his way to the submarine.

Bill and Janet sat in the kitchen having a second cup of tea, still not able to believe their tremendous good fortune.

CHAPTER FOUR

Back on the submarine, Captain Graf (aka Captain Tony Stewart) drafted his first message since leaving port. It was encrypted and sent in the radio room.

FROM: U 69
TO: ADMIRAL COMMANDING U BOATS

ARRIVED AND MADE CONTACT

SHORT SIGNAL END.

Graf called his officers together to brief them on his meeting with Bill Sullivan. The first watch officer was Heinz Weber. He was a bachelor, a year older than Graf, and *U-69* was his third boat. He had been passed over for captain twice and was anxious to impress Graf so that he would not be passed over a third time. Weber was a stickler for detail and inflexible when following protocol. There was no one better at dealing with the routine of a submarine and the textbook attack, but when innovation was required he was slow to react.

The second watch officer was Helmut Becker. He was 24, married with no children, and this was his second boat. He was well-liked by everyone in the crew except Weber, who was jealous of the respect he got from the crew. If there was a criticism of Becker it was that he was too friendly with subordinates. His leadership style was rated as being persuasive, hardly the kind of leadership expected of a U-Boat officer.

The engineer was Bernhard Muller. At 31, he was the oldest of the four officers. Muller was married with three children and this was his second U-Boat, although he had been serving on surface ships for nine years. Muller was quiet, got along well with everyone and did not actively seek promotion. He was content to remain a U-Boat engineer and to serve the

Fatherland in that capacity. Of the four officers, he was the only one who spoke English with a heavy German accent.

Graf and his officers met in the hallway outside his cabin. There was no need for secrecy and there was nowhere they could meet without other sailors around.

"So, how did it go, Captain?" Becker asked.

"It went well. Very well indeed. This is an isolated community and it is the first time people here have ever seen a submarine. We probably could have surfaced here without the modifications and wearing our uniforms and they would not have known the difference."

"Dumb Englishmen," Weber said.

"I don't know if I would go so far as to say that they're dumb. They may know there's a war on, but they certainly have no involvement in it," Graf said.

"Until now," Muller said.

The others laughed.

"Okay, let's get ready to set up a base. Sullivan has agreed to rent a room in their church so we can set up a radio monitoring station there. Even when we're at sea and submerged we'll be able to keep in touch with the Admiralty. The message that is being prepared is the only message we will send from the boat while in port. Under no circumstances is anything to be sent from the station ashore. It will receive only."

Graf turned to Weber. "I've got Karl and Peter set up for shore duty. Except for me, they will be the ones most in contact with the villagers."

"Yes, Captain," Weber answered.

"Good. Bernhard, find Gerhard and Gustaf for me," Graf ordered.

Muller got up from his bunk and made his way aft. He had only taken a few steps when he spotted the two sailors and waved for them to join him and the others.

The taller of the two was Gerhard Schafer. He was 28 and had never been on a U-Boat before. He had been in the Navy for two years. Educated in England, he returned to Germany and enlisted at the outbreak of the war. Because of his command of English and his knowledge of England, he became an intelligence officer. His alias was Dan Blair and he would be the village's new schoolteacher.

Gustaf Bauer was a 35-year-old Catholic priest who ministered to the sailors in St Nazaire and had enlisted in the navy at the outbreak of the war. He'd gone to school in the United States, but returned home to Germany after deciding to become a priest. He had never been on a

U-Boat before. His alias was David Lake and he would be the village's new priest.

"Dan and David," Graf addressed them by the names the villagers would know them. "I trust you are ready for tomorrow when we will put you ashore and you can begin."

"Yes, sir," they said in unison.

"Good. Our contact will be minimal. After all, we are supposed to be merely the people who brought you here. The primary part of your mission is to ensure there is no outside contact."

"Yes, sir, we understand that completely," Lake said.

"Good," Graf said. "I think that should do it for now. Now, let's toast to our imminent success. Heinz, where's that bottle of schnapps?"

Weber stood up and waved at the chief bosun who shortly afterwards appeared with a bottle of schnapps and shot glasses. Weber passed out the glasses and half-filled each one.

"To our success," Graf said, as he lifted his glass and the others joined him.

CHAPTER FIVE

The next day, Bill and his son Ray were getting the boat ready to go out fishing just as the sun was coming over the horizon. As it got brighter they looked across the harbour at the submarine and could see that it was sitting very low in the water. The only thing above water was the wheelhouse. They gave the boat a passing glance as they slowly made their way out of the harbour and towards the fishing grounds. Within the next fifteen minutes, all of the rest of the fishermen would be on their way.

Bill and his brother Walt fished with a thirty-two foot wooden boat constructed almost completely from spruce. The gunwales were made of birch and all of the seams were chinked with oakum. Their father had built the boat ten years earlier and they had carefully maintained it so that it was in very good condition. The boat was powered by a 6-1/2 horsepower Acadia engine affectionately known as a 'one lunger,' a reference to its one cylinder. The engines were very popular with fishermen because they ran even when they were soaking wet, which they often were. The engine was housed in a small wheelhouse with a cot and room for the crew to huddle in inclement weather.

The trap fishery had ended a month earlier and now the men were fishing for cod using trawls, long ropes weighted on both ends with closely placed, baited hooks attached at intervals. Bill and Walt had six tubs of trawl and they "hauled the trawls" once or twice a day depending on how successful they were.

The rest of the Sullivans were up by 7 a.m. An hour later, breakfast had been cleaned up and Janet was doing the laundry. Mary took her bucket and her cleaning rags and made her way to the church. Everyone in the community took turns cleaning the church once a week. This was the Sullivan's day to do it.

Mary had grown into a very good-looking young lady. She had cut her blond hair short but left it long enough to cover her ears. When she threw back her head and laughed, which she did often, her hair touched her shoulders. She had long legs like her mother and her lips were full.

Her clothes hid a very shapely body, and she deliberately dressed to hide her large breasts, a predominant feature in her mother's family. She had a beautiful smile with perfectly straight white teeth, and her blue eyes sparkled when she laughed. She was tall like her father and her face was tanned by a combination of sun and wind.

Mary had forgotten the sailors were at the church until she opened the door and heard the radio crackling. She heard a voice using words she didn't understand. As the door closed behind her, a sailor suddenly appeared.

"Who are you?" he shouted.

"My name is Mary Sullivan and I'm here to do the cleaning because today is my family's turn. And I ask that you not shout at me, please."

He paused as a younger sailor appeared. The second sailor's jaw dropped at the sight of such a pretty girl and he simply stared at her.

"What did you hear?" the older of the two asked.

"I heard a voice speaking a language I didn't understand and a radio crackling," she replied.

"That was radio talk," the handsome younger sailor finally managed. "We have a special language that we use. For anyone who has never heard it before, it sounds foreign. May I ask your name?"

"I've already told the rude person there that it's Mary Sullivan and I've come here to clean the church. Now, if you'll let me get to my business, I will do my job and leave you to your radio talk."

The sailors looked at each other and then at Mary. The older of the two spoke. "I'm sorry, Miss Sullivan. It's just that we have to be very careful."

"I understand," she said, as she walked into the main area of the church. The handsome sailor followed her.

"My name is Karl," he said. "My friend does not have good manners. I'd like to apologize for the two of us. Please accept our apologies."

Mary stopped her dusting to look at him. She didn't think she had ever seen a man as handsome before. He was tall, with blonde hair, fair skin, and a smile that lit up the church. He was dressed in a white shirt and black bellbottom trousers.

"Your apology is accepted," she smiled. "But I'll wait to see what your friend has to say."

Karl laughed. "I don't blame you," he whispered, "but Peter is a nice person and you will realize that after you get to know him."

"I have no desire to get to know him, or you, for that matter," Mary said haughtily.

"We got off to a bad start," Karl smiled. "Let's start over."

Peter had retreated to the radio room and closed the door and nothing could be heard.

"So," Karl asked, "is this what you do here, clean the church?"

"No, it is my family's turn to clean the church this week and Mom is doing the laundry so I said I would come do it. There is not much to it. Just a bit of dusting. Don't you have something to do besides watching me?"

"It's a lot more fun watching you," he smiled. "I haven't seen a girl in over three months and I don't think that I have ever seen one so pretty."

Mary's face turned as red as the beets in her mother's garden.

"I'm sorry," Karl said quickly. "I didn't mean to embarrass you. Surely the other boys in this place must have told you how pretty you are, unless they're blind."

"No, they're not blind," Mary snapped, "but they have better sense than to go around telling girls they don't know that they're pretty."

"I'm sorry again. It appears that no matter what I say I upset you. That was not my intention. Can we start over again?"

Mary stopped and looked at him. "You sure do a lot of starting and stopping."

"My name is Karl. I am a radio man on *HMS Sea Shark* and I am very pleased to make your acquaintance, Miss Sullivan." He bowed.

"You can call me Mary, but I don't want you talking all that mushy stuff."

"Message received and understood," Karl said. He clicked his heels, lifted his right hand in salute, and quickly drew it to a position touching his right eyebrow, with the palm turning outward.

Mary returned to her cleaning under Karl's watchful eye.

"What do you do for fun here?" he asked, after a few minutes of silence.

"We go swimming and picking berries and we have picnics and take walks on the beach," she answered.

"That sounds like a lot of fun. May I ask you how old you are?" he said shyly.

"I'm sixteen, almost seventeen," she said. "How old are you?"

"I'm eighteen."

"Where did you come from before you pitched here?" she asked, as she sat on one of the benches.

Karl laughed.

"What are you laughing at?" she asked.

"I'm laughing at the way you talk. You have a funny accent," he said. Moving to the bench in front of her, he knelt on it and looked at her.

Mary stood up. "I won't sit here with you if all you're going to do is make fun of me," she said.

"Sit down, Mary. Please sit down," he pleaded, as he reached for her hand. "I'm not making fun of you. I love your accent and the way you talk. It's just different."

Mary looked at him and sat down.

"We've been at sea for over three months but my home base is in London," Karl said when she was seated beside him.

"Wow!" Mary said. "London, England. You're a long way from home."

"Yes, I am. But I signed on to be a sailor, and I knew that when I did I would be at sea for extended periods."

Mary continued her work as Karl leaned against a pew and watched her.

"I have to finish my cleaning here and get back home to help Mom with the washing and the other chores. I've already taken too much time talking to you."

"I'm sorry. I didn't mean to take you away from your duties. Maybe I could talk with you sometime when you don't have to clean."

"I don't know about that," Mary answered.

"How about this evening? If you'd like to come back after supper, we could sit outside the church and you could tell me all about yourself."

"There's not very much to tell you about me," she laughed. "You know everything there is to know. My name is Mary Sullivan. I live in Three Rock Harbour and I'm 16 years old."

"Mary Sullivan who is 16 and lives in Three Rock Harbour! There's a lot more about you than that," Karl said. "Please. We'll sit outside the church and talk about everything and nothing. I'll tell you about England, and you'll tell me about this place. Okay?"

Mary paused for a few seconds. "Okay," she said, "but I won't be able to stay very long. Now go away and let me finish my cleaning."

"Great, I'll see you this evening."

Mary finished a few minutes later and left the church. As she walked down the hill she couldn't help smiling as she thought about the handsome young sailor she had left behind.

When Mary had left, Peter came out of the radio room.

"I'm going to the boat to get a bolt to put on that door," he said. "We can't have anyone walking in on us again. If the captain finds out that she was here while we were broadcasting, he will shoot the two of us."

Peter returned an hour later and put a deadbolt on the inside of the door. He explained to Captain Graf that he felt such a lock was necessary to prevent people from coming into the church unannounced. He did not report that someone had already come in, unannounced.

After supper, Karl went outside to wait for Mary. He couldn't get her face out of his mind. Peter was opposed to their meeting, but Karl convinced him he was making much ado about nothing. Peter was the senior of the two and could have ordered Karl not to see her, but Karl subtly indicated perhaps he should include in the daily communications diary that they had been interrupted by one of the local girls when they were broadcasting. Peter agreed to the liaison in exchange for the diary omission.

Karl trained his binoculars on the Sullivan house and waited for Mary to come out and make her way up the hill. It was nearly 6:30 before he saw her coming towards him.

She had changed her dress and put a ribbon in her hair. The closer she got to the church, the more often she stopped to straighten the belt around her waist and brush the hair out of her face. Karl hid the binoculars before she arrived.

He met her halfway down the hill.

"Hello again, Mary Sullivan from Three Rock Harbour," he said.

"Don't be silly," she laughed.

They walked up towards the church together. There was a big rock in a grassy area near the front of the church and they made their way towards it.

"Thank you for coming," Karl said. "I've been looking forward to it all day."

They sat on the grass with their backs to the rock, facing out towards the harbour.

"What do we do now?" Mary asked, after they were settled.

"We sit and talk and find out things about each other," Karl said.

"So I see that you've done this before," she grinned.

"That's not what I meant at all. For the last three months the only other human companionship I have had is with a bunch of unwashed submariners. I'd just like to sit and talk with someone who smells clean, dresses nice, and has a smile that lights up the entire place."

"So that's why you asked me here, because I'm clean?"

"Don't be so difficult to get along with," Karl snapped playfully.

"I'm sorry," Mary said as she reached and touched his hand. "I'm just not used to sitting and talking with boys."

Karl put his hand on top of hers. "Well, get used to it because I'd like to do this every day until we leave here."

"Tell me what it is you do here," Mary said, changing the subject.

"You know that I can't talk about what I do. I'm a radioman and you should be able to figure out that I work with radios. I don't want to talk about what I do. I want to talk about you. All I know is your name, your age, and where you live. Tell me everything."

Mary paused for a few minutes. "Well, I've got one more year of school and then I want to go to St. John's and work. Mom and Dad don't want me to leave. They expect me to find someone here, marry him, have half dozen or so youngsters and live happily ever after. I can't think of a single boy in Three Rock Harbour that I'd like to have one child with let alone a half dozen."

"Not even me?"

"Now you're being silly again," she said.

"Sorry. Tell me more," he encouraged her.

"I'd like to become a teacher, but we don't have the money to pay for my room and board and for me to go to teacher's school. So, I plan to go to St. John's, get some kind of a job, save my money, and then train to be a teacher. I've already saved up thirty-two dollars."

"I see that you've got your entire life planned. Does getting married and having children fit into your picture at all?"

"I don't think so. But after I'm a teacher and I find a rich doctor with a big house then I might consider it," she laughed.

Karl laughed with her.

"Tell me about you," she said. "All I know about you is your name and what you do."

"You know my name and age and what I do. I've been in the navy for three years now."

"Three years," she said. "That would mean that you were only 15 when you joined."

"I lied about my age. You see, my father and my mother were killed in London by a German bomb attack. I was at school when it happened and when I went back home the entire flat was destroyed."

"What's a flat?" Mary asked.

Karl laughed. "That's what we call an apartment," he said. "Anyway, my parents and sister were killed and I had to go live with my aunt in Liverpool. I only lasted a few months before we both got sick of each other. So she signed my enlistment papers and here I am. I spent a year or so on a destroyer and then I applied for the submarine service. I was accepted six months ago."

"Wow, you've sure had a lot of things happen to you. I'm so sorry to hear about your family. I don't know how I would deal with it if something were to happen to my family."

"I'm slowly getting over it. Time heals all wounds, so they say."

They looked down in the harbour and Mary was surprised to see bubbles began to appear around the submarine.

"What's going on?" she asked.

"They've started the engines and are leaving and going out on patrol. They'll be gone a couple of days. That means I won't have so much work to do and we can spend more time together."

They watched as the small rowboat was thrown off the submarine and three people got in it and began rowing ashore.

"Who are they and why are they coming ashore?" Mary asked.

"I believe they're your new priest and your schoolteacher," Karl said. "Your father must have met with Captain Stewart and they're coming ashore now to do whatever it is schoolteachers and priests do. Where do the priest and the schoolteacher live when they come here?"

"The schoolteacher boards with Mrs. Cull. The priest usually only stays one night and sometimes it's with Mrs. Cull too. Seeing that he's going to be here as long as the teacher I guess they will both stay with Mrs. Cull."

The boat made its way to the wharf. Two people got out and the remaining one rowed back to the submarine. "That's Dad on the wharf meeting them," Mary said.

"He'll be bringing them over to Mrs. Cull, I'd bet."

The men from the submarine carried heavy suitcases as they followed Bill, and he did indeed lead them to Mrs. Cull's house.

"Can we go for a walk instead of just sitting here all evening?" Karl asked as the men disappeared between the houses.

"Sure, where would you like to go?" Mary asked.

"I don't care. Anywhere, as long as you're there and we can talk."

"How about we take a walk up the brook path to Gull Pond? There should be lots of trout jumping up there this evening."

"Great," he said. He jumped up and held her hands as he pulled her to her feet. Mary brushed off her dress and straightened the ribbon in her hair. Side-by-side, they made their way up the hill towards the pond.

The two men from the submarine introduced themselves to Bill. Dan Blair was the schoolteacher and David Lake was the priest. They apologized for not coming ashore sooner, but said the crew had a little send off for them at suppertime and they wanted to say their goodbyes. As they walked to Mrs. Cull's house they chatted. They told Bill they were Canadian Naval Officers stationed in Halifax. Dan Blair was Lieutenant Blair, a Sea Logistics Officer and David Lake was Lieutenant Lake, a Catholic Chaplain. They said they would not tell their students and parishioners in Three Rock Harbour that they were military officers.

Mrs. Cull was a warm, matronly lady. She was about 60 years of age, and her husband had drowned in a sealing accident nearly ten years earlier. Her children were grown with families of their own, and she had agreed to provide accommodation for the schoolteacher and the priest.

She met them at the door. She was over 200 pounds, with grey hair tied back in a bun. A white apron covered the entire front of her dress, leaving only the sleeves visible. She had a beautiful smile and rosy cheeks that didn't need rouge.

"Hello," she beamed, as she opened the door after the first knock. "Welcome to my home. I'm Freda Cull and it's obvious by the collar that you're the Father," she pointed at Lake. "And you're the schoolmaster," she said, pointing at Blair. "Come in. Come in."

"Pleased to meet you, Mrs. Cull," Lake said, as he walked in.

"Now there'll be no more of that Mrs. Cull stuff. I'm Freda and that's that."

"Hello Freda," Blair said as he extended his hand to her. "And you must call me Dan."

"No, that's not the way it works. You are paying guests in my home. So it's Mr. Blair and Father..."

"Lake, David Lake," he said, also extending his hand.

"Mr. Blair and Father Lake. Let me show you to your rooms. Have you had supper yet?"

"Yes," they said in unison.

Bill stayed downstairs while she led them up to their rooms.

"They're getting settled," she said, when she came back down.

"Good," said Bill. "I'll be off now." He went to the bottom of the stairs and shouted out to Blair and Lake. "You know where the church is? I'll be on the water tomorrow morning when you get up so you can make your way up there and look around for yourselves."

The men appeared at the top of the stairs and said that was fine.

Bill said goodnight as he left to go home.

CHAPTER SIX

The following days were busy ones for the people of Three Rock Harbour. They got to meet their new teacher and priest. Now, they had a priest who would be with them every day and not just the occasional Sunday. It was still few days before Sunday, and the day after that school would begin. No matter what time school started, the older boys had to stay with their fathers until the fishing season was over in the fall. The girls could start school anytime. But when their fathers came ashore with a load of fish they would have to go and help out.

Word was not long spreading that the teacher and the priest were staying at Mrs. Cull's. The women of Three Rock Harbour decided they would have a meet-and-greet social at the church that evening, so everyone could meet the new additions to the community. There would be tea, sandwiches and sweets and every woman in the harbour would try her best to ensure that at the end of the evening there would be no doubt as to who was the best cook.

By 11 a.m. the fishermen had returned with their morning catch and the work of cleaning the fish began. Mrs. Cull encouraged Blair and Lake to go down to the wharf and help out. "There's no better way to get to know people than to work side by side with them," she told them.

They were intrigued by the process and marvelled at how everyone worked together to get things done. Before long, they were dressed in the appropriate gear and pitching in as needed. It was such a novel sight that in no time at all the entire community, except for those who had to remain home to cook and look after small children, were down on the wharf looking at something they had never seen before in their lives: a priest and a schoolteacher up to their elbows in fish slime.

Everyone had something to say as they watched the unusual sight.

"It's too late to save his soul, Father bye."

"Make him sit up straight, teacher, before you cut his throat," another yelled out.

Every comment brought peals of laughter. None of it seemed to bother Lake and Blair, who seemed to be immensely enjoying themselves. Whenever they spoke, everyone looked and listened to what they had to say.

Bill gave Shoot a salmon to carry up to Mrs. Cull to cook for the men's lunch.

"Wait until supper and I'll send up a good feed of cods' heads," he said, when they said thanks.

That intrigued them. "You actually eat their heads?" Blair asked.

"Yessir we do," Bill answered, "and if it was up to me, that's the only part of the fish I'd ever eat."

"I'm sure that I couldn't get past the eyes," Blair said.

There was a slight pause after he spoke, and then everyone broke out in laughter. Bill laughed too.

"Pass me a head," he said to Walt. "Come here," he motioned Blair and Lake to come over to the splitting table.

Walt passed Bill a fish head.

Bill took the head and stood it on the table so that its mouth was pointing skyward. He took a knife, drove it into the fish's eye, and drew the blade down to the table. He turned the fish around and repeated the process on the other side. As the two men watched, he turned the head over so that the mouth was facing the table. He drew the blade of the knife down to the mouth, and then repeated the process on the other side. After separating the top of the head from the bottom, he threw the top over the side of the wharf.

"This here is the part that we eat," he said, spreading apart the lower part of the cod's head. "This here is the tongue which is like a scallop, and the side of the head is likely the best tasting fish there is. After the missus rolls it in a bit of flour and fries it in the pan, my sonny byes, you'd think you had died and gone to heaven. Excuse me, Father, no disrespect."

"No disrespect taken," Lake said. "I'm looking forward to trying it for supper this evening."

After the fish had all been cleaned, the fishermen got ready to go out again. There was always an early morning fishery and another where they left the harbour around 4 p.m. When there were fish about, they had to be caught.

That evening, at the social, after everyone had drank their tea and eaten their sweets, Bill Sooley took over as master of ceremonies. People moved from the school up to the church, where Sooley sat behind the pulpit, with the priest and the teacher on chairs to his right. As soon as Sooley stood up, the room went quiet.

"I'd like to thank everyone for coming here this evening," he began. "First, I'd like to thank all the women for putting on such a wonderful spread. I'm sure that if the grub is any indication, our two guests will leave with bellies on them like mine."

Everyone laughed as he patted his ample belly.

"Second," he said, "I never thought I'd see the day when some of you men would come to church at all, let alone on a Friday evening."

Again, everyone laughed.

"Enough with the foolishness now," he continued. "I'd like to introduce Mr. Dan Blair. He's our new schoolteacher and I'd like to ask him to say a few words."

Blair walked to the pulpit and stood beside it.

"Thank you, Mr. Sooley," he said. "I know many, if not all of you, had a great laugh at Father Lake's and my expense this morning as we attempted to help clean the fish." He paused as several people whispered to each other and smiled.

"I thought you were pulling our legs when you told us you actually eat cod heads. But now that we've tried them, I have to say that I prefer salmon."

Blair paused as laughter filled the church yet again.

"I have been here for less than a day and I can truly say that if the rest of my stay is as enjoyable as this first day, then you may be stuck with a teacher for a long time."

Everyone wanted to clap, but it wasn't appropriate in church.

"Your government passed the School Attendance Act a little while ago and it means that all children between the ages of 7 and 14 have to attend school. I know that some of the older boys are working with their fathers, but we're going to have to make every effort to get their schooling completed. Both sides are going to have to give a little.

"I'm very much looking forward to being the schoolteacher and getting to meet, not only all of my students, but all of you as well. I trust that we will all learn from the experience and again, if my first day is any indication, then I certainly have a great deal to learn."

The congregation couldn't restrain themselves. They all clapped. No one remembered ever clapping in church before. Sooley stood up as Blair moved away from the pulpit. He made faces as he tried to impart the message that clapping in church was a sin.

"Now, I'd now like to introduce our new priest, Father Lake." Sooley said.

Lake walked to the pulpit and stood behind it with his hands resting on top.

"Like my colleague, Mr. Blair, I too had a wonderful time today, and I'm sure that he would like to join with me in thanking you all for it," he said.

With that, he stepped back from the pulpit and began to clap. Blair immediately jumped to his feet and began clapping too. Clearly, clapping was not a sin in Father Lake's church.

"I look forward to our time together. I intend having morning and evening masses every Sunday. And, while I know it's tradition to take up a collection during services, I am suspending that tradition."

Sooley eyed him strangely.

"Our navy friends are paying us very handsomely to use the church, and it will be more than enough to cover all of our expenses. If the navy should leave in the near future we will address that when we come to it. But for now, I'd like everyone to attend church without worrying about whether or not they have anything to put in the collection plate.

"I have noticed too that our wood supply is quite low. If we are to have services here this winter then we will need more than our Lord's Spirit to keep us warm. I will be asking Mr. Sooley to organize a wood donation drive sometime in the next few days. We will, of course, need wood for the school stove too."

He paused for a moment and then continued. "I look forward to meeting with all of you in the near future in your homes and I trust that we will have a good year." With that, he bowed his head. "Thank you Lord for bringing me to this place and for giving me the opportunity to spread your word. These are God-fearing and hard-working people, Lord, who, like your Disciple Peter, are fishermen. Keep them safe on the ocean and off the ocean. Guide them from the shore to the sea and back again safely. Fill their nets with fish, their hearts with your love, and their minds with the faith of life eternal. In your name we pray, Amen."

A chorus of 'Amens' followed as Father Lake stood back and was replaced by Sooley.

"Thank you, Father Lake and Mr. Blair," Sooley said, looking in their direction. He turned back to the congregation. "It looks like there are still a few things left to eat so let's get it cleaned up and we'll see you all back here Sunday."

Everyone stood up. Lake and Blair mingled with the congregation. By then, though, everyone was anxious to get home. Tomorrow would be another day of fishing and early to bed meant an early rise.

Bill and Janet gathered up their family and made their way down the hill to their house. There was a slight chill in the air and they wanted to get home and light the stove before it got too cold. Mary was also anxious to listen to the *Gerald S. Doyle News Bulletin.* It came on the radio every evening at 8 p.m.

At home, Bill quickly gathered up wood to stoke the fire in the kitchen stove, and Mary looked impatiently at the alarm clock on the mantel over the stove. It would take a couple of minutes to warm up the radio tubes. Everything had to be timed perfectly so that the radio would only have to be on when the news was on so as to preserve the batteries. Mary was quite an expert at it now. Right on time, the news began. The Sullivans were quiet as they heard the three familiar sounds that preceded every broadcast.

"Welcome to the Broadcasting System of Newfoundland." The announcer said as he pronounced every syllable in Newfoundland.

"This is the Gerald S. Doyle News Bulletin sponsored by Gerald S. Doyle. Always use Aspirin conveniently available in the 10-tablet family package or the 12-tablet individual tin.

Today is September 5, 1942. Unfortunately, I have some very bad news to report to you this evening. We still don't have all of the details, but I am able to report to you that German U-Boats have struck again. I am sad to say that two ships were sunk off Bell Island earlier today.

The SS Saganaga was hit early this morning and it is with a very heavy heart that I tell you this evening that 29 souls perished after the boat was hit by two torpedoes.

Later in the morning the SS Lord Strathcona was sunk and I am pleased to report that there was no loss of life in the second sinking. But the loss of both of these ore carriers will no doubt have a detrimental effect on ore shipments from the mines.

We also have a report that damage was done to the conning tower of the U-Boat in its encounter with the second ship. The extent of this damage was not known at news time but as details become available we will pass them on to you, our loyal listeners."

There was a break as other items were advertised and then the family announcements began:

"Bill would like to let Winnie in Ship Harbour know that he has arrived safely in St. John's and began work yesterday. To Martha from Herbert, discharged from hospital today. Will start making way back home tomorrow."

The family announcements were a very big part of the Bulletin, especially important in rural areas that lacked telephones or any other form of communication.

Everyone listened to the messages even though they rarely knew any of the people concerned. When someone left a community, the last words were usually: 'Let us know what's happening by putting a message on the *Bulletin.'*

The rest of the broadcast dealt with death notices and other mundane issues. Mary then agreed to turn the radio off to save the batteries.

"I wonder if Captain Stewart and his crew were able to help out in Bell Island," she said to her father.

"I don't know. Mary, it depends on where they headed when they left here last night," he said. "By the way, was that you I saw up by the church when I was bringing the priest and the teacher over to Mrs. Cull's?"

Mary looked at her father, surprised that he had noticed her.

"Yes," she answered warily.

"Who were you with?"

"One of the sailors who works on the radio at the church. I met him when I went there to do the cleaning."

Her father became very serious.

"Mary, you are no longer a child. You're a young woman and a very pretty young woman."

"Oh Dad, don't embarrass me."

"All I'm trying to say to you is that these people are only here for a short while and I know what I was like when I was his age. You're a good girl and I want you to act like one. I don't want you getting into any relationships with these people. Do you understand what I'm trying to say?"

"Yes, Dad. Don't worry. We're just friends. It's nice to talk to someone who hasn't spent their entire life in Three Rock Harbour. We're friends. Just friends."

"Okay, but be careful," he finished.

Mary went to bed thinking about what her father had said and about the walk up to Gull Pond with Karl. She had barely known him a day, and yet she had feelings for him unlike those she had for any of the boys in Three Rock Harbour.

Karl's hands were soft. The other boys' hands were like sandpaper from being in the salt water so much. Karl talked nice and he had interesting things to say. Once, on their walk up to Gull Pond, she thought he wanted to kiss her but he didn't. She wasn't sure how she would have reacted if he had. She had never kissed a boy before and she wasn't sure how to do it. She wished there was a book she could read or someone she could ask about all that kind of stuff. She certainly couldn't ask her mother. There were times she wished she had an older sister to talk to. Her friends were the same age as her and they didn't talk about those kinds of things. She wasn't even sure it was something she could talk about with the nurse when she arrived in the fall.

Mary fell asleep with more questions than she had answers for. She had, however, made up her mind that if Karl tried to kiss her, she would let him. But that was it. A kiss was all she would ever permit.

CHAPTER SEVEN

Three Rock Harbour. September 4, 1942

U-*69's* mission was to patrol the region around Conception Bay, particularly St. John's. Graf's orders were to engage the enemy, especially supply ships, and sink them. Three Rock Harbour would provide a safe place to hide after an attack. The Americans might start looking in deserted coves. but they would not look in places that were inhabited. At least, that was what the German Admiralty had concluded.

It was 2100 hours when *U-69* prepared to get underway.

Graf gave the order to leave Three Rock Harbour.

The submarine would be gone for a few days and that would allow time for the new teacher and priest to get familiar with people in the community. They would also ensure there was no contact made with the outside world.

Graf ordered that the submarine use its batteries to manoeuvre out of the harbour. He didn't want to draw attention to their departure, and by using the batteries there would be little noise. Outside the harbour a few hundred feet, he ordered a switch to the engines and proceeded on at full speed. *U-69* would travel to St. John's on the surface of the water and then begin the hunt.

Graf immediately felt much better. He felt trapped in the harbour, and realized if the submarine was discovered he and his crew were helpless to defend themselves. Their only hope would be to convince whoever discovered them that they were British. That might give them 24 hours leeway before the British confirmed the boat was not theirs. After that, all hell would break loose. Confined to the harbour, the submarine would be a sitting duck.

U-69 made good progress in the calm sea and by early morning had arrived outside Conception Bay. Lookouts reported a steamer going into St. John's harbour and Graf quickly made the decision to follow it. He knew that travelling into a strange area at night and on the surface was very dangerous. There were rocks above the surface as well as below and only by traveling in the wake of a ship could he be assured of getting into a harbour safely. He estimated the ship he was following to be about 3,000 tons. He kept far enough behind to remain undetected.

"Where exactly are we now?" Graf asked his navigator, CPO Fischer.

"This is the main port, St. John's, Captain," he answered. He produced a map. "There's a narrow entrance to the harbour. I would suspect that there's a net."

Lieutenant Weber joined them.

"They have guns on the cliffs overlooking the harbour, Captain," he said. "I would strongly advise against going into the harbour."

"I agree," Graf said. "We don't need to go in. We can wait to see what comes out."

"There will be a destroyer escort for anything coming out," Weber said. "Look at the charts, Captain." Weber spread one out on the table. "There's not much water there. We couldn't go very deep to get away from the charges."

"Point taken," Graf said. "And St. John's is not our target anyway. We'll hide until tonight and then go up to periscope depth and get a good look at what is going on."

"That's Bell Island there," Becker offered, pointing to a small dot on the map. He had been looking for an opportunity to add to the conversation. Weber glared at him.

"Bell Island," Graf expanded, "is a small island that produces iron ore. Before the war, Germany was one of Bell Island's biggest buyers of iron ore. But now, Bell Island is producing iron ore that is turned into steel to make weapons to try and destroy us. Bell Island is our target."

Fischer called out orders to the helm as *U-69* moved deeper into Conception Bay. Graf could see the lights of Bell Island and used them as a beacon to move closer before giving the order to dive. The submarine slowly slid below the surface and began the descent. They would spend the night in 24 metres of water.

On September 5, at 0630 hours, Graf gave the order to begin the ascent to the surface. He wanted the ascent very slow and controlled to prevent bubbles being noticed. He positioned himself behind the periscope and waited for the submarine to break the surface. As it did, he lifted his hand and the switch on the ballast tanks was closed. All eyes were on the captain as he turned the scope to line it up.

"Damn," he said. "The fog is as thick as pea soup, I believe that is how the British put it. Take us back down and we'll wait for it to clear."

U-69 repeated the process a couple more times. Finally, at 1100 hours, it surfaced to periscope depth and the fog had cleared.

Graf turned the scope in the direction of the port.

"I can see our enemies," he said.

Weber moved into position ready to give the orders to aim the torpedoes.

Excitement spread throughout the boat. Graf checked to see if there were any destroyers nearby that could give chase after they had completed their mission.

"Ready torpedoes," he called out.

"Ready torpedoes," Weber repeated. The words were repeated several more times. Weber called out instructions to the helm to line the boat up for the attack.

"I want to move in to 350 metres. She's British. I'd estimate 9,000 tons. *Saganaga*," Graf spelled the name out. "Two should do it. Fifty metres. 25 metres." A slight pause. "Fire torpedoes."

His orders echoed through the boat. The two torpedo men pushed the buttons, releasing the weapons.

"Torpedoes away," the radioman confirmed. "They're sunk, Sir," he shouted excitedly.

"They've what?" Weber asked.

"Sunk, Sir."

"Did they change the switch from charge to fire?" Graf shouted, as he kept his eyes glued to the target. Seconds later, he got the response he didn't want.

"They didn't set the switch, Captain," Weber confirmed.

"Ready torpedoes," Graf shouted again, and two more torpedoes were readied to fire.

"It will take 10 minutes to get them loaded," Weber informed the captain.

"Keep us from drifting, Helm," Graf ordered. "I want those torpedoes loaded in record time, Lieutenant."

Weber left his position and raced to the torpedo room.

Graf continued to monitor their position, pleased to see they had apparently not been observed. The fog had been their friend.

The wait was excruciating, but Weber finally arrived back in the control room.

"Ready, Sir," he said, as he took his position.

"Set the switches," Graf ordered, and the command went through the boat.

"Switches set, Captain," Weber confirmed.

"Fire," Graf shouted. He immediately received confirmation the torpedoes were away.

Graf followed their progress from the bubbles. In seconds, an explosion rocked the U-Boat and everyone knew that the torpedoes had hit their target. A cheer went up.

"Keep those goddamn people quiet," Graf shouted. He didn't wait for a response as he yelled a change of course order to the helm.

Graf watched as all hell broke loose in the harbour.

U-69 had moved in closer than he liked.

The water was very shallow and there was very little room to manoeuvre. He gave the order to surface so that they could switch to engine power and get out of the harbour as quickly as possible. A sudden shudder went through the boat.

Graf turned the periscope. "We've been hit," he said. "We've been rammed." He yelled a course change to the helm. "Ready aft torpedoes."

A few seconds later, he got confirmation the aft torpedoes were ready for launch.

"Set the switches. *Strathcona.*" He spelled out the letters in the name of the second target ship. "Fire torpedoes," he ordered.

Seconds later, the vibrations confirmed *U-69* had its second kill.

"Put lookouts up and get us out of here," Graf ordered, as he moved away from the periscope and Weber took his place. Weber called out orders as they left the harbour, keeping an eye on the chaos behind to ensure they weren't being followed. He steered a course that took them out of the shipping lanes and into an isolated cove. Three hours later they were safely tucked away.

Two nervous torpedo men were soon standing at attention in front of Captain Graf. Chief Bosun Schneider stood beside them.

"You two endangered the lives of everyone on this boat," Graf said to them as he paced the hallway. "There is no excuse for your failure under fire. How could you forget to set the switch from battery to fire?"

The torpedo men didn't speak. They both stared straight ahead.

"Not one, but both of you, forgot to set the switches. Two torpedoes are now sitting useless and wasted. I don't know how much they cost but you can bet you'll pay for them."

For the next ten minutes, Captain Graf gave the two young submariners the dressing down of their lives. When he was finished, he had a similar conversation with Weber in private.

"You are the firing officer on this boat and you failed me," he said. "I will not tolerate a mistake like this again. Do I make myself clear?"

Graf knew Weber would be even less popular with the crew after this incident as he would drill them relentlessly until their next encounter.

The only one pleased with what had happened was Becker. He didn't want any harm coming to his crewmates, but anytime Weber made a mistake it made him look better in the captain's eyes.

Muller confirmed that damage to the conning tower was minimal and could wait until they returned to Three Rock Harbour. When darkness fell, they surfaced and returned to their pen in Three Rock Harbour.

CHAPTER EIGHT

When the fishermen of Three Rock Harbour went out to the fishing grounds the following day, they noticed that the *Sea Shark* was back at her mooring. There were a couple of sailors on the deck keeping watch and a couple more doing repairs. The sailors waved as the fishermen left the harbour. It was still barely daylight.

By 11 a.m. the fishermen were beginning to arrive back in the harbour.

When Bill passed by the *Sea Shark*, he stopped when he saw Commander Stewart.

"Good morning," he called out.

Stewart was supervising some work taking place on the top of the boat. The centre of the boat was surrounded by a covering of some kind and there were welding sparks flying off the side and down into the water.

"Good morning to you too, Bill. I trust that you did well."

"Yeah, not bad. Not bad at all. Would you like a few for your dinner?"

"Yes, thank you. I think my crew would enjoy that very much."

"Good, just a second and we'll move over beside you," Bill said.

"No," Stewart said quite suddenly. "That's fine. Go over to your wharf and I'll join you in a few minutes."

"It will only take a second to move close to you," Bill countered.

"No, no," Stewart said. "The skin on this boat is very thin. One rogue wave and we've got a problem. I'll be over there shortly."

"Okay," Bill said, as he turned the boat toward the wharf.

"I guess he just doesn't want us touching his boat," Walt said when they were out of earshot.

Bill laughed.

Twenty minutes later, Stewart and two sailors tied up to the wharf.

"Help yourself," Bill said when he saw them. The sailors threw a half dozen fish into the little boat and headed back to the submarine.

Stewart moved toward the splitting table and tossed a few coins into the can nailed on the edge of the table. It was there for people in the community who wanted to buy a fish, but there was seldom any money in it.

Janet convinced Stewart to have lunch with them and he agreed. Afterwards, as they congregated on the wharf to clean up the fish it was clear there was a job for everybody.

"I can see now that this is really a family affair," Stewart said as he saw all of Bill's family were involved in some part of the cleaning up process.

"Everyone works or no one eats," Bill said.

"So what do you do with all of this fish?" Stewart asked.

"It's salted and then at the end of the fishing season the boat comes in and gives us credit for it," Ray answered for his father.

"I'm not sure I understand what you mean by salting," Stewart said.

"Go up to the end of the wharf and have a look for yourself," Bill pointed the way.

Stewart walked up to the end of the wharf and the stage house built there. He walked over, looked inside, and recognized Janet.

"Hello Mrs. Sullivan," he greeted her.

Janet was startled. She turned quickly and said 'hello.' Shoot was there with her and said hi.

"So, this is salting," Stewart said. Shoot looked like he was about to say something but Janet held up her hand to silence him.

"Yes, we wash the fish after Bill finishes splitting them and then we lay them on the floor of the stage and cover them with salt. After 21 days we take them out of the salt, wash them, put them up there on the flakes to dry, and then store them until the boat arrives."

"There's a lot of work to this," Stewart said.

"You're right," Janet laughed. "But I don't know of many jobs that don't require work."

Stewart laughed. "You know, I can't argue with that. And now that you mention it, I had better get back to my boat."

"I see that you've really got the sparks flying out there this morning," Janet said. "What are you doing, building a piece on?"

The others in the stage laughed.

Stewart laughed too. "No, we're always doing repairs. There's always a leak to fix or an engine to repair. Good morning, Mrs. Sullivan."

Stewart walked to the wharf and waved at his boat. Seconds later, the rowboat was put in the water and a sailor began making his way to pick up the captain.

"There were a couple of ore boats sunk off Bell Island yesterday morning," Bill said as he came up behind Stewart. "Did you see any of that action?"

The question caught Stewart completely off guard. His thoughts were all over the place.

"No," he managed. "We were busy in the other direction. We were sent up to the west coast of the island."

"That's too bad," Bill said.

"How did you hear about Bell Island?" Stewart asked.

"Mary likes to listen to the *Gerald S. Doyle News Bulletin* every night before we go to bunk. We were listening to it last night and we got the news."

"Oh, that's right, you have a radio," Stewart said. He feared the worse. If Lake and Blair had let anyone communicate with the outside he would shoot them himself.

"Yes, we do," said Bill. "One of the older people here died a few years ago and left Mary his radio. The batteries are getting low now so we don't listen to it for very long. When the batteries finally go dead, I doubt whether I will have the money to buy new ones."

"I think we might be able to come up with a few batteries for you before we leave," Stewart said, as he stepped down into the rowboat that had just arrived at the wharf.

There was a sudden splash that got everyone's attention.

"What was that?" Bill shouted.

Everyone looked around.

"Was that one of the youngsters? Who's looking after the youngsters?" Bill yelled.

There was a scream from the other side of the wharf and everyone ran in that direction. Stewart scrambled back onto the wharf.

The woman continued to scream.

"Someone save my baby. Someone save my baby."

Bill ran to the side of the wharf and looked down. He watched as a little boy of about three thrashed around and slowly began sinking to the bottom.

"Who can swim?" he yelled.

Before the words were out of his mouth, there was another splash. A man dove into the water and everyone watched in total awe as he came up underneath the sinking boy. With a single kick, he forced himself and the boy to the surface as the mother continued to scream.

Holding the little boy above the surface of the water, Captain Stewart made a couple of kicks and was beside the wharf. Quickly, he climbed up on the ladder and passed the child's lifeless body to Bill.

Once Stewart was up on the wharf, he grabbed the boy from Bill. As he placed him face up on the wharf he began pressing down on his chest. After the first few compressions, the little blond boy with the blue eyes and sunburned face lifted his head and coughed. A gush of seawater spewed out, followed by a whimper.

Everyone finally began to breathe. The mother stopped screaming and someone helped her to her son. Stewart passed the child to her. When she was sure the boy was okay, she began a tirade.

"How many times have I told you to stay away from the edge of the wharf? How many times have I told you that you're going to fall over and the sculpins are going to eat you? You little devil," she ranted, as she made her way up the wharf.

Suddenly she stopped, and every eye was upon her. She made an about face and marched back to Stewart. The child's feet barely touched the wharf as she dragged him along with her.

"Thank the man for saving your life, although I don't know why he would bother," she said.

The boy didn't look up but managed a very weak, "Thank you."

"You're welcome, young man," Commander Stewart answered, "Just listen to your mother the next time."

"There won't be a next time," she snapped. "If he ever falls off this wharf again, I'll drown him."

Everyone smiled but no one laughed.

"Thank you, Sir," the woman said before she turned away. "If you'll come up to the house I'll get you some dry clothes."

"No, that's fine. I have a change of clothes on the boat."

It didn't take long for word to spread that Commander Stewart had saved the life of the young Sparkes boy. Those on the wharf who had witnessed the event offered their congratulations. Many were heard saying they should learn how to swim. They said too that had it not been for Commander Stewart the new priest would be holding his first funeral service.

When the fish had been cleaned and salted, the tables washed down, and the boats cleaned, the fishermen went home to rest before they went out again. Stewart returned to his submarine to supervise the work being done on the deck. For a couple of hours, everything was quiet in Three Rock Harbour.

Mid-afternoon, Mary went to the church to do some dusting, even though there was really no need to dust. She just wanted to see Karl again. She combed her hair, thought about changing her dress, but didn't want her mother asking questions, and so just smoothed out the wrinkles. She told her mother she was going up to the church to make sure everything was ready for the Sunday service. Her father raised his eyebrows in response. He knew the real reason she was going to the church.

"Remember what I said, young lady," he warned, as she was leaving.

Mary made her way up the path to the church and lifted the latch. It wouldn't open. That had never happened before. She wondered why there was a lock on the church door. She knocked a couple of times. In a few minutes, Karl opened the door.

"Hello," he said, obviously surprised to see her. "I didn't expect to see you here this afternoon."

"I don't have to check with you when I want to come and clean the church," she said.

"No, that's not what I meant," he replied.

"Why is this door locked? The church door has never been locked?"

"We didn't want anyone disturbing us when we are working on the radio," he answered. "We have to keep our communications secret."

"Even if one of us heard something, who would we tell?" she laughed.

Karl laughed too. "That's a good point," he said. "I guess we never thought of that. I suppose it's the nature of our business to always be suspicious."

"Fine, then let me in to do my cleaning," Mary said. Karl looked behind to ensure that the door to the radio room was closed before holding the door open for her. Mary brushed by him as she went in.

With Karl watching, Mary dusted off the benches, wiped the window ledges, and swept the floor.

"Don't you have something better to do then to watch me?" she asked.

"I like watching you," he said. "I like watching you very much. I told you that all I get to see are sailors, and when I see a pretty girl I like to look as long as I can."

Mary couldn't remember anyone ever calling her pretty beside her father. She was a little embarrassed.

"You shouldn't be saying things like that in church," she said.

Karl laughed. "So, should I be saying that you're ugly?"

"That's not what I meant. This is the Lord's house. We don't say things like that here. Anyway, I bet you've seen a lot of girls who are prettier than me."

Karl paused for a few seconds. "No, I don't think that I have. In fact. I know that I haven't."

"You're making fun of me now," Mary said.

"No, honestly I'm not. From the first time I saw you I was convinced you were the prettiest girl I had ever seen."

Mary smiled and kept on dusting.

"Can we go outside for a while and look at the harbour? I don't think there is much dust because it would be afraid to come in here," said Karl.

Mary laughed. "Okay, but just for a little while," she said. "I have to go home soon to help Mom with supper. Dad and my brothers will be going out on the water in a little while."

Karl held the door for her as they went out to sit by the rock they'd sat by before. As they looked down at the harbour they could see the boats tied up at the wharves, bobbing up and down.

"It sure is quiet here," Karl said. "This must be a wonderful place to grow up."

Mary laughed. "You have got to be joking. There's nothing here but fish and boats. There are no places to go, nothing to do, and nobody new to see. I can't wait to finish school so I can go to St. John's and go to work."

"I could live here for the rest of my life," Karl said. "I love the peace and quiet and the open spaces. And I haven't met a person yet who didn't say hello and ask me how I was. When you leave here you are going to see what it's like on the outside. People don't talk to you even if they live next door. They would rather steal from you than talk to you and you'll wish you were back home."

"You must have been raised in a horrible place," Mary said.

"It certainly wasn't as nice as this and there certainly weren't people there as nice as you."

He looked at her and she looked at him. He was taller than her and they both had the same colour hair. He looked a little skinny. She would try and remember to bring him some good home-cooked food the next time she came to the church.

"What are you eating anyway?" she blurted out.

"Wow! Where did that come from?" he laughed.

"Oh, sorry. I didn't mean it to come out like that. It's just that you need a little more meat on your bones." she said, as she reached to pinch him.

"Ow," he said, as he grabbed her hand and held it. "Your hands are so nice and soft."

"Soft? One minute my hands are scrubbing dirty clothes and the next minute I'm cleaning fish. You might say a lot of things about my hands but they're not soft," she said.

He didn't say anything as he held her hand. He slowly pulled her towards him. She watched as he closed his eyes and she closed her eyes too. He was going to kiss her, and she had already decided that she would let him. Should I moisten my lips, she thought? What do I smell like? Do I stink of fish? His mouth moved towards hers and it seemed natural that she should open her mouth a little. His kiss was gentle and for the first time she realized how sensitive her lips were. She made a pleasurable sound and felt so overwhelmed with emotion it was like she was floating on air. Then he moved a little closer and his hard body pressed against her chest. Her nipples were so erect she was sure he could feel them through her jacket. His lips against hers and the feeling of his body against her body filled her with sensations she had never thought possible.

Karl suddenly pulled away from her. "You have never been kissed by a boy before, have you?" he laughed.

"There's no need to make fun of me," she snapped.

"I wasn't making fun of you, honest. I don't know why I said it. But I'm glad because I will always be the person who gave you your first kiss. Nothing can change that."

They heard a sound coming from behind the rock. It was an unmistakeable snicker. Mary jumped to her feet and looked around the rock.

"Shoot, you little devil," she said, as she saw the source of the snicker. "What are you doing up here?"

Shoot was sitting with his back to the rock and his face buried in his hands.

"I asked you a question. What are you doing up here spying on me? I should give you such a licking that you won't be able to sit down for a week."

Shoot took his hands away from his face and stood up. "I'm sorry Mare." He always called her that. "Mom told me to come tell you to come down and help with supper. I came up the back way so that I could surprise you. Surprise," he said meekly.

Karl laughed.

"I'm not laughing," Mary said, as she reached for the back of his shirt and began leading him down the hill. She didn't even stop to say goodbye to Karl.

"What did you hear?" she asked Shoot when they were away from Karl.

"I didn't hear nothing," he answered.

"Anything," she snapped. "You didn't hear anything. Then why were you snickering?"

He didn't know what to say.

"Answer me," she demanded.

"You were talking mushy stuff," he said, as he got ready to start crying.

"Don't you dare cry," she ordered. "We weren't talking mushy stuff. We were just talking."

"Okay," he answered.

"I don't want you telling Mom and Dad or anyone else about this. Do you understand?"

He nodded.

"Who was that person," Shoot asked after they had walked a little while.

"He's one of the sailors from the boat. Now remember, I don't want you talking about this and we agreed. Right?"

"Right, Mare," he answered.

They continued the walk home and as they did Mary put her fingers to her lips. Shoot couldn't have seen us kiss because he was behind the rock, she thought, as the tingling feeling returned. So that's what a kiss feels like, she thought.

Once home, Mary helped her mother with supper. They were having moose soup and her mother had already begun the work of chopping the vegetables. As the turnip and carrots were chopped, Mary threw them into the boiling pot. Her father particularly liked parsnip in his soup and so she peeled one, chopped it, and threw it in. She finished peeling and chopping the potatoes and left them soaking in a bowl of water. They would be the last to go in the pot. The soup would be ready for the 4 p.m. meal.

The smell of the soup filled the house. Janet was darning socks and Bill was on the daybed having a nap. The rest of the family were scattered around the house and garden. Mary set the table and put the freshly baked bread away in the breadbox. She put two loaves on the table. They would be devoured at supper, and possibly even a third loaf.

Fifteen minutes later, Mary threw the potatoes in the pot. A half hour after that, all that remained were bread crumbs, dirty bowls, and moose bones scattered all over the table.

Bill and his sons then made their way down to the boat. This time, Bob was allowed to go because the sea was calm. Before Bob left, his mother gave him orders to make sure he stayed away from everyone when they were working. She said if he fell over and drowned she would kill him when he got home.

Janet and Mary and Shoot cleaned up after supper. Shoot always protested doing what he called woman's work to no avail. "Soon, I'll be able to go out in the boat," he would say as he dried the dishes. He muttered to himself as he worked and occasionally his mother would tell him to stop acting like a baby. She'd say she couldn't wait for the day she didn't have to listen to his mumbling anymore. All the while she was praying that he would never grow up and go out on the water where she would have to worry about him as she did the rest of her family.

Janet loved her family and her life in Three Rock Harbour. She could ask for nothing more. But every time the boat left the wharf she worried about not seeing her family again. She hated it when they all went out in the boat together. She took consolation in the fact they were never out there by themselves. There were always other fishermen in the area and they could see each other. Today, the wind was calm and the seas were calm and she wouldn't worry as much. But she would still be relieved when she saw the boat return.

The men had a good catch and by 8 p.m. they had everything salted and ready for the morning. As Bill watched the setting sun he was certain it would be a fine day. Wind was the fishermen's curse. The wind could come up without warning, making them scatter to the closest shelter. Sometimes, they had to spend days waiting out a storm in some cove while their families waited, not knowing if they were dead or alive until they saw them coming back into the harbour.

This day, however, everyone was safe in Three Rock Harbour. As the kerosene lamps were blown out only one remained lit. The one in the church where one sailor slept and the other sat with headphones on, listening to ships talking to each other and making notes in a language that made sense only to them and their fellow sailors. Messages were passed on to Commander Stewart who then decided whether or not the submarine stayed in the harbour or went to sea. The sleeping sailor was dreaming of Mary and her first kiss. It had not been his first, but it certainly had been his best.

CHAPTER NINE

School started at 9 a.m. on the Monday after Labour Day. It was a warm day and so there was no need to light a fire in the potbelly stove in the centre of the classroom. When school started, all of the students entered through the main door of the church and it became necessary to keep the door to the radio room closed all the time. The students had been told to stay away from the areas where the radio room was located. Mr. Blair reminded them of that on their first day.

The students were in one room in the church. Everyone had a slate to write on and there was a blackboard at the front for the teacher to use. There were 43 students. The older students were expected to help the younger ones when they were finished with their own work. The older the students, the less time the teacher spent with them.

Mary was the only senior student. This would be her last year, and Mr. Blair had already told her he had reviewed his predecessor's reports and she would be more of a teacher's assistant than a student. This would assist her greatly when she got her first teaching job. He said he could also help her find a school where she could teach when she finished school. The thought intrigued Mary, but it frightened her more than anything. She would have to give it a lot of thought.

Captain Graf and his sailors had finally finished doing the work topside on the submarine and were getting ready for another patrol. They were very much aware that they had to be very careful with their radio communications and ensure they kept their transmissions brief. No one knew they were in Three Rock Harbour. They had become aware that the United States Naval Coast Guard had set up a top-secret radio receiver and transmitter at Mouse Island near Port Aux Basques on Newfoundland's west coast. It was part of the LORAN (Long Range Navigation) system being installed throughout Newfoundland. Besides Mouse Island, other locations included Sandy Cove on Fogo Island, Battle Harbour in Labrador and Fort Pepperell in St. John's. The system's primary mission was to monitor U-Boat activity and provide navigation aids to Allied vessels. All of the plotting data was sent to Fort Pepperell for analysis. Based upon a ship's radio signals, its location could be determined.

Even though Graf was sending coded information to his German superiors there were very few people who knew about his mission. Transmissions from the radio room in the church were forbidden. So, whenever Graf needed to communicate with his superiors he did it at sea and then quickly moved to a new location. The role of the radio room in the church was to listen and determine the location of enemy shipping.

During *U-69's* last patrol, to Bell Island, the crew had picked up a passenger. He was Captain Martel of *PLM 27*, a free French ship under the orders of General De Gaulle. Graf was aware that Martel was likely a spy who was providing information on enemy shipping locations. Martel had a wealth of information, and for the past few days he had been undergoing debriefing sessions aboard the submarine. During *U-69's* next patrol, Martel would be returned to his ship. Before leaving his ship, Martel had advised his crew that he would be away for a while and could not reveal his orders. The crew were to remain in port and await his return.

Martel was an expert on the new, more complex Triton Code equipment that had replaced the Hydra Code equipment in February of that year. He provided some necessary training to *U-69's* communication staff. He also knew how to read the enemy's code, and he provided the necessary training for that as well.

On the evening of September 13, *U-69* left Three Rock Harbour on its second patrol. The plan was also to drop Martel off at a discreet location where he could rejoin his ship.

Thanks to the previous evening's *Gerald S. Doyle News Bulletin*, everyone in Three Rock Harbour knew the boat from Trepassey would be arriving the next day to pick up the fish that was ready for shipping. An agreement had been made with Captain Stewart that they could sell their catch, but he said he would credit them an equal amount for what they sold. Everyone was praying that the price of salt fish would be up this year, but that was something completely out of their hands. Since the war, the price of cod had increased. They'd heard on the *Bulletin* about some of the prices other fishermen were being paid. But the merchant who bought their fish always had a reason why he didn't pay that price. Money never changed hands and all they ever received were credit notes in Paul Arns store.

The fish would have to be taken from the stages and wheeled down to the wharf to be loaded aboard the ship, where it would be graded and weighed. Few of the fishermen could read or write. They had to depend on their children to make sure everything was counted and recorded correctly. Fish was graded by size and quality. The bigger the fish and the better the quality, the higher the price. Fishermen were given a price per quintal (112 pounds).

It seemed the merchants would do anything to do the fishermen out of what was rightfully theirs. The problem was that if a fisherman couldn't sell his fish he and his family would starve. So, whatever the merchant offered they had to accept, as no one else would come to Three Rock Harbour to buy fish. The merchants all had their own clearly delineated territories. These monopolies made them very rich men at the expense of the fishermen.

In addition to grading the fish using their own rules, the merchants artificially determined the price. Some went so far as to adjust their scales so that the established weight of a quintal was changed significantly without the fisherman's knowledge. Fishermen could be credited for 112 pounds of fish when they were actually selling as much as 125 pounds. All the fishermen got for their fish was a credit note in the merchant's store where prices for everything, including the salt they needed to cure the fish, were inflated, costing many times higher than in St. John's. If someone had to leave the community for medical treatment, the only way to get cash money was to go to the merchant's store and ask for a loan from their credit note. The fishermen were always at the merchant's mercy.

On the day that the ship from Trepassey arrived, the men did not go fishing. Everyone in Three Rock Harbour pitched in to help with the transporting and the weighing of fish.

Mary, who earned a few extra dollars selling her jam to the cook on the ship, stood by as the fish were graded and weighed. She kept a tally on her slate, and when all was finished she matched her total to that on her father's credit note. There was a one-quintal difference and she mentioned it to her father, but he said 'shush.' It would serve no purpose to argue as his catch was now mixed with the other fishermen's fish.

Mr. Blair and Father Lake watched the proceedings from a safe distance. It was their job to ensure there was no mention of the submarine. Every person in the community knew that one slip meant that the submarine would have to leave and with it would go all the extra money they had been promised.

By mid-afternoon, all the fish had been loaded and the community shop re-stocked. Credit notes were issued and balances on overdrawn accounts reduced. Small credit balances remained, but by the time the merchant came to buy fish again, the accounts would be overdrawn. The fishermen were always indebted to the merchant.

The technician who could fix the radio transmitter in Arns' shop was on the ship from Trepassey. As the fish was being loaded aboard, he set to work repairing the radio transmitter. By mid-afternoon, it was working and he returned to the ship to help with the loading.

As the technician went out one door, Karl came in the other. His job was to ensure there were no unauthorized transmissions. While Arns was down at the wharf, Karl removed one of the tubes from the radio transmitter. The transmitter could now be used intermittently. The Americans at Mouse Island would notice the signal from Three Rock Harbour and discount it. If there were ever a need for the Germans to use their radio transmitter, the Americans would think it was the one in Arns' store. Later that day, Karl would explain to Arns how things were going to work. After all, he'd say, he and Arns were on the same side in this war.

In late October, the ship from Trepassey would return on its final call for the year. Once the latest load of salted fish was picked up, the fishermen would haul up their boats. Only the dories would remain close to the shore so that they could hunt for seals, their main source of meat for the winter.

The rest of this particular day was spent tending to the vegetable gardens. The wind had come up and Bill decided he would stay on shore until the next morning.

In another week they would be digging potatoes and putting them in the cellar. Later the carrots and turnips would be dug and placed in bins in the cellar too. But it wasn't until the snow was on the ground that the cabbage was cut and put with the other vegetables.

Blueberries were already being picked and turned into jam. The store had run out of sugar a few weeks earlier, but now that it was restocked jam could be made again. Bakeapple jam had already been made and the jars filled an entire shelf in the cellar. By the end of the month, partridgeberries would be ripe and they too would be turned into jam.

Several buckets in the Sullivan cellar were filled with salt and pieces of moose that would be a welcome winter treat, boiled in the same pot with the vegetables. Chickens would be killed when they stopped laying eggs. For Christmas, they would slaughter a lamb. Bill would also put a salt lick in the woods and when the moose got accustomed to going to it, he would be able to place a snare and trap one. He had a rifle, but bullets were in short supply.

Mary had observed Karl going to Arns' shop and leaving with something wrapped in brown paper. After supper she walked up the hill to the church and knocked on the door. Karl answered.

"This is an unexpected pleasure," he said.

"That will depend on your answer to my questions," she said sharply.

Her response caught him off guard. "What's the matter?" he asked, as he held the door open for her to come inside.

"I saw you go into Arns' store and leave with a package. What did you steal?" she asked.

"I didn't steal anything," he answered.

"You didn't have the package with you when you went in and you had it with you when you came out. So, you had to have taken something from the store. That's stealing."

"You don't understand," he tried to explain.

"Well then, explain it to me. I'm not stupid. I may not have sailed all over the world but I'm not stupid. Tell me how you can go into a place with nothing and come out with something and it's not stealing."

"It was a radio tube."

"So you stole a radio tube," she said.

"I didn't really steal it. You see, we have to control transmissions from here. We can't let it slip that we are here. I was acting under orders. I was given an order that as soon as the radio transmitter was fixed, I had to take control of it. Arns will still be able to use the radio transmitter. It's just that either Max or I have to be there when it's being used. So, you see, I didn't really steal it." His eyes pleaded for her understanding.

Mary paused for a few seconds before speaking. "I don't know whether to believe you or not. If I thought that you stole something from Mr. Arns I would never forgive you. But your story, as ridiculous at it sounds, is probably true."

"Thank you," Karl said, with obvious relief in his voice. "I will be meeting with Arns later to let him know what I've done."

"Good," she said, "and sooner rather than later."

"Don't I get a goodnight kiss?" he asked.

"Not tonight," she said, as she turned and left without looking back.

Karl followed her with his eyes until she was below the hill and then he closed the door. When he turned around, Max was there. Max Adler had replaced Peter.

"I don't know what you're up to with that girl," said Max, "but all you're letting yourself in for is trouble. And if the captain finds out, there will be hell to pay."

"The captain is not going to find out unless you tell him. And if you tell him then it will be the sorriest day of your life."

"We're going to be leaving here someday so why do you want to get yourself all hot and bothered over a little tramp like her?" Max said, with a smirk on his face.

The words were barely out of his mouth before Karl punched him and he fell to the floor. "How dare you talk about her like that? If you ever mention her name again, I'll kill you. You understand?"

Max got up from the floor, rubbing his jaw. "You really are screwed up," he said, as he turned and went into the radio room.

CHAPTER TEN

Captain Graf ordered his men to harbour stations to begin the process of leaving Three Rock Harbour. As before, he moved out of the harbour under battery power. When safely out of earshot, he ordered the main engines started.

The diesel engines came to life. Puffs of smoke billowed from exhaust vents as the oil was burned off. Slowly, the boat moved forward towards the open sea. Several sailors stayed on the deck to make sure there was nothing floating, dead logs and the like, that could strike the boat and cause damage. The sun was rapidly setting and there was a full moon so it was easy to navigate to open water.

"Ready for sea, Sir," Graf heard one of the officers yell from the belly of the boat.

"Take her out," he called back, holding on tightly as the increased power made the boat vibrate as she surged forward.

U-69 had a range of 5000 nautical miles at 17 knots while surfaced, and a range of only 56 nautical miles at two knots when submerged. It could crash dive in 25 seconds. The diesel engines were inoperable when the submarine was submerged. The only way to propel the boat then was by batteries and as a result the batteries were drained very quickly. When and where possible the boat traveled on the surface of the ocean, only submerging when it was absolutely necessary. The batteries were always being charged when the diesel engines were operating. The sub had a special pipe installed that allowed it to sink to periscope depth and still have the engines running. However, with the constant swell of the Atlantic Ocean, it made running in that situation often times impractical.

U-69's main eyes and ears were its hydrophones, two pairs of underwater microphones that listened for propeller noises. By measuring the time it took for sound to travel to each of the microphones, the device could tell the type and location of another vessel, but not its range or speed. Because sound travels much farther underwater, hydrophones could pick up ships up to a 100 kilometres away. To be totally effective, though, the submarine had to stop all engines in order to listen.

All that separated the sailors from the ocean was the sub's steel hull. When submerged and under attack from depth charges, the sailors had to be very careful not to touch the hull. The vibration from the explosion could extend into their bodies and kill them instantly. On a submarine, the difference in temperature between the cold exterior and the warm interior resulted in condensation. Sailors used electric heaters to get rid of moisture when going to bed. They covered themselves with oilcloths. In the morning, the folds in the oilcloths were filled with water.

Commanders had to be particularly careful when firing torpedoes because the weight of the torpedo leaving the boat affected its buoyancy. Ballast tanks had to be constantly monitored. Buoyancy was also affected by the salinity of the seawater; something that remained constant in the Atlantic Ocean, except where major rivers flowed into it.

It was dark by the time *U-69* left the harbour and, with a remote chance the boat could be detected, it ran on the surface. The crew's mission was to deliver Captain Martel to a point where he could get to his ship. *PLM 27* was moored in Harbour Grace. It would take approximately 15 hours to travel to Harbour Grace, which meant the boat would have to travel on the surface for an extended period. That would not be advisable considering the number of ships in the area, so at dawn Graf would seek out some isolated cove and spend the daylight hours there.

By 6 a.m. the submarine was nestled in a little cove in Great Island. Graf had adjusted the buoyancy so that only a small portion of the boat was above water, making detection very difficult. The radioman constantly monitored the area. If anything was seen or heard, the boat could submerge very quickly.

At 8 p.m. they were ready to get underway again. Giving St. John's a wide berth, they dropped Captain Martel off near Carbonear. He would make his way to Harbour Grace overland.

U-69 was badly in need of fuel and provisions. During their last encounter with the enemy, six of her torpedoes had been used and needed to be replaced. The Germans had set up a covert fuel dump where fuel drums and other items were stored on Baccalieu Island, off the northernmost tip of the Avalon Peninsula. Food and mail was also stored there. Graf had been there before and knew that it was an isolated spot and the chance of being observed by anything other than birds was remote.

U-69 arrived at its destination shortly before dawn, but had to stay offshore until evening because there were several fishing boats in the area. When the area was finally clear, the crew went ashore and located the cache of supplies.

They had to be very careful not to leave any record of their visit. The oil drums were left in place and a hose run from them to the boat. Fortunately, it was calm and the transfer was made without incident. Food and mail were loaded on next. The most difficult part of the transfer was the torpedoes.

The five metre long 'cigars' were hard to handle even with proper hoisting rigs, but to do it in the dark and from a rock at the edge of the North Atlantic made for a very challenging event. Once the torpedoes were loaded, the boat moved away from the area and Graf found a place to hide until the following day.

Communications from all ships in the area were constantly monitored to determine the location of enemies or Allies. German U-Boats always ended their messages with a report on their fuel consumption. The Allies could tell when they decrypted their messages how far they had traveled since their last message was sent. *U-69* had the ability to decipher messages and search for targets. But now, after restocking the submarine, the crew was given a chance to rest and read their eagerly awaited mail.

No one knew *U-69's* location so they could not be given direct orders to seek out and destroy. And, fearing their messages might be deciphered by the enemy, Graf did not communicate with his German superiors. There was reasonable assurance of the security of their system based on the last code change, but he wanted to be absolutely sure.

During the evening meal, Graf was contacted by the radioman.

"I have a contact, Sir," he reported.

Less than ten minutes later, they were underway.

The radioman had intercepted a message from Allied communications that a U-Boat was being pursued. As *U-69* headed for the battle scene, the crew readied for combat. However, they didn't communicate with their sister U-Boat. *U-69* assisted with the battle and slunk away like a deadly wolf.

Two days later, when *U-69* arrived back in Three Rock Harbour it was two torpedoes short of its complement. Graf and his crew had sunk another enemy ship. They were all in high spirits.

When Bill and his boys left for the fishing grounds on Saturday morning they could see the submarine was back in the harbour. There was a night watch who waved at them as they left. Bill determined that when he returned he would invite Commander Stewart to the Saturday evening get together.

Once a month, on Saturday evening, a social was held in the school. People came together to socialize and dance. Roger Foley played the accordion while his brother Sam played the fiddle. The women made sandwiches and cookies. The men had enough moonshine to lift their spirits.

Earlier that afternoon, Karl had asked Mary if she would accompany him to the dance and she agreed.

By 7 p.m. the party was in full swing. The men had stashed their liquor outside the school, and when the women wanted to dance they went looking for them. It was acceptable to drink the liquor outside the church but not to bring it inside.

By 8 p.m. when Commander Stewart arrived, everyone was in high spirits. Bill met him at the door.

"Good evening," he slurred.

"Good evening, Bill," he responded with a smile. "I see that you're enjoying yourself."

"Yes, I am. Maybe I could interest you in a drink."

"I'd like that," he said, as Bill took his arm and led him outside.

Bill had a half-filled bottle near the fence and he headed for it. He picked it up and passed it to Stewart who took a look and drained nearly one quarter of it.

"I see that you are no stranger to moonshine," Bill laughed.

Bill didn't know it, but U-Boat captains often went ashore in Newfoundland and attended dances posing as British sailors. Once there, they got a wealth of information about shipping.

Stewart wiped his mouth with the back of his hand and passed the bottle back to Bill.

"We have something very much like that in my country," he said, "but we call it by a different name."

"No matter what you call it, it still warms your insides," Bill laughed. "Let's go inside and see if we can find a widow so you can have a scuff."

Bill looked at him. "Scuff?" he asked.

"Dance, bye, have a dance," Bill laughed.

The two men headed for the door. Stewart was able to walk in a straight line but Bill had difficulty doing the same. Janet was waiting as they entered.

"It looks like the best you'll be able to manage is to sit down," she said to her husband. "Would you like to dance with me, Commander Stewart?"

"I'd be honoured if your husband doesn't object," he said.

"No, no, go ahead. Dance with her," Bill laughed. "See if you can keep up with her because I can't." He made his way to a chair near the wall and sat down.

The musicians began playing a waltz and Stewart took Janet's hand and led her to the floor. He led her around the dance floor as others paused to watch.

"You dance beautifully," he said.

"You're not so bad yourself," she said. "It's quite a change from being pulled around the floor like a sack of flour by Bill."

"Oh I don't think it's that bad," he said.

"My Bill is the most wonderful husband, father and provider in the world but he's also the worst dancer," she laughed.

Janet flitted around the dance floor and never felt lighter on her feet. "Don't you go away, Commander Stewart, because before this night is over we are going to dance again," she said after the waltz.

"It's Tony, please," he said, as he escorted her back to where Bill was sitting.

At that moment, Stewart saw something that immediately caught his eye. He'd thought the only submarine crew at the social were himself, Blair, and Lake, but now he spotted Karl sitting with a very pretty young girl whom he recognized as Sullivan's daughter. Karl stood up as soon as he saw his captain. Stewart indicated he wanted to see Karl outside. Karl excused himself and followed his captain.

Stewart walked away from the others with Karl following followed him. When they were far enough away that they couldn't be heard, Stewart stopped to face him.

"What the hell do you think you're doing here?" he asked.

"I was invited here by Mary?" Karl lied.

"Why did she invite you? How did you meet her? Are you out of your goddamn mind?" The captain could hardly keep from shouting.

"I met her here at the church when she came to clean it," said Karl.

Stewart was fuming. He wrung his fists in frustration.

"Is it your intention to jeopardize this entire mission? You know how sensitive this is and we could be discovered at any time. Just one slip and you could endanger us all. Is that the regard in which you hold your fellow crew?"

"No sir. I didn't think it would do any harm. It's just that it's been so long..."

Stewart cut him off. "I don't care how long it's been. But I will tell you one thing. It's going to be a lot longer. You get your ass back to the boat and I don't want to see you ashore again until this mission is over. You don't go anywhere but directly to the boat. You don't speak to that girl or to anyone else in this village. Am I clear?"

"But, Sir, I was just dancing with her. Nothing will slip. It will be fine," Karl tried to argue.

"If you say another word I will have you shot. No, I will shoot you. Now about face and get back to the boat and I will deal with you there. Make sure that someone returns the rowboat for me. I will talk with the girl's mother and tell her about the mistake you have made."

Karl reluctantly turned and headed down the hill toward the boat as Stewart returned to the dance and walked over to Janet.

"Mrs. Sullivan," he said, "I just ordered one of my crew back to my boat. He was here with your daughter and..."

"It's Janet and I've told you that several times," she broke in. "Yes, I saw that and my husband said it was okay but I was against it. Thank you very much for doing what you did."

"You're welcome. I trust you will explain to your daughter that such a liaison is not appropriate and that her friend will be confined to the ship for the rest of his stay."

"Yes, I will do that," she said.

"Thank you. Now, I've had a very difficult day and if you'll excuse me, I'll return to my ship after I say goodbye to Bill and a few of the other men. Thank you for the lovely dance and hopefully we can do it again sometime."

"You're welcome, and yes, I hope that we can do it again sometime in the future."

Stewart left as Janet went over to speak with Mary.

"I just spoke with Commander Stewart," she said, as she sat next to her daughter. "The young man has been ordered to return to his ship and that's where he will remain until they leave."

Mary looked at her mother incredulously. "Why?" was all she could manage.

"Because it's not right," Janet answered.

"What was wrong with it? We were here dancing like everyone else. He wasn't drinking like every other man here. He wasn't fighting and he was just here talking with me."

"He's older then you and I don't want you getting attached to someone who'll be leaving here one day and you'll never see again. He's a sailor for goodness sake. He has a girl in every port."

"He doesn't have a girl in every port and he's only a little older than I am. Dad is five years older than you. It's not as if we were getting married or anything. We were just talking and dancing." Mary jumped up from her chair and stormed out of the school mumbling to herself.

She continued mumbling as she walked down the hill towards her house. Without warning, Karl stepped out from behind a house. She was about to scream when she recognized him and quickly covered her face with her hand.

"I'm sorry, Mary, but I've been ordered back to the boat," he said.

"I know. Mom told me," she said. "But why?"

"The captain doesn't want me associating with you because he's afraid I might say something that would let you know what our mission is."

Mary laughed. "Even if I did know, who could I tell? You could be men from Mars and it would make no difference."

"We're not from Mars, Mary. That's something I can tell you for certain," he said, smiling. "But there are things about us that if you knew, it would change a lot of things."

"What things?" she asked.

"I can't tell you about it. I've got to go. I don't want to go but I've been ordered to return to the boat. Mary, I don't know what I'm going to do if I can't see you anymore."

"I'll miss you too, Karl. I have to be honest with you. You're different than any boy I've ever met."

Karl took both of her hands in his as he leaned forward and kissed her. She didn't resist. He let go of her hands and embraced her. This time he kissed her more passionately and she responded.

"Oh, I'm going to miss you," he said.

"Me too," she said. "But you'd better get back to your boat before the captain sees you and you'll really be in trouble."

"Yes, you're right. I have to go. But I'll want to talk to you." He paused for a few seconds as he moved away from her. "I'll get a message to you. I don't know how but I'll get a message to you." He took a few more steps. "I know," he said. "I'll have to do night watch as punishment. You keep a lookout for me on the deck. I will stop every few minutes and wave. Then you'll know it's me. I'll write to you and put it in a container and throw it over the side when the tide is in. Then you can get it. Okay?"

She nodded her head and watched as he ran down the hill toward the rowboat. "Goodbye," she whispered.

Commander Stewart said his goodbyes before going to the radio room where Max was on watch. He banged on the door.

"So you finally decided to relieve me," Max said as he moved to the door and opened it. When he saw his captain, his mouth dropped. "Sorry, Sir. I thought it was Karl. Sorry, Sir." Max snapped his heels together and saluted.

Stewart stepped inside and closed the door.

"Did you know Karl was seeing that young Sullivan girl?"

"Yes, Sir," Max answered.

"Then why in the hell wasn't it reported?" he demanded.

"I have no excuse, Sir."

"Are you doing the same thing with some other girl?" Stewart asked.

"No, Sir. I just do my duty, Sir."

"I hope so," Stewart said. "I will be sending a replacement ashore and I warn you that if this happens again you both will be shot. Is that clear?"

"Yes, Sir. Perfectly clear."

Stewart turned and left the radio room. The father of the boy whose life he'd saved was waiting outside. Like Bill, the man had been drinking and it took five minutes for Stewart to get clear of him. Finally, Stewart was back at the wharf where a member of the crew was waiting to row him across to the submarine. He would be glad when this day was finally over.

CHAPTER ELEVEN

As the days grew shorter, the weather turned colder in Three Rock Harbour. There were more bad days than good days, and it was during the bad days when they couldn't go fishing that the fishermen repaired their nets and other gear. The downside of the bad days was that when they weren't fishing they weren't making any money.

As winter approached, a change came over Three Rock Harbour. The grass turned brown, the leaves of the birch trees created a kaleidoscope of colour and everything prepared for the winter sleep. But just as nature was entering its dormant cycle, Mary Sullivan was becoming more vibrant, more alive, and more desirous of companionship. Not the companionship of family and friends, but the companionship of the opposite sex.

Mary had turned 17 and there wasn't a boy in Three Rock Harbour who would not have given anything to be with her. In school, all the boys sought her help just to be near her. Even some of the married men discreetly expressed their thoughts about her to each other, but never when Bill was around.

Mary, however, thought only of Karl. None of the other boys in the community interested her. Karl's soft touch, his kind words, and gentle manner stirred feelings in her that she really didn't understand and that she couldn't discuss with her mother.

After the social, Karl was punished and had to spend the night on deck as a guard. Mary got up from her warm bed and made her way down to the shore. When he saw her, he waved.

Most nights now when she went to sleep she could see him standing on the deck of the submarine. When she waved at him, he returned the wave. He sent his first note to her via the tide a few days after the social.

It was dark and Mary was on the shore just a hundred feet away from the boat when he threw a can into the water. Within a few minutes the tide brought the can to her. She had difficulty getting it and decided the next time she would bring a dip net. When she finally had the can in her hand she wanted to call out to him, but dared not for fear of alerting the others. She waved as he blew her a kiss and she scurried home with her precious package.

She crept into the house, careful not to awaken the others. She lit the lamp in the kitchen and kept the wick low to create just enough light to be able to see. The fire had gone out in the stove and she shivered a little, even though she had her coat on.

She examined the can. There was no picture on it and it had writing on it in a language she didn't understand. It was sealed with green tape. She tore the tape away carefully, praying that no water had seeped in. When the tape was removed she reached into the can and removed a piece of paper.

Hello Mary Sullivan from Three Rock Harbour, (Mary smiled, remembering how he'd addressed her that way during one of their first meetings).

Although I have only known you a short time, I miss you more than I thought I could ever miss anyone. I think of you when I first open my eyes in the morning and yours is the last face I see when I close my eyes at night. I close my eyes and I remember kissing you for the first time and for the last time and I long for the time when I will get to do it again.

When you wave to me before you go to bed every night, it makes my life bearable. I think of you lying in your warm bed, alone and asleep, and I'm happy that you live in a place where war never came until we arrived. I see you sleeping and I try to imagine what it would be like if I could leave this prison and go to your room and kiss you without you even knowing that I was there.

I want so much to be with you that it hurts. I want us to be able to sit with our backs to the rock and look at the harbour for the rest of our lives. I don't want you to be mad at me for saying this but I think I love you. I know we have only known each other for a short time, but if it isn't love I'm feeling for you then I don't know what it is. I hurt so much when I can't be with you. I worry when I think of you so close and yet so far away. I see you going to school in the mornings, coming home for your dinner, and I wish that I could be there with you.

I don't know if you have feelings for me like I have for you. If you don't, then I understand, but if there is something I have to change or do to make you care for me the way I care for you then you need only say it. If it is within my power to do, I will do it.

Mary, please tell me how you feel about me. You can send me a message the same way I am sending it to you. Put your message in this can and throw it to me. I will use the boat to row to it when the rest of the crew are asleep.

Please Mary, write to me and tell me how you feel. If you tell me you don't care for m, then it will break my heart, but I will not bother you anymore. Tell me you care for me and I will do anything to be with you.

Good night my love

Karl.

Mary read the note twice and held it to her breast. She looked at his name. She thought that it began with a 'C' but she had obviously been wrong. She could feel her heart pounding and she had difficulty swallowing. A tear trickled down her cheek as she tried to picture his face. The colour of his eyes and his hair and everything about him slowly came back to her. It was as if they were back sitting with their backs to the rock.

She read the note again. Of course she had feelings for him. She didn't understand them either. She put the note to her lips and kissed it. She wished it were Karl. She wished she could be with him, have him put his arms around her, and hold her tight. She shivered again but it wasn't from the cold. Her breasts hurt and her nipples were hard and erect like she was cold, but she wasn't. When the paper touched her lips she ran her tongue across them and it felt good. Oh how she wished there was someone she could talk to. Even a book might give her the answers she wanted. If her teacher had been a woman she might consider asking her.

Reluctantly, she got up from the bench and carefully folded the note and put it in the can. She blew out the lamp and looked out through the kitchen window and towards the boat. She could see the lone soul on the deck.

"Good night, my love," she said, as she blew Karl a kiss.

Mary went back to bed but she couldn't sleep. All she kept thinking about was the letter from Karl. She could see the can on her bureau and she tried to remember everything he had said to her. Whenever she closed her eyes all she could see was his face. Finally, she could not stand it any longer so she got up, lit her lamp, found some paper and a pencil, and answered his letter while sitting up in bed.

Dear Karl,

Thank you for the lovely letter. I miss you too and I wish that you did not have to spend all your time on the boat but could be still working in the church. That way I could see you every day.

Yes, you are right. We have not known each other very long but I also have feelings for you. I don't know what those feelings are but I think of you all the time. I'm sitting here in my bed and I can't sleep after reading your letter so I had to write to you to tell you how I feel.

I wish I could tell you how I feel, but I don't know how to describe it. My feelings are not like any I have had before. All I know is that when I'm with you I feel like I'm in a different place. A place where I feel safe and comfortable and I don't ever want to leave there. I don't know if that makes any sense to you because it really doesn't make any sense to me.

I like it when you kiss me and put your arms around me. When that happens, I close my eyes and I think that nothing could possibly be better than this.

Do you think that the captain will let you come ashore again? Would it do any good if I asked my father to speak with him? Dad would speak to him if I asked him and I think that might help.

I'm going to stop writing now because I want to go and throw my letter over to you. I will return again tomorrow night at the same time and you can let me know if I can ask my father to speak with the captain.

Love,
Mary

Mary finished writing and went over to her bureau and got the can. She removed Karl's letter and put hers inside. She used the tape to seal the top, and when she was sure it was watertight she put her clothes back on, blew out the lamp, and left the house.

There was a full moon so she could easily see to walk along the side of the shore, across from the submarine. She could see Karl on the deck, leaning against a ladder. She waved to him a couple of times but couldn't get his attention because of the noise of the waves crashing against the shore. She found a small rock and threw it with all her might. It splashed down halfway to the boat. Karl looked up. His eyes swept the shore and he caught sight of Mary.

He immediately ran to the side of the boat and waved frantically at her. She returned the waves and held up the can, motioning she was going to throw it. He nodded. She threw the can and it landed less than half the distance the rock had gone. With the tide not in her favour, there was no way the can would reach Karl on its own. She felt instant despair. Karl's actions indicated he too was disappointed by the throw. He looked around to see if anyone was watching. Convinced that no one was, he placed his rifle up against the ladder and stepped into the little rowboat. He untied it and quickly rowed towards the can. Within a minute or so he reached it and scooped it out of the water. He paused to look at Mary and blow her a kiss before he quickly headed back to the boat. Mary made her way home, pausing to watch as Karl climbed onto the submarine and tore the tape from the top of the can.

Karl strained to read the note by the light of the moon, but there was not enough light. He would have to wait until morning, and it would be the longest wait of his life.

Mary made it back home and fell asleep thinking about Karl. She was relieved he had her letter and knew how she felt. She tried to keep from smiling but couldn't. She fell asleep praying she would dream about him.

For the next couple of weeks, she and Karl exchanged letters every night, except when the seas were very rough or it was raining. Karl didn't want to have Mary's father speak to the captain because he felt would do no good. The captain, Karl explained, was very strict and any interference from an outsider might make matters a lot worse.

In his letters, Karl talked about deserting but he knew that if he deserted and got caught he would be shot. Also, where could he go? The only place he could go was into Three Rock Harbour, and Commander Stewart and the rest of the crew would search every house until they found him. He couldn't leave the ship and go anywhere without Mary. She wanted to be with him too, and the longer they were separated the more their love grew. They openly expressed their love for each other in their letters.

The submarine would sometimes leave for a few days, and not knowing when they would return was very difficult for Mary. On one trip, the sub was gone for five days and Mary thought she would never see Karl again. During the first week of October, the weather was extremely bad and they only exchanged letters once. That was after the submarine had left Three Rock Harbour for one day, and Karl's letter to Mary on his return expressed his frustration at not being able to see her.

My dear Mary,

I don't know how much longer I can live like this. Not being able to see you, to be with you and to be able to put my arms around you is too painful to describe. I love you so much that my heart is going to break if I'm not soon with you. I could leave the boat and be with you for just one embrace but if I get caught then I won't be permitted to even go on deck again. I would be forced to remain below deck until we leave and then for sure I would never see you again.

I would rather be dead than to live like this. The pain is so unbearable. I actually thought of killing myself so that I wouldn't have to be in such pain any longer.

Oh Mary, I have just had such a wonderful idea. What if I did kill myself? Then I wouldn't have to be on this boat any more. What if I killed myself but really didn't kill myself only everyone thought I did? Then they wouldn't have to search for me. I have an idea Mary. I think it will work.

If everyone thinks that I fell overboard and drowned they might think it was an accident. But what about a body? They would need to find my body. If there was a big sea then maybe my body would be carried out to sea and be lost forever. Yes, that would work.

I will have to tell some of my shipmates that I can't swim and that I'm afraid of falling overboard some night and there will be no one there to save me. This can work, Mary. You would have to find me a place to hide until the boat left. I think we are scheduled to leave before Christmas and after that I will be okay. Can you find me a place to hide until then? It would have to be a place where no one would ever see me. No one could know but you and me.

Oh Mary, I think this could work.
With all my love,
Karl.

Mary read Karl's letter and felt more excited than she had ever felt in her life. Finally, there was hope that they could be together. But where could she hide him? It would have to be a place where he could be warm and she could get food to him without anyone knowing. Soon there would be snow on the ground and some places around the community would only be accessible by using snowshoes. If people saw snowshoe tracks going to the same place all the time, they would be suspicious.

She racked her brain and knocked her head with her knuckles to see if she could shake an idea loose. It didn't do any good and she was about to give up in frustration.

Then it hit her. What about the hay barn? Her father had a barn that was filled with hay only. It was near the root cellar and you could actually get into the cellar from the barn. It was used when all the other hay in the closer barn was gone. There were footprints around it all winter long, and in January they would start using the hay there for the animals. That would give her lots of time to hide Karl. And he could get food from the cellar if there was ever a problem with her getting to him.

It would be perfect. The hay would make a perfect bed for Karl and she could get him a few blankets and he would not be cold. She quickly got out a pencil and paper and scribbled him a note telling him of her plan. He answered her the next night and said it would take him a week or so to spread the word among his shipmates that he was afraid of falling overboard and drowning. Then he would have to wait for a big sea that would toss the boat around a little and make the story about his falling overboard the more believable.

During the first week of October, Karl sowed the seeds of his fear amongst the crew. They listened and laughed at him. When he asked that he not be made to do the night watch, the seed was planted with the watch commander. At the start of the second week of October, a very strong wind developed around noon and there was talk about going to sea to weather the storm. But the submarine crew attached another couple of moorings to the boat to keep her steady and away from the cliffs. The sailors drove spikes with eyes in them into the walls of the cliffs and used ropes to secure the boat. Karl knew when he saw the ropes and the wind and the waves that tonight would be his chance. He would send Mary a message that he would leave the ship at 4 a.m. and she would have to be there to meet him.

Karl went up on deck at midnight. Not long afterwards, Mary appeared and he threw her the can. She retrieved it and a few minutes later she appeared on the veranda and waved the lamp a couple of times to show Karl she had understood his message.

Karl examined the ropes attached to the cliff. If he cut one of them it would be very obvious. It would not be possible to pull the spikes out of the cliff so there had to be another way. He examined where the ropes were tied onto the boat. Each was tied to the base of the deck gun. The welder had welded hooks there earlier. He knew the welder. He was sloppy and careless and many times did not clean the areas he was welding very well and the result was that the welding let go.

Karl looked and, sure enough, he could see lumps of welding material instead of the smooth stream indicative of a good job. Karl stuck the barrel of his rifle in the loop and pried it. It gave way a little.

"Thank you for being such a horrible welder, Heinz," he whispered.

Mary could not sleep. She was afraid if she did, she would not awaken in time to meet Karl. She sat up in her bed and watched the clock.

Karl paced the deck. He too monitored the time very closely and as each hour passed he knew he was closer to freedom. At 3:30 he saw Mary on the cliffs above him. She waved and he waved back. He didn't have to wait until 4 a.m. He moved to where the rope was attached and put the barrel of the rifle in the eye and lifted. He had to time it perfectly because as soon as the rope was free the boat would be pulled towards the opposite cliff. He looked around. What would he do with his rifle? He couldn't leave it on the deck. It would have to be thrown overboard. Which side? It would have to be on the side where the rope broke free because the boat would pull in the opposite direction, which would cause him to fall overboard and lose his rifle at the same time.

Earlier, he had been to the galley and when the cook wasn't watching he'd been able to squeeze a little blood from some pork he was cooking for dinner. He put it in a small container and kept it in his pocket for just the right time. Carefully he removed it, and using his finger smeared a little on the side of the conning tower. He next pulled a few hairs from his head and stuck them into the blood. Hopefully, it would seem as though he had hit his head and fallen overboard.

He had also taken a few letters from his parents and put them in his pocket. He removed them now and threw them over the side. Graf and the others might think they had fallen out of his pocket. He moved to the eye and used the rifle barrel to finish breaking it clear. Almost instantly the boat swayed away from him and even though he was expecting it, he almost fell overboard. He recovered and threw the rifle in the water. He would have to be quick because someone below might feel the sway and come on deck.

He was wearing a life jacket and a special suit designed by German engineers to keep the body warm for extended periods in the event their ship was sunk.

He dived into the frigid water and it was as though a million needles had stabbed his body. His boots and clothes weighed him down and made swimming very difficult. He would only have to swim a hundred feet or so, and he was glad because he could feel the strength leaving his body.

Mary stayed high up on the cliffs, out of sight. Karl made it to the shore and she watched as the first sailor appeared on the deck of the boat. The sailor immediately noticed the rope that had broken clear and yelled out to the others below. Mary could not make out what they were saying.

Karl reached the rocks and paused to look behind him. No one was looking in his direction, and the moon was behind the clouds so it would be next to impossible to spot him. He climbed up on the rocks and began making his way towards the beach. Out of sight of the crew, Mary made her way down towards him.

She ran to him and they embraced. Karl was shaking like a leaf. It was below zero and with the wind the cold was nearly unbearable. Their lips met and they kissed. Karl could not stop shaking.

"Come on," Mary said. "Let's get you to the barn and out of these wet clothes before you freeze to death."

Behind them, the crew quickly realized that Karl had been swept overboard. They would search for the body, but with the winds and the tide he could be long since swept out to sea.

Back on shore, Karl's clothes were nearly frozen to his body as he and Mary made their way to the barn. Mary tried to assist him but all she did was get in his way. She gave up after the first hundred feet and just ran beside him, whispering encouraging words. She constantly looked around to see if she could see anyone watching them but was unable to tell.

Ten minutes after leaving the water, they were at the barn. Mary arrived first. She pushed open the door and waited for Karl. They couldn't risk lighting a lantern. Once they were inside, Mary told Karl to wait while she climbed up the ladder to the loft and opened the upper doors. The little light there spilled in and she called out to Karl who stood shivering below.

"Come up here," she called. "Follow my voice."

Karl carefully made his way towards her. She had blankets and dry clothes for him, and as he approached he began stripping off his wet clothes. He removed his jacket and his shirt and fell to the hay as he tried to undo his boots. The combination of the darkness, his numb fingers, and the frozen laces made it an almost impossible task. Mary threw a blanket over his bare back.

"Cover yourself," she said. "Let me try and undo your boots."

Karl fell back into the hay and pulled the blanket around him. Mary began trying to untie his frozen laces. Gradually she was able to loosen one and pull it off. She poured out the water and threw it to one side. His sock came off with the boot. She then set to work on the second boot and soon had it and his sock off.

"Take off your pants and underwear," she said, as she got up and turned her back.

Karl stood, undid his belt, pulled the wet clothes from his body, and let them fall to the hay-covered floor. He pulled the blanket around him.

"Okay," he said. "Did you bring any clothes for me?"

"Yes. I brought some of Dad's old clothes. I don't think he will miss them."

She passed him a heavy shirt and he turned his back and pulled it on. The blanket fell to the floor and she looked at his nakedness. She had never seen a naked man before.

Karl turned, and she passed him a pair of pants. He pulled them on, then sat down and put on the socks.

"Oh my," Mary said.

"What is it?" Karl asked.

"I forgot a coat. You'll freeze to death tonight."

Karl laughed as he reached and pulled the blanket around his shoulders.

"This is fine. I will wrap myself in this, cover up with the hay, and I'll be fine. My coat will be dry in a day or so anyway."

"I'm sorry," Mary said. "I'm so sorry."

Karl moved towards her. "You saved my life. Without you, I would have frozen to death. Without you, I would still be on that boat. Don't be sorry."

His lips touched hers. She returned his kiss. His face was cold as he broke the kiss and embraced her.

"I love you, Mary Sullivan from Three Rock Harbour," he said.

"I love you too, Karl." She paused. "I don't even know your last name," she said as she pulled away to look into his eyes.

"It's Smith. Karl Smith," he said.

"Hello, Karl Smith from *the Sea Shark*," she laughed.

He kissed her again, only this time it was much longer than before. Even though his face was rough and he was still shivering a little, Mary thought it was the most wonderful kiss she had ever experienced. She was having feelings she had never had before. If this was love then it was wonderful.

Karl broke away from her again. "Aren't your parents going to miss you?" he asked.

"Oh my," she said. "Yes, if they wake up and find me gone they won't know what to think. I had better get back home. I don't want to leave you. You know that. But I have to go. Don't go outside and if you hear someone coming to the barn make sure you keep perfectly quiet. There's no need for anyone to come up here. It will be a couple of months before this hay will be needed. Don't let anyone see you here. I will come by in the morning with some food before I leave for school."

She went to the two open doors and pulled them closed.

"Don't open these for any reason," she warned. She moved towards him and once again they kissed before she pushed herself away. "Hang up your wet clothes away from the hay. I will see you later this morning," she said as she went down the ladder. She carefully opened the door and closed it behind her.

Mary hurried along the path to the house. She took a quick glance at the light on the *Sea Shark* before opening the door and going inside. As she was closing the door, trying to make sure no one heard her, she suddenly heard a voice.

"Is that you, Mary?" she heard her father say. "What in the name of God are you doing out this time of the morning?"

Mary had not been expecting anyone to be awake. Her father's voice startled her. "Ahh," she mumbled. "Ahh, I saw the light on the *Sea Shark* and I wasn't very sleepy so I went down to see what was going on." She lied to her father for the first time ever.

"Yes, I saw the light too. It looks like they are looking for something. Do you have any idea what is going on?"

"No," she lied again. "All I could tell was that there was a lot of shouting and I figured they were being attacked by a giant codfish or something." She laughed.

Her father laughed too. "They're a weird crowd and it wouldn't surprise me," he said. "Go to bed out of it. It'll be morning soon enough."

"Good night, Dad," Mary said as she made her way to her bedroom. She fell asleep, secure in the knowledge that Karl was finally off the boat and safe with her.

CHAPTER TWELVE

The crew of *U-69* began searching as soon as they realized that Karl had fallen overboard. It wasn't long before they found the blood and the hair on the conning tower and came to the conclusion that when the welding broke and the boat heaved, Karl had hit his head and fallen over. The little rowboat was launched and they tried to search for him but even in the harbour it was very rough. They tried calling out his name but there was no answer. Graf was reluctant to use the big light on the deck because he feared drawing attention from passing ships or aircraft. The crew searched until daylight but could find no trace of Karl.

He awakened early. As he huddled in the cold loft with the blankets wrapped around him and peered out between the crack in the two doors, he saw the diver from his boat slip into the water. He wasn't submerged very long before he appeared with the rifle. He passed it to another sailor who passed it to Graf. He examined it for a few seconds and passed it off to someone else. Karl watched as the order was given to launch the rowboat and a couple of sailors began searching the shoreline.

Bill and his crew were up at their usual time. The wind had died down and they would be able to tend to their trawls. Bill and his brother Walt met on the wharf. A little while later they were ready to leave. Graf noticed them as soon as they walked on the wharf and signalled the rowboat to return to the U-Boat and pick him up.

"Good morning, Tony," Bill said as the boat approached. "It looks like you had a busy night last night."

"Good morning, and yes we did. One of our mooring ropes broke free and it looks as if one of my crew has fallen overboard. I suspect the worst."

"That's too bad," Bill said. "Anything we can do to help?"

"Yes, I was wondering if there were a couple of boats available we could use to search for the body."

"Yes, bye, that's not a problem." By this time several other fishermen had joined them on the wharf and were getting ready to go out fishing. "In twenty minutes anything left here you can use. They'll be the boats that belong to the hangashores and they won't need them."

"I'll be sure to thank Mr. Hangashore when I see him," Stewart said.

Bill and the others laughed as they explained that a hangashore was a name for someone too lazy to fish. Before Bill left, Stewart asked him if he would have a lookout for the body and if he found it to take it aboard.

"If the tide took him out of the harbour then he's gone," Bill said. "There was a strong tide last night and the tide here can almost suck the bottom out of the harbour. George Humby's trap up on Southern Point might hold him up if he sank. But if he's afloat he won't come ashore till he reaches Ireland."

The fishing crew spent an hour or so scouring the harbour and one lone boat went out in the bay. They were still looking when Karl heard the door to the barn opening. It had to be Mary, he thought, but he kept perfectly still and waited.

He heard her coming up the ladder and then her smile lit up the loft.

"Good morning," she greeted him. "I see that you didn't freeze to death."

"Good morning to you too," he said as he stood and kissed her.

She moved away from him.

"I boiled a couple of eggs for you and brought some blueberry jam bread. I couldn't get you any tea without raising suspicion but I'll get you something hot later. I have to go now. I told Mom I was just running over to Sarah's house for a second. I'll see you when I come home from school."

With that, she turned and went down the ladder.

Karl opened the canvas bag and took out the food. He didn't realize how hungry he was until he began eating. As he ate he watched his crewmates search for him. After a couple of hours, they gave up. He hoped his death would be officially recorded in the boat's log as drowning at sea.

Mary brought him fried fish and potatoes for his lunch as well as warm clothes. She also managed to bring him some hot tea. For supper, she brought him moose stew and sat with him as he ate it. They talked and because it was dark they were able to open the doors to the loft and look out at the harbour. Karl piled hay for them to sit on.

They talked about everything and anything and laughed a lot as they huddled under the blanket, noting it was much warmer than it had been the previous evening. As they talked, they noticed the activity around the submarine had increased.

The mooring lines were thrown off and the rowboat was lashed to the deck. Everything on deck that shouldn't be there was removed and taken below.

"They are getting ready to get underway," Karl said.

"You mean they're leaving?" Mary asked.

"Yes, that's exactly what I mean," Karl said.

"Are they leaving for good?" she asked.

"No, that's too much to hope for. I think they're just going out on patrol for a couple of days and then they'll be back, unfortunately."

As they huddled under the blankets they watched as the boat came out from the rock tunnel and made its way out into the open ocean.

"I won't be sorry the day that she leaves forever," Karl said.

"Same here," Mary said.

They watched until the boat was out of sight.

"What will you do when they leave forever?" Mary asked.

"I haven't really given that much thought," Karl said. "I suppose I will have to tell everyone and hope they will let me stay."

"You'll be a deserter from the Royal Navy," Mary said. "The people here might have a little bit of a problem with that. They love King George and you had better have a good story about why you left. I just pray they won't decide to do something that we'll both regret."

"I never dreamt the people here would care so much about the war." Karl said, and paused before continuing. "Maybe I will have to tell the real truth about why we're here."

"What do you mean, the real truth?" Mary asked.

"Oh, I'm just thinking out loud. Why don't we talk about something else? I think we'll have to cross that bridge when we get to it."

He leaned towards her and kissed her. "Okay?" he asked.

She put her hands on his face while she kissed him and then they playfully fell back into the hay, where they moved closer together and their kisses became much more passionate.

They forced their bodies toward each other and the blanket fell away. They wrapped their arms around each other and rubbed each other excitedly. Karl touched her cheek as they kissed and then moved his hand down to her chest. She was still wearing her heavy woollen coat. Carefully, and without her resisting, he undid one button to her coat and then another.

"What are you doing?" she asked, as she pushed away from him.

"I am taking off your coat so I can feel your body against me. It's warm and soft and I like it."

Mary sat up, finished undoing the last couple of buttons, and threw her coat on the hay beside them. Finished, she lay back down and snuggled into him.

"That's better," he said, as they resumed their original position.

Karl moved his hand back to her face and then moved it down to her neck and to her breast. She gasped as he squeezed it gently. He could tell she was excited because her nipples were as hard as rocks. He continued to massage her breasts and then slowly moved his hand inside her sweater. She didn't resist, the more he massaged her the more she matched his gyrations.

"Would you take off your sweater for me?" he asked as he pulled back a little and looked at her.

"I have never done this with anyone before," she said.

"It will be alright," he said. "I just want to look at your body and to touch it. You excite me more than anything?"

"Have you ever been intimate with another girl?" she asked.

"Yes, once," he admitted. "I have to be honest with you. But it was only one time."

"My Dad said that all you sailors have a girl in every port."

He laughed. "That might be true of the other sailors but it's not true for me. I have only been with one another girl. She was a prostitute."

Mary sat up and slowly pulled her sweater up over her head. Underneath, she wore a white singlet. Despite the darkness, Karl could see her erect nipples stretching the material.

"Take off the shirt too," he said.

Mary paused as if trying to make up her mind. "I'm afraid," she said.

"What's there to be afraid of? There's just the two of us here. It's okay."

She reached for the bottom of her singlet. "You won't laugh, will you?" she asked.

"Mary, my love," he smiled. "Of all the things going through my mind, laughing is not one of them. Take off your shirt."

She turned her back as she took off her singlet and tossed it with her sweater and coat.

"Turn around," Karl said.

She turned and knelt before him with her arms across her chest.

"Take away your hands," he whispered.

Slowly Mary removed her hands. "They're magnificent," Karl gasped. "I never dreamt that breasts could be so beautiful."

She continued kneeling before him. Her breasts were large and the colour of buttermilk. Her nipples were huge and surrounded by a perfect circle of brown. He couldn't take his eyes off them. Slowly he moved toward her and placed both of his hands on her chest. His hands were cold and her hard nipples pressed into his palms. She withdrew a little and took a deep breath. He removed his hands and embraced her. Then he moved his face down to her chest and took one of her nipples in his mouth. He gently flicked his tongue on the nipple as Mary threw back her head and took deep breaths. He moved his mouth to the other and tried to force even more of it into his mouth. She made an unrecognizable sound of pleasure.

He pushed her on her back and she threw her hands over her head as he buried his head in her chest. As he sucked and massaged her breasts his manhood grew so large that it hurt. She began to make even more unrecognizable sounds and used both of her hands to help him suck and massage her breasts. She began to pant and cross and uncross her legs. Then she straightened out like someone with rigor mortis. She bit her bottom lip as she gave a muffled squeal.

Karl sat up and looked at her. "Are you alright?" he asked, as she finally appeared to relax.

She opened her eyes and looked up at him. "I have never felt anything like that before in my life. I can't describe it. It was like I was going to explode and then I did."

As she began straightening her clothes, she looked up at Karl and said, "I love you."

"I love you too, Mary."

She stood up. "I have to go now," she said. "Mom and Dad will be wondering where I am. I hate to leave but I have to go."

Karl embraced her. They kissed and then she moved away without speaking. "I'll see you after breakfast and I'll try to bring you something to eat," she said, when she was on the ladder.

She paused for a moment. Then he heard her close the door behind her.

Mary dropped by to bring him something for his Sunday morning breakfast, but she didn't get back again until almost suppertime. At that time, she apologized and said she had to return home to help her mother with supper because they had people coming over. She also had to help Shoot and John with their school homework.

Karl said he understood and ate everything that she had brought him. They kissed goodnight and Mary said if she could sneak away later, she would come and see him. She never did get the chance and it was morning before they saw each other again.

CHAPTER THIRTEEN

Three Rock Harbour. October 1942

Captain Graf received new orders to travel to the west coast of Newfoundland. There were reports that ships travelling out of Halifax were heading across the Cabot Strait towards Port aux Basques and then traveling up along the coast. His mission was to intercept these ships and sink them.

It was 2000 hours when the battery-powered motors moved the U-Boat out of the harbour and into the open ocean. Safely outside the harbour the diesel engines were started and *U-69* began making its way towards the west coast. Weber took command when they got underway and he immediately began drilling his torpedo crew. There was not going to be a mistake like they had at Bell Island.

For a couple of days, the submarine patrolled the area without sighting any ships. Graf was beginning to think the report he had received from the German Admiralty was not factual. Weber was in command and Graf was in his bunk when he got a call at 0230 hours on October 14 that they had spotted two freighters.

As soon as he arrived at the command post he was briefed.

"We are approximately 25 miles from Port Aux Basques, Captain. There's no moon and swells of about three feet. We've spotted a freighter and there's a destroyer behind her, approximately one-quarter mile. We are at full alert, Sir," he finished.

"Thank you, Lieutenant. Take your position," Graf ordered.

Weber moved to a position in the conning tower and Graf joined him. He spotted the two ships and came back down the ladder. He called out an order for CPO Fischer to move the boat into position for a starboard attack on the freighter.

"Watch crews on deck," Graf ordered and eight seamen scrambled up the ladder to the deck. Each crew was responsible for covering a 90-

degree arc and scanning for activity. The spotters on the deck reported positions to the captain below as the freighter followed a zigzag course.

"*S.S. Caribou*," one of the spotters called down and its name was immediately recorded. Although the ship was traveling in blackout conditions, a brief break in the clouds allowed the spotter to see her name.

"In position, Sir," Weber called out. "Range 400 metres. Speed 10 knots."

"Ten knots," Graf called out to the helm. "Load torpedoes," he spoke into the tube and received word seconds later that the torpedoes were loaded.

"Set switches."

"Switches set."

Graf continued to give commands to the helm until he was satisfied that they were in position. "Fire one," he ordered.

"One away," he heard.

The torpedo was ejected from the U-Boat with a burst of compressed air. Then its counter rotating propellers came to life, driving it toward the *Caribou* with a speed of over 30 miles per hour. The only sign that the torpedo was on its way was a string of bubbles as it headed for its unsuspecting target.

"On course," Weber called from the conning tower.

Everyone waited in silence. Graf looked at his watch. It was 0330 hours. Seconds later, he heard the explosion as the torpedo struck the *Caribou* and tore a huge hole in its starboard side. Graf went up the conning tower to observe the explosion.

Unknown to Graf, the *Caribou* was not a freighter. It was a passenger ferry that took passengers from North Sydney, Nova Scotia to Port aux Basques, Newfoundland. On board was a crew of military and civilian passengers as well as 50 head of cattle.

Because of a fear of U-Boat attacks, the RCN minesweeper, *Grandmere,* captained by Lt. James Cuthbert, had been ordered to act as escort for the *Caribou.*

On the *Caribou*, the engine room crew and a large number of passengers and other crew were killed immediately when the torpedo with its warhead of high explosives tore into the ferry. Two lifeboats and the radio room were destroyed at the same instant. All below deck lights went out and the remaining survivors were plunged into darkness. The boilers exploded immediately after that and the ferry began sinking.

Confusion ensued and although Captain Tavenor immediately realized what had happened he was virtually helpless. Passengers and crew attempted to reach the deck from the darkened passages. Those who did make it immediately launched the two lifeboats from the port side. Unknown to them, the seacocks on both boats were open. As soon as they were launched they began to fill with water. The problem was quickly fixed on one of the boats. But the other was so overcrowded, it could not be fixed and the boat capsized, spilling the passengers out into the freezing Atlantic water.

The crew who made it to the deck attempted to launch the stern lifeboats, but they were full of panic-stricken passengers who refused to get out and let the crew launch them. Many were still there as the *Caribou* began to slowly sink below the surface.

Back on the *Grandmere,* the crew saw the explosion and the U-Boat on the surface. Cuthbert ordered full speed ahead with intentions of ramming it. Graf realized his intention and ordered his boat to dive. "Dive, dive, dive," Graf yelled as he scrambled down the conning tower, followed by the others.

"Full to port," he ordered his helm and the boat began to turn as it sank below the surface. Once he was below the surface and hidden from the minesweeper he gave the order, "One hundred and eighty degrees to starboard," and the boat turned towards the passengers in the water where the *Caribou* used to be.

Behind him, he could hear the depth charges as the *Grandmere* chased off in the direction Cuthbert had seen the U-Boat turn as it slipped below the surface. Graf ordered his boat to sink to four hundred and fifty feet and wait.

On the surface, Cuthbert searched in vain for the U-Boat. In the meantime, the passengers who had not been killed by the explosions were bobbing up and down in the water. Cuthbert was torn between hunting down the U-Boat or rescuing survivors. His orders, however, were specific. U-Boat hunting was his top priority. But, in the following hours, he was able to take on board 103 survivors. Two died before reaching port, bringing the death toll to 136.

When he was satisfied that the minesweeper had given up, Graf began slowly moving the submarine away from the area. An hour later he surfaced and *U-69* began making its way back to Three Rock Harbour.

CHAPTER FOURTEEN

After the submarine left, Mary and Karl developed a routine. They had a signalling system in which Mary would leave a piece of cloth on the fence where Karl could see it. When it was there it meant she was thinking of him but couldn't come because of other commitments.

Although they kissed a lot, Mary was wary about the heavy petting that had occurred during their first get together in the loft. She had experienced feelings of pleasure and regret that she didn't understand. There was nothing more enjoyable than being with Karl, but she still didn't want to engage in anything other than kissing and hugging.

Today, she brought him supper and said she would able to visit with him later that evening. At 8:30 she showed up and her distress was evident.

"What's troubling you, Mary," Karl asked as he greeted her with a kiss.

"The most horrible thing has happened," she said, holding back tears.

"What's wrong?" he asked as he took her hands and they sat down on the hay.

"We were just listening to the *Doyle Bulletin* and we heard that the *Caribou* was sunk and more than 100 people drowned."

"I assume that the *Caribou* is a boat," he said.

"Yes, she's a passenger ferry that operates between Newfoundland and Nova Scotia. She was sunk by a U-Boat. Why would the Germans want to sink a ferry? Why would those heathens want to murder women and children who have no involvement with the war? I wish that I were a man so I could join up and go over there and kill every one of them. I will hate the Germans until the day I die."

Karl looked at her as she vented.

"Maybe it was a mistake. I know that sometimes destroyers are around the ships. Maybe they intended to sink the destroyer."

"That's no excuse," Mary snapped at him. "They still killed over a hundred innocent people. I'm so mad now that if I saw a German I would kill him myself. Why are you making excuses for them anyway?"

"I'm not making excuses, Mary. It's just that there's a war going on and things like that happen. I'm shocked about this too, but I don't think you should hate all the Germans because of the actions of a few."

"Just because we live in Three Rock Harbour it doesn't mean that we don't know about the war," Mary said. "We didn't start this war. Germany did."

Karl paused. "Why are we talking about this? We are not going to solve the problems of the war."

"That's not what I'm trying to do," Mary answered. "I just don't understand why someone would kill innocent people. I can understand soldiers killing soldiers but to just blow up a ship with people on it who are not involved with the war, that's not war."

"I agree, Mary. I understand. That's the part of my job I hated the most. Never seeing the enemy. Never meeting the enemy. Just killing them because the captain said to kill them. Seeing all the bodies floating in the ocean after a successful mission and not being permitted to save them from drowning when all we had to do was to throw them a life raft. I hate this war more than you can ever imagine. I left my boat because of you, Mary, but I could just as easily have left it because I hate it. The captain even keeps a record of his kills."

"But you are one of the good guys," Mary said, as she moved a little closer to him. "You didn't blow up innocent people."

Karl stopped and looked into her eyes. He got up and walked over to the open loft door and stared out into the harbour.

"Is something wrong? Mary asked.

"Do you love me, Mary?" he asked.

"Yes, Karl. I love you," she answered.

"Well, I can't lie to you anymore. I have to tell you something and if after I tell you, you want to hate me and you want to tell everyone in Three Rock Harbour, then I will understand."

Mary looked at him with an obvious confused stare. "What are you talking about?" she asked.

"It's been a lie, Mary. One great big fat lie."

"What's a lie?"

"We are not who we say we are," he answered, as he turned his head and moved away from her.

"What do you mean you're not who you say you are?"

"You think that we're the *Sea Shark*. We're not the *Sea Shark*. We're *U-69*."

"So, you're not the *Sea Shark*, you're *U-69*. So who cares what your name is?" she said, trying to smile.

"You don't understand, Mary. The *Sea Shark* is a U-Boat, a German submarine. I'm not a British sailor. I'm German. My name is Karl Schmidt."

Mary paused as if a film had been running and it had stopped and the camera light was about to burn through it. Blood rushed to her face and she was turning a beet red. Her eyes and her mouth opened and at the same time she tried to mouth something but nothing came out. She finally managed to stand up and she stood looking at him.

"You're a what?" she almost screamed.

Karl looked around and listened. Someone had to hear her. Mary stared at him and suddenly turned and headed for the ladder.

"Where are you going?" he asked.

Mary paused at the ladder. "I'm going to tell someone. I can't believe this. A German U-Boat in Three Rock Harbour and we're helping you to kill our people. We're all going to be thrown into jail after this is all said and done. Ooooh!" she said in frustration.

"Please don't leave. Let me explain," he pleaded as he moved toward her. "You can't leave. You must listen to what I have to say."

"You lied to me. You all lied to everyone. Commander Stewart, or whatever his name is, came into our house and sat down with mother and father and lied to everyone. You're Germans. You're filthy, murdering Germans. I hate them and I hate you. How could you do this to me?" she said, as tears streamed down her cheeks.

"It's not like it sounds. I don't know how it sounds. Please don't hate me, Mary. You said you loved me. Nothing has changed. I'm still Karl and you're still Mary from Three Rock Harbour." He tried to smile.

"You're German and that thing is a U-Boat? You've been hiding here and going out and sinking our ships?"

Karl nodded.

"How could you do that? How could you sink ships and kill innocent people? My God!" she suddenly remembered. "It must have been the *Sea Shark* or whatever it is, that sank the *Caribou*."

"We don't know that," Karl suddenly said. "We don't know that at all."

"We don't know that she didn't, either," Mary said. "And speaking of sinking, did you have anything to do with the boats that were sunk near Bell Island?"

Karl just hung his head.

"I asked you a question," Mary said very sternly.

Karl looked up at her and nodded. "But I wasn't on the boat. Remember. I was in the church. I didn't go out when the boat went out."

"My God," she said. "My good God in heaven. You have been here all this time and we didn't suspect a thing. We actually started to like you. You're German!"

She walked to the other side of the loft and walked back again. "What about Father Lake and Mr. Blair? Are they Germans too?"

Karl nodded again.

"How? Why? I don't understand. Why would you do something like this?"

He just shook his head.

"Is that your real name? Are you really Karl?"

"Yes."

"And I suppose that Commander Stewart is not really Commander Stewart?"

"No, his name is Captain-lieutenant Ulrich Graf," he answered, pronouncing the captain's name using the proper German accent.

"But you all speak English and you look English," she said.

"Not all of us speak English as well as I do. My mother is English and my father is Austrian. We spoke English at home as much as we spoke German. Captain Graf went to school outside of Germany and the others have similar stories."

"So even our teacher and our priest are German?" she asked.

"Yes, we are all German."

Mary stood and stared. Karl stayed in the same spot. Occasionally he would look at her and turn away. Finally Mary broke the silence.

"So this entire thing was a lie. A lie to hide your true identity so that you could leave here and go out and murder innocent civilians. I don't have any words to describe what I'm feeling right now."

"I think I know how you're feeling. I'm a sailor, or rather I was a sailor. I didn't like my job. But if I didn't do it I would be shot. If they found out I deserted they would murder my entire family. I don't know what I can say to change your opinion of me, but Mary, I left them and I've told you what I am. I don't know if you can ever forgive me, but I'm still Karl. I'm still the person you met and who you told just a little while ago that you love. I'm not a murderer. I would do anything to change all of this, but I can't. If there is anything I wouldn't change though, it's meeting you. You may not love me anymore but I love you and I will always love you."

Again Mary paused before answering. "I never said that I stopped loving you. I don't know what I feel," she said in frustration. "Our entire relationship is a lie. You're supposed to be my enemy. I'm hiding you. That makes me a criminal. I could probably be sent to jail for what I'm doing."

"No one is going to send you to jail. You haven't done anything wrong. I would think the Allies would want to talk to me. I've got things I could tell them that they would want to know."

"What kinds of things?" Mary asked.

"Secret stuff. I am a radio operator. I know how to operate the Enigma."

"What's the Enigma?"

"That's the code machine we use when we send and receive messages. We use it to encode messages that we send and decode messages that we receive," he explained.

"If you co-operated with the Allies you would become a traitor," Mary said.

"I know." Karl looked sad. "But I'm willing to do that to be with you. And Mary, I'm not a true German. As I told you, my mother is English and my father is Austrian."

"That might be a way out. If you were willing to co-operate then they would not punish me and you would be allowed to stay here. Don't you agree?"

"Yes, I definitely agree with you, but who are we going to tell? There's nobody here to tell. There's a radio, but Max has one of the tubes and it won't work without it. There's no way to tell anybody anything. That's why the boat is here in Three Rock Harbour. It's perfectly isolated."

"So what are we going to do? We can't allow the boat to return here, stay for a rest and then go out again and kill more innocent people. We have to stop it. There has to be someone we can tell and some way we can stop it."

Karl was about to say something but Mary held up her hand to silence him. "Don't say any more. Don't say anything at all. I have to think about all of this. I have to try and figure out how we are going to get us out of this mess without everyone here getting killed. I can't believe we were so stupid as to let ourselves get fooled like this. I have to tell father."

She fell silent and Karl left her to her thoughts. Finally, after what seemed forever to him, she spoke. "I have to go. I have to be alone to figure out how we're going to get out of this mess." With that said, she left.

CHAPTER FIFTEEN

Mary did not sleep very well that night. There were so many things going through her mind that sleep was out of the question. There was a German U-Boat in Three Rock Harbour and the Germans were using it as a base to sink ships. She was in love with one of the crew who had deserted and she was hiding him in her father's barn. Her teacher and her priest were Germans. The promise that Commander Stewart had made to all of the fishermen would not be kept because one morning they would wake up and the boat would be gone. When they contacted someone from the outside looking for their money, no one would have a record of the *Sea Shark* being there. Eventually, it would be discovered the boat was in fact a German U-Boat and life for people in Three Rock Harbour would never be the same again. They would be considered traitors and stupid and just the thought of it caused her to shiver. And, when they realized that Mary had been hiding one of the crew and she knew they were German, they would probably throw her in jail and throw away the key.

The windup alarm clock on the dresser beside her bed ticked the night away. All she could think about was Karl, the U-Boat, and her father's reaction when she told him. If she told him, what would he do? Would he do something that could get him killed? She didn't know what to do.

When Mary walked into the classroom the next morning, Mr. Blair could tell that something was bothering her. She looked at him as if he had two heads. When he asked if she was feeling okay, she shrugged her shoulders and went about her duties. Throughout the morning she kept looking at him and listening to him talk to see if she could detect that he was German. He had a bit of an accent but unless someone knew that he was German they couldn't tell by listening to him. At least as far as she was concerned.

Mary couldn't concentrate. Every time she looked at Mr. Blair the voice of the announcer on the *Doyle Bulletin* kept echoing in her head. Blair was just as responsible for the deaths of the people on the *Caribou* as were the rest of the crew. By mid-morning she could not bear to be in his presence any longer and said that she was sick and going home.

Her mother was surprised to see her, but could tell that something was bothering her. Mary hated lying to her mother but she couldn't tell her what she knew. She couldn't tell anybody because if they knew what could they do? She went to her bedroom, lay on her bed, and began to consider her options.

The U-Boat was not back yet so the only Germans in Three Rock Harbour were Karl, Mr. Blair, Father Lake and the two radio operators. If she told her father, he could tell the other fishermen and they could overpower the Germans, take control of the radio and call for help. The Germans would have guns and there was a good chance that someone might get killed. The other problem with that plan was that the U-Boat would certainly hear the message being sent and would not return to port. So the people responsible for the sinking of Allied ships would get away to sink other ships. That was simply not acceptable to her. There had to be a way to capture the boat and its crew and punish them for what they had done.

If there was a way for her to get a message to the outside without the Germans knowing about it that could be the solution. But how could she get a message to the outside? No one was allowed to leave. Then an idea suddenly came to her.

She got up from her bed and went downstairs. Her mother wasn't around which was good so she made her way to the barn where Karl was. She would have to tell him her plan. She carefully opened the door, went inside, and up the stairs.

"Gee, what are you doing here this time of day?" he asked once he had seen her. He had been hiding behind a pile of hay.

"I told Mr. Blair or whatever his name is that I was sick and I went home from school. I have been in my bedroom lying on the bed trying to figure out how we're going to stop this from continuing. And I think that I've come up with a plan."

"What is it?" he asked excitedly.

"I have got to leave Three Rock Harbour," she blurted out.

"How are you going to manage that? They will stop you. No one is allowed to leave."

"There is no other way. If I tell Dad, he and the other fishermen will overpower them and send a message. Someone might get hurt and your boat will hear the message and escape."

"I wish you wouldn't call it my boat, Mary. I've left the boat and I won't ever go back to it," he said.

"Sorry, but you know what I mean. So, that's out of the question. I want them caught and I want them punished for what they did. I will have to go to St. John's and tell someone. Then they can send an army or something and capture everyone."

"If that happens then there will be people getting hurt. Captain Graf is not going to let your army take his boat without a fight," Karl said.

"I understand that but the people getting hurt won't be my father and the other people in Three Rock Harbour. They will be people who are trained to fight. They won't be fishermen."

Karl paused for a few seconds. "But you still haven't answered my question about how you are going to get to St. John's."

"I'm going to get sick. I'm going to get a horrible pain in my stomach and Dad is going to have to take me to Salmonier to see the doctor. When people here get sick we have to go into Salmonier. From there we travel to St. John's. Once I'm there I will find someone and tell them about the U-Boat. Then they can send people to capture it. I'm already home from school because I'm sick so for the rest of the day and up until tomorrow morning I am going to get worse. I hate having to take Dad away from his fishing but I have to do this. I'm not asking for your permission, Karl. I'm just telling you that this is the only way I see to fix this. That is, unless you have a better plan?"

Again, Karl paused before answering. "No, I don't have a better plan. But I can't see them letting you leave. You know about the boat, and Blair and Lake won't let you leave. I'm sorry but I don't know their real names either. They will do anything to keep you here. Captain Graf is not here so they will have to make a decision and I'm afraid that they will kill you rather than let you leave."

A sudden look of horror came over her. "They wouldn't do that," she said with her statement sounding like a question.

"Yes, they would. This is war, Mary. These people are the enemy and they have a perfect situation happening here. No one suspects a thing. They won't let anything jeopardize it. Take my word for it."

"But we can't let this continue. We have to stop them," she said.

"Yes, I know, but I don't want to lose you. I love you."

"And I love you too, Karl, but are our lives worth the lives of the hundreds of other people who will be killed if we don't do something?"

"No, but…" he said before she cut him off.

"There is no 'but' about it. I have to do this. I have to take my chances. I can't tell Dad and I can't tell anyone. So, once I commit to this, I will have to make sure that I protect myself as best I can. I will just have to make up a plan as I go."

"I'm afraid for you," Karl said.

"I'm afraid for me too," she said. "Now, if this works I might be gone a few days. You will have to be on your own. I won't be able to bring your food. But you will be able to get to the root cellar without being seen. Go there in the nighttime and make sure that whatever you take Mom won't notice that it's missing. Do you understand?"

"Yes, I understand but I'm still afraid for you," he said.

Mary walked toward him and they embraced. She withdrew a little and they kissed. "I have to do this," she said as she pushed herself away. "I have to do this."

She left and went down the ladder as he followed her with his eyes. "Be careful," he called to her as her head disappeared below the floor.

Mary was unnoticed as she went into the house and upstairs to her bedroom. She lay on her bed with her mind made up that she had to get out of Three Rock Harbour. She put her hand on her stomach and moaned. It wasn't loud enough for anyone to hear downstairs but it was a start. She got undressed, put on her nightgown, got into bed, and waited. Half an hour later she heard a noise downstairs.

"Mary, are you okay?" she heard her mother call.

"I'm up here," she answered, trying to sound sick.

Her mother came up stairs and into her room.

"Are you still sick?" she asked.

"Yes, I am," she answered.

"What's wrong?"

"I have terrible pain in my stomach. It started this morning in school. I had to leave school and come home."

"It's not your woman's time, is it?" she asked.

"No that finished two weeks ago."

"Did you have anything different to eat?" her mother continued with her questioning.

"No, Mom. I ate what everyone else ate."

"Okay, I'll go get you a good dose of salts to clean you out. We'll see if that clears this up."

She left and went downstairs and returned a few minutes later. She had a glass half-filled with water and a small can. She placed the glass on the night table, scooped a spoonful of salts into the glass, stirred it and passed the glass to Mary. Mary took it and drank it down in one attempt. She then passed the glass back to mother. Seconds later she burped loudly.

"Excuse me," she said.

"That should help," her mother said. "You just rest and I'll check on you a little later." She turned and went downstairs.

Mary lay in the bed and occasionally moaned. She made sure they were loud enough for her mother to hear. Over the next hour the concern was obvious on her mother's face. Around 1 a.m. she came to say that her father was back in the harbour and she would go down on the wharf and speak with him. She remembered him saying at supper that he would be moving his trawls today and would be late getting back.

Nearly fifteen minutes passed before Mary heard her father coming up the stairs. He didn't stop to remove his oil clothes or his boots.

"What's wrong, Mary?" he asked as he paused in her bedroom door.

"It's nothing, Dad," she said, trying to sound brave and weak at the same time.

"Your mother says that you have a pain in your stomach. Is it something that needs a doctor?" he asked.

"I don't know, Dad." She moaned again for effect.

"Have you had pain like this before?"

She shook her head.

Her father stood looking at her. Mary hated what she was doing. "Your mother said that she gave you a dose of salts. Why don't we wait for an hour or so and see what happens? We'll go clean up the fish. If you are still sick then we'll go to St. John's."

"That will ruin your afternoon fishing and it's such a long way."

"It makes no difference about the fish. It's late so we may not get out this after. Your getting better is all I'm worried about. You rest easy now and I'll see you again in a little while."

Mary stayed in bed while her family went down to lunch. She listened until they had finished eating and left to clean up the fish.

Word quickly spread throughout the community that Mary was sick and her father was considering taking her to Salmonier. Father Lake heard the news and went looking for Blair. He was at his boarding house having dinner. Lake walked in.

"Come on and have your dinner?" Freda Cull said when she saw him.

Lake hung his coat on the hook in the porch and went into the kitchen where Blair was seated at the table, eating. They exchanged greetings.

There was a big soup tureen in the centre of the table and surrounding it was a loaf of sliced fresh bread. He began to help himself.

"I'm going down on the wharf to see if I can get us a salmon for supper. You help yourselves and the teapot is on the stove. I'll be back in twenty minutes," Freda advised them.

As soon as they heard the door close, Lake spoke. "The Sullivan girl is sick and her father is talking about bringing her to Salmonier to see the doctor. What are we going to do?"

"I knew she was sick because she didn't look well when she came to school this morning. I didn't realize she was so sick that she needed a doctor," Blair said.

"When is the boat due back?" Lake asked.

"Not until tomorrow and that's too late. The captain's orders are that no one is to leave here," Lake said. "I don't know if he ever thought about the possibility of someone getting sick."

Lake continued eating without speaking. He filled his bowl for the second time and then spoke.

"We have to stop her from leaving."

"How do you propose that we do that? Go over to her house and shoot her?" Blair said sarcastically.

"Do you have a better idea? We have to do something." He stared at Lake. "She's a very bright kid. If we spoke with her and told her not to mention anything about the boat because if she did and outsiders found out about it, then we'd have to leave and that would cause all of the people here to lose a lot of money. What do you think?"

"I don't know," Blair said. "You know how pissed off the captain was when he found out about Karl and the girl. I wouldn't be one bit surprised to hear that he made away with him and it wasn't an accident that he fell over and drowned. He wants this mission to succeed and he'll do anything to ensure its success. If Graf were to come back here and find her gone, he might do away with the two of us. Well, maybe not the two of us, but me for sure."

"Okay, but how do we explain to Bill Sullivan that we're not letting him take his daughter out of here? There's just the four of us. If he gets those other fishermen behind him, we won't have to worry about the captain killing us. If you remember when we were being briefed on this mission, I asked about a doctor and was laughed at. Now, if we had a doctor here, this wouldn't be a problem."

"It's no help talking about what we could have done," Blair said.

Lake reached out to fill his bowl with soup. "I've got it," he said. "I think that I've got the solution and nobody will be any the wiser."

"What is it?" Blair asked as he stopped eating.

"We don't know for sure that she'll have to go. But if she does then I'll go with her. I'll tell Bill that as her priest I feel obligated to go. I'll stay with her all the time and I'll make sure that no one is with her unless I'm with her. The doctor won't mind I'm sure."

Blair returned to eating. "It might work," he said. "I'll be the one telling the captain so I'll be the one who'll be closest to him if he doesn't approve. So, convince me that she won't get to speak to anyone."

"She won't. I'll be with her every minute. I won't let her out of my sight. If she has to stay in the hospital I will make arrangements to stay in the room with her," Lake said.

Blair finished drinking his soup. "Okay. But if when the time comes for you to return and you find that we're gone, then you'll be on your own because the captain has decided that it's just too risky."

They finished eating their lunch and took their tea to the living room.

"Go see her," Blair said. "If they're taking her to St. John's make sure that you convince the family that you want to go. Let me know what's happening. I have to go back to school. As soon as you find out what's going on, let me know. Come up to the school if I'm still there."

Lake finished his tea and left for the Sullivan's house. He went to the wharf first and saw the Sullivans busy on the wharf. He approached Janet. "I hear that Mary is sick," he said to her.

"Yes, she has something wrong with her stomach. We're going to see to her once we finish with the fish. If she's no better Bill is going to have to bring her to Salmonier."

"May I go see her?" he asked.

"Yes, sure. She's in her bedroom. Just go up the stairs. You'll find her.

"Thank you," he said. as he walked up the hill to the house.

He opened the door, walked in. and went up the stairs. Mary heard someone come in and make their way up the stairs. She guessed it must be her mother. She moaned for effect.

"Mary," Lake sang out.

Mary thought her heart would stop. Karl's words began to echo in her head. He was here to kill her. All her family were down on the wharf and she was alone. They would come home and find her dead. He would probably put a pillow over her head and nobody would ever know.

"Mary," Lake called again. "This is Father Lake. I spoke with your mother and she said it was okay for me to come and visit you."

So, he spoke with Mom, Mary thought. He wouldn't dare kill her now because her mother would know. Or was that a lie? Maybe he didn't speak to her mother at all. What was she going to do? Suddenly her mind was made up for her.

"How are you feeling, Mary?" he asked, as stepped into the doorway of her bedroom.

Mary stared at Father Lake. She didn't know what to say. Her heart was beating so fast and loud that she could actually hear it.

"Okay," she finally managed to say.

"It looks like your father may have to take you to Salmonier. Are you feeling any better?"

She shook her head.

"You rest. I will speak with your mother," he said. "If you have to go to Salmonier then I'll go with you to make sure you are looked after," he said as he left.

Mary had a new problem. She was going to St. John's to tell someone about the U-Boat, but how could she tell anyone if Lake was with her all the time? That must be their plan. To make sure that she didn't say anything, they would have someone stay with her all the time. Maybe she would just have to get better on her own because this plan wasn't going to work. Mary stayed in bed as she tried to sort out her predicament.

Lake left the house and went down to the wharf. He spoke to Janet again.

"I've seen Mary and she said she is not feeling any better."

Bill walked over to where Lake and Janet were standing.

"Did you see her?" he asked.

"Yes, and she says she's no better."

"Okay then, it's settled," Bill said. "As soon as we finish here, we'll get underway.

"I'd like to accompany you," Lake said. "I'm her priest and I could stay with her and make sure she is okay. If they admit her to hospital I'll be with her. And when she's ready to come home, I'll put a message on the *Doyle Bulletin* for you."

"You'd do that?" Janet asked.

"Yes, of course I will," he answered.

"That makes me feel a lot better," Bill said, as he took his hand and shook it. "We'll be getting underway within the hour. I suggest you pack a bag. Janet, go get Mary ready."

Mary was still in bed when she heard her mother return. She had made up her mind. She would go to St. John's and try to get a message to someone. As long as she stayed in Three Rock Harbour, there was nothing she could do. At least in St. John's she would have a chance. She moaned as her mother approached.

"Your father is going to take you to the doctor," her mother said, as she went to her dresser and got her a change of clothes. "Get dressed and dress warm because it's going to be cold, even in the cabin of the boat. Father Lake is going to go with you. That's a load off our minds. He's a good man."

If she only knew, Mary thought. If she and Bill only knew what kind of man Father Lake really was they certainly wouldn't let him go with her.

Mary got out of bed and began dressing. She moaned occasionally for effect and hated herself for the game she was being forced to play. But there was no other way to deal with the situation. She prayed that she would be able to get a message to someone in St. John's.

The weather was surprisingly good for mid-October. It took nearly three hours to get to Salmonier. Were it not for the help of Father Lake, Bill would have had to tie up his boat, hire a taxi, and take his daughter to St. John's, six hours away. Then he would have to wait for her. He would lose several days of fishing as a result. But thanks to Father Lake he could just drop them off at the wharf and head back to Three Rock Harbour right away. He had to get back to Three Rock Harbour before dark and before the wind came up. He dropped Mary and Lake off at the wharf and made Lake promise to let them know what was happening via the *Bulletin*.

Lake carried their bags as he and Mary stepped off the boat onto the wharf. There was a group of men milling about and he inquired about hiring someone to take them to St. John's. St. John's. They were told where the man who provided the taxi service lived and twenty minutes later they were on their way to St. John's. Lake had told Bill earlier that he would look after the expenses and they could discuss the costs after they returned. This was just another reason why the Sullivans were indebted to Father Lake.

It took six hours to get to St. John's and another half an hour to weave through the city to St. Clare's Hospital. Mary had never been to St. John's and she couldn't believe that so many people could live in the same place. There were houses and people everywhere and even though it was dark when they arrived, the lights from the homes lit up the city so that it was like daytime.

They arrived at the hospital and were greeted by one of the nuns who provided the nursing services. She showed them to a waiting area where a half dozen or so other people were waiting to see the doctor. There was a nun behind the counter, checking in patients. Lake was wearing his collar and that meant special treatment.

"Hello," the nun greeted him as soon as he approached.

"Hello, I'm Father Lake from Three Rock Harbour. Mary Sullivan has been complaining about severe stomach pains. I wonder if she could get to see the doctor."

"Yes, that won't be a problem. There are six people in front of her. It will be a wait of approximately twenty minutes," she said.

Lake went to sit down and give Mary the news. The wait was closer to thirty minutes and finally she was called. She got up and followed the nun. A man of about 50 was waiting in his office. He held the door as she approached.

"Hello Mary," he said as she approached. "I'm Doctor Chaytor. I'm told you're having stomach pains. Is this your father?" he asked. He quickly noticed the collar, but before he could apologize Mary spoke.

"No, this is Father Lake," she answered.

"I'm pleased to meet you, Father Lake," the doctor smiled as he extended his hand.

"I'm pleased to meet you too," Lake said.

Mary walked through the door, and Lake tried to come with her.

"I promised her family I wouldn't leave her for even a second," he said.

"You won't be able to keep your promise, I'm afraid," Doctor Chaytor said. "There are only going to be two people in the room when I examine this young lady. And unless you have a medical degree you're not going to be one of them. Sister Peach," he called out. "See that Father Lake is comfortable."

Lake tried to say something else but Doctor Chaytor smiled and closed the door. Mary's heart was beating madly.

"Now young lady, I want you to take off your coat, get up on my examination table and let's see if we can find out what's wrong with your stomach," the doctor said.

Mary waited a moment to ensure that Lake was out of earshot.

"Doctor," she said very excitedly, "there is nothing wrong with my stomach. My name is Mary Sullivan from Three Rock Harbour. That man is not a Father. He's German. There's a U-Boat in Three Rock Harbour and it comes and goes. It was the one that sank the *Caribou.* They have been making out that they are a British submarine called the *Sea Shark,* but actually it is *U-69* commanded by Captain-lieutenant Ulrich Graf. They hide in Three Rock Harbour and they go out for a few days and then come back. They are due back tonight or tomorrow. You have to help us, Doctor."

Doctor Chaytor stood staring with his mouth open.

"I'm not crazy, Doctor. This is the only way I could figure out to get a message out to help us. No one knows, only me. No one, not even my family, knows the truth."

Doctor Chaytor still didn't speak.

"Doctor, please say something. "I didn't think that he was going to let me be alone. We don't have much time."

"I'm going to give you a shot," Chaytor finally managed.

"I don't need a shot, Doctor. Please, you're our only hope. Check out my story but don't let anyone know what you're doing. He says his name is Father Lake. Check and see if he exists. And our schoolteacher is Dan Blair. He's about 40 and has a British accent. Check him out as well. Our radio transmitter is not working. That's because they took away the tubes so we can't transmit or receive. They have convinced everyone that they are on a secret mission and they are really British. Please, Doctor."

Doctor Chaytor finally sat down. "If all of what you have told me is true then how come you're the only one who knows who they really are?"

"That's complicated but I will tell you quickly. One of the German sailors is a radio man and they have a radio station set up in our church. I used to go to the church and clean it and we met and talked. We sort of got to like each other, if you know what I mean. Right now I love him. His captain saw him at a dance with me and he got really mad and sent him back to the boat and he was not allowed to leave. He was put on late night guard watch and he made out he fell over and drowned. I have been hiding him in my father's hay barn for the past few days. When I told him how much I hated Germans after I heard about the sinking of the *Caribou* on the *Bulletin* he told me who he really is. Then we made up this plan. Doctor, you have to believe me. I'm not crazy. I know it sounds like I'm crazy. Please."

"So you're saying that a German U-Boat is masquerading as a British submarine and hiding out in Three Rock Harbour," he said. 'Where is Three Rock Harbour? I don't think I have heard of it before."

"It's a fishing community on the Southern Shore. It's about three hours from Salmonier," she answered.

"I see, so you're convinced that they're German and they are in a U-Boat?"

"Yes, Doctor, that's exactly what I'm saying. They asked everybody to keep the secret and when they leave before Christmas they will pay everybody a lot of money."

"My God, the story is so wild that it just might be true. But how am I going to help?"

"You have to check out my story without anyone suspecting anything. Blair and Lake are part of the U-Boat's crew. Blair is our schoolteacher and Lake is our priest. Find out where our regular teacher is. Find out why the priest has not been visiting once a month like he should have. If Blair and Lake are really who they say they are then somebody has to know them. Please, Doctor. My family is all back there. You are our only hope."

"Okay, let's say the incredible story you're telling me is true. What am I going to do?" he asked.

"You are going to have to say that I'm sick. You have to say I must stay here, at least overnight. Put me in hospital or something. Check out my story, but for God's sake be careful. When you find out that Blair and Lake are fakes you will know. Then you will have to tell someone about this. You must know someone in the army or the navy. And you can't use a radio. They have radios and if they hear it they could hurt or kill the people in Three Rock Harbour. I don't know what you have to do," Mary said, as tears began to stream down her face. "You have to know someone. You have to know what to do. You just have to."

"Now, now, don't go crying on me. I think I believe you and that will make me as crazy as you if what you're saying is not true. But it's so crazy a story that it has to be true. Okay, I will tell your keeper that I suspect appendicitis. That will give us some time to deal with this. While we are getting you ready for surgery, I'll be able to check out your story. My brother-in-law is a lieutenant in the navy and I will speak with him after I check out the teacher and the priest. If they don't check out then I'm having you admitted for a psychiatric analysis."

"Thank you, Doctor. Thank you." She ran to him and embraced him.

"Okay, that's fine. Now you get up on the table and stay there until I return," he said, as he left the room.

Lake was waiting for him and he had a very concerned look on his face. "How is she?" he asked.

"I believe she has appendicitis," he said. "I'm having her checked into the hospital so we can do some tests. You may go and wait with her, if you wish."

"Thank you, thank you very much, Doctor," Lake said as he left and hurried to where Mary was.

Chaytor gave instructions that he would not be seeing any more patients for the rest of the evening. He said he had some matters he had to attend to immediately. The nursing sister was to ensure that Mary was admitted to the hospital and he would return later to make all of the necessary arrangements.

Chaytor went to his office and closed the door. He picked up the telephone and asked to be connected with the Basilica. A few minutes later he was speaking with Father O'Brien.

"Father O'Brien," he began. "My name is Dr. Chaytor and I'm here at St. Clare's. I was wondering if I could ask you a couple of questions."

"Yes, Doctor," he answered immediately.

"You supply or provide, I'm not sure what the correct expression is, the priest for Three Rock Harbour?"

"Yes, Doctor, that's correct. We have Father Lake there or rather we used to have Father Lake providing pastoral care for that community."

"I'm not sure I understand what you mean, used to provide care," he said.

"Father Lake was the victim of an unfortunate accident a couple of months ago," said O'Brien. "He had his own boat that he used to travel to the various communities in his charge. He was based in Trepassey and was doing his rounds when he ran into a storm. His boat was found washed up, but we never did find his body. We have been trying to get another priest back into service for the few communities there but it's a difficult process. It's getting late in the year now and so it will be spring before we can assign another priest to the region."

Chaytor couldn't believe what he was hearing. Clearly, whoever the Father Lake was with Mary, he was not the priest he said he was. He thanked O'Brien for the information and hung up the receiver.

Chaytor was friends with the superintendent from the school district who provided the schoolteachers for the southern shore. They played bridge together once a week. He found his home number and called him.

"Hello, Doc," he answered.

"Hello, Ray," he answered, "I'm looking for a bit of information."

"Yes, sure, if I have it," Ray answered.

"You provide the teacher for Three Rock Harbour from your staff, don't you?" he asked.

"Yes, I do," he said.

"What teacher is there now," he said.

"Let me think," he said. "Ahh, Dan Blair, I think it is. Yes, that's right, Dan Blair."

"Are you sure?" he asked.

He paused for a few seconds. "Yes, I remember him because this is his first assignment. He's only a few years older than his students. Why do you want to know, Doc?"

"Oh," he stammered, "I have a young patient and she has done nothing but talk about him since I admitted her. He was the one who insisted that she come into St. John's to get checked. I just wanted to let you know that I appreciate what he did and if you're his boss to let you know that you have a fine young man there."

"Thank you for that. I'll be sure to make a note in his file," he said.

They said their goodbyes and reminded each other about the next bridge date. Chaytor hung up the telephone and reflected upon the conversation.

He couldn't believe what he had just heard. The Blair who was described by Mary was about 40 with a British accent. My God, he thought, she's not crazy, she's telling the truth.

Chaytor picked up the telephone and called the base in Fort Pepperell. He left a message for his brother-in-law, Lieutenant Ken Sears, to call him. He explained that it was very urgent and he wanted to be contacted immediately. If he weren't at work they would have to track him down and have him call. It took nearly thirty minutes but then the telephone rang.

"What's up?" Sears asked when Chaytor answered. "Is Rosemary okay?" Sears was married to Chaytor's sister.

"She's fine, Ken. She's in good health. That's not why I called you."

"Good," he answered. "I was worried. What can I do for you?"

"I'm at St Clare's. I need to speak with you immediately and I can't discuss it over the telephone. Whatever you are doing right now drop it and come here. I can't be any more specific than that. I don't care how you do it, just come here. Don't wear your uniform and don't introduce yourself using your military rank. I will leave a message at reception and you just give your name as Ken Sears when you arrive? Do you understand?"

"What's this all about, Doc?" he asked.

"I can't give you any more information and there is no time to waste.

Just get the hell over here right now," he said, raising his voice.

"Okay," Sears answered. "I'll leave immediately."

Chaytor hung up the telephone and got up from his chair. He went to the reception area and gave instructions to the Sister that he was expecting a visit from a Mr. Ken Sears.

"Show him to my office and then find me," he said.

He left and went to the admitting area and found out that Mary had been assigned a room. He went to it and saw she was in bed and Lake was sitting in the chair beside the bed. He stood up as soon as Chaytor entered.

"So, I see that they've got you settled in. How are you feeling?" he asked as he approached her and lifted her hand to feel her pulse.

"I'm still having a lot of pain," she lied, as she placed her hand on her stomach.

"I'm waiting for the surgeon to arrive to get his opinion. He won't be long." He turned to Father Lake. "Father, could you just wait outside for a couple of minutes? I'd like to give her another examination."

Lake stood up. "No, I don't mind," he said, smiling as he stood up and went outside.

Dr. Chaytor rolled down the sheet and put his stethoscope on Mary's stomach.

"I have spoken with the Basilica and they said that Father Lake was killed when his boat sank. I spoke with the school authority and they told me that Dan Blair is a young boy and this is his first teaching assignment. I suspect the Germans sank Lake's boat, and I don't know what they did with Blair. But it looks like you're telling the truth, young lady."

"Thank you," she smiled. "Thank you very much. What do we do now?"

"I have called my brother-in-law who is in the navy. He is on his way. I will bring him here when he arrives and we'll tell the priest that he's the surgeon. I'm going to tell him to come back in now so that we don't raise his suspicions. Okay?"

She nodded her assent and Chaytor went to the door and called Lake in.

"I think she is going to need surgery," he advised Lake when he returned. "I know her family is worried about her so perhaps you'd like to call the *Bulletin* and have a message broadcast for her family to hear tomorrow night. You can use the telephone in my office if you'd like? We have to wait for the surgeon to arrive, so we can do that now."

"Yes, that's a good idea," Lake said.

"We're just going to my office, Mary," Chaytor said. "You'll be fine until we return. Doctor Sears should be here soon and he'll do a very thorough examination and determine whether or not you need surgery. Okay?"

"Yes, thank you, Doctor," she said.

"I know that you're hungry," he added before leaving. "But if we're going to have to do surgery then you can't have anything to eat or drink. It won't be long now before we know what we're going to do."

Chaytor took Lake to his office and they called the radio station and left a message to be put on the *Doyle Bulletin*.

For the Sullivans in Three Rock Harbour. Mary arrived safely. Being assessed by the doctor. Will know if surgery is required shortly. Will advise further.

After the message was sent. Chaytor suggested they go to the cafeteria and see if they could get something to eat. Lake didn't have to be asked twice. He had not eaten since lunch and was hungry. They went to the cafeteria. Late at night there was only one person working in the cafeteria. But there were sandwiches and coffee available. Just as Lake was getting his food, a Sister advised Chaytor that the person he was expecting had arrived. He told Lake to finish his meal and then come to Mary's room.

Chaytor followed the Sister to reception where his brother-in-law was standing. He was dressed in civilian clothes as requested.

"Thank you for coming," he said, as they shook hands. His brother-in-law tried to say something but Chaytor put his finger to his lips.

"Follow me," he said as they went in beside the counter. "Give me your coat," he said and took it and threw it across an examination table. "Put this on." He passed a lab jacket to him and Sears put it on and raised his eyebrows to express his confusion.

When the jacket was on they left the examination area and made their way towards Mary's room.

"What's this all about?" Sears asked, when there was no one around.

"Just be patient for a minute or so until we get to where we're going," Chaytor asked.

They were in Mary's room a few minutes later and locked the door.

"Mary Sullivan, this is Lieutenant Sears. I want you to tell him what you told me," Chaytor said.

Mary sat up in bed. "I'm from Three Rock Harbour," she began. "A couple of months ago, a submarine appeared in our harbour. The captain said his name was Commander Stewart and the name of the boat was the *Sea Shark*. He said they were there on a secret mission to help patrol the area for German U-boats. They didn't want anybody talking about them being there. They gave us a teacher and a priest and they set up a radio station in the church. They took away the tubes from our radio transmitter so that we couldn't transmit anything to anyone. They said they would be staying until Christmas and then they would pay everyone money equal to what they would get when they sold their fish. They stay for a few days and then they leave for a few days. I know that they are really a German U-Boat and the captain's name is Ulrich Graf. The submarine is the one that sank the boats near Bell Island and the *Caribou*."

"What?" Sears said as he looked at Chaytor. "Is this some kind of joke?"

"This is no joke, Ken," Chaytor said. "There was a man who accompanied her here and he says his name is Father Lake. I called the Basilica and was told that Father Lake's boat was sunk around the time the U-Boat arrived in Three Rock Harbour. He's from the U-Boat. I called the school superintendent and he says that the schoolteacher they sent to Three Rock Harbour is a young kid. The person who is there is a middle-aged man. He was also supplied by the U-Boat."

"How do you know all this?" Sears asked.

Mary looked at Chaytor. "I'm hiding one of the crew in my father's barn. They think that he fell overboard and drowned. He told me everything."

"My good God. This is just unbelievable. There is actually a German U-Boat hiding there?"

Mary nodded.

Sears paced around the room.

"I don't know what to say. If I go to my superiors with this they are going to think I'm nuts." He looked at Chaytor and at Mary. "Tell me that this isn't some kind of a joke," he said.

"This isn't a joke," Chaytor said.

"Describe this thing you think is a U-Boat," Sears said to Mary.

Mary began describing it. She closed her eyes and tried to remember every detail. When she was finished she waited for Sears's response.

"That's what a U-Boat looks like," he admitted. "Tell me about this sailor that you're hiding."

"They set up a radio unit in the church. I used to go there to clean and we started talking. We were at a dance and the captain saw us and ordered him back to the boat. We used to send each other messages in a can. He didn't want to stay with them so he faked his death and I have been hiding him."

"He was a radio person?" he inquired.

"Yes," Mary answered.

"Do you believe him?" he asked.

"Yes, I believe him. And he told me something that you should know about. He says that he knows how to operate the Enigma machine, whatever that is," she said.

Sears's jaw dropped. "What?" he shouted, as he approached her.

The sudden rise in Sears' voice startled Mary. She stared at him.

"Repeat what you just said," he ordered.

Mary still did not respond. She looked at Dr. Chaytor.

"Answer him," he said.

"He said that he knows how to operate the Enigma machine, I think that's what he said the name was."

"My good God Almighty," Sears said. "This is true. This young girl is telling the truth. Do you know what an Enigma machine is, Doc?"

Chaytor shook his head. "No," he answered. "What's an Enigma machine?"

"Exactly," Sears said. "What's an Enigma machine? You don't know what an Enigma machine is. Mary doesn't know what an Enigma machine is. Outside of the military, there aren't a dozen people in Newfoundland who know what an Enigma machine is. So, how could a young girl from Three Rock Harbour know what an Enigma machine is? How would she have even heard about an Enigma machine?"

"You're rambling, Ken. What's going on?" Chaytor asked.

"This is unbelievable," Sears said.

At that moment the door to Mary's room opened and Lake entered. Chaytor reacted quickly.

"Father Lake, this is Doctor Sears. Doctor Sears, this is Father Lake."

They shook hands.

"Father, could you give us another couple of minutes please," Chaytor asked.

"Yes, sure," Lake said as he left the room.

"Is that him?" Sears asked in a very low voice.

Mary nodded.

"Okay," Sears said. "I have to get this information back to my superiors immediately. I will be in contact." He was flustered because he had so much to say and so little time to say it.

"Go," Chaytor said. "I will talk with Lake. Get back to me as soon as you can."

Sears left the room, and almost immediately Lake appeared.

"The surgeon has gone to check on the operating room situation and will get back to us. It appears as if she is going to need surgery," Chaytor lied. "I also have a few things to check on. I'll be back shortly, Mary."

Chaytor caught up with Sears as he was taking off the lab coat.

"I'll be in contact," Sears said as he pulled on his own coat. "Don't breathe a word of this to anyone. I'm going to see my boss and I just hope that he doesn't have a heart attack after I give him this information. For God's sake, be careful, Doc. This is big. This is really big."

Sears left, almost running from the hospital. Chaytor took the lab coat and threw it in a laundry basket. He sat down and breathed a loud sigh of relief.

"Why me?" he managed.

CHAPTER SIXTEEN

It was after midnight before Sears finished at the hospital and made his way east to Fort Pepperell, an American base in the capital city. An agreement between the United States and Great Britain signed two years earlier on 2 September 1940, the Destroyers-for-Bases deal, resulted in the site being chosen for an American base. In May of 1941, a local labour force began construction at the site.

During the Battle of Britain and the Battle of the Atlantic, Britain became desperate for more war supplies and went looking to the United States for these supplies. Because Britain was unable to finance the purchases, they made a deal with the Americans giving them 99-year leases on land to build their bases in Newfoundland. Newfoundland was thought to make an attractive beachhead for Nazi aggression against North America, as it was lightly populated and defended.

In January of 1941, the transport ship *Edmund B. Alexander* arrived in St. John's with the first American troops to occupy wartime Newfoundland. Ken Sears was a communications specialist who accompanied the engineers. There was no accommodation for the American troops in St. John's so they stayed on board the ship until May of 1941 when they were moved to a temporary installation of tents called Camp Alexander. In November, the troops moved to newly built Fort Pepperell. During his first year in St. John's, Sears met and married Rosemary Chaytor.

Initial plans for Fort Pepperell included accommodations for a garrison of 3,500 troops; however, the military increased the figure to 5,500 early in 1942. The garrison was designated the Newfoundland Base Command and its duties included the defence of United States bases, St. John's harbour and area, and the airfield at nearby Torbay. In order to do this the Army established harbour defence fortifications on Signal Hill and a radio intelligence station at Snelgrove on Portugal Cove Road. Seacoast defence facilities, infantry sites, and searchlight batteries were located along the coastline at Red Cliff Head, Middle Cove, Torbay, Pouch Cove, Cape Spear, Flatrock, Robin Hood Bay, Logy Bay, Outer Cove, and White Hills. The Army operated a filter centre at Fort Pepperell for data collected from radar air warning sites at Cape Bonavista, Allan's Island, Cape Spear, St. Bride's and Fogo Island. Lieutenant Sears was Commanding Officer of the filter centre.

The new base in St. John's was operated by the United States Army Air Forces (USAAF). At the same time that construction was underway in St. John's, the United States Navy was building a base in Argentia, and the USAAF was building a base in Stephenville.

The primary lodger unit at Pepperell was the 6604th Air Base Wing, which operated and maintained Fort Pepperell. The Royal Canadian Air Force established RCAF Station Torbay on December 15, 1941 and shared the facility with the Americans as well as the Royal Air Force. Colonel Paul N. Starling had replaced Lt. Colonel J.J. Yates as officer commanding Fort Pepperell on December 2, 1941. There were currently about 5,500 troops stationed there and all were heavily involved with exercises and manoeuvres.

Sears knew he would have to contact Colonel Starling immediately and impart the information he had. He drove up to the entrance of Fort Pepperell, showed his identification to the guard, and drove on in to headquarters. He located the duty officer and was told that Colonel Starling was in his quarters. Ten minutes later, Sears was knocking on his door.

A maid opened the door and invited him in. A minute or so later he was shown into the colonel's study. Starling was sitting behind his desk. He pointed to a chair in front of it.

"What brings you here at this time of the morning, Lieutenant?" he asked.

Sears sat down. "I've just returned from St. Clare's Hospital where I met with Dr. Chaytor and a young girl from Three Rock Harbour."

"These people sure do give the names of their communities colourful titles," Starling laughed. "Where's Three Rock Harbour located?" he asked.

"It's across the bay from Salmonier," Sears answered. "Directly across the peninsula from Argentia."

"Okay, I think I know where it is," he said.

"Colonel, this is going to be one of the most outrageous stories you will ever hear. Believe me, Sir, I'm not drunk, and I believe that every word of what I am about to tell you is true."

"Well, you certainly have my attention, Lieutenant. Continue."

"Dr. Chaytor is my brother-in-law. He called me earlier this evening and asked me to come over to the hospital. There I met a young girl from Three Rock Harbour. She told me a story which has been somewhat verified and, if true, and I think it is true, will turn this base on its head."

"Go ahead," Colonel Starling said.

"She says a couple of months ago a German U-Boat came into their harbour."

"What?" the colonel shouted.

For the next ten minutes Sears related the story to his commanding officer. The colonel hung on every word and occasionally interrupted an expression of total shock. Finally, Sears finished story.

"This is just too outrageous to be true," Starling said. "Surely to God these people would not have the balls to try something like this. This just has to be one big misunderstanding."

"Colonel, you know the Germans are using Enigma machines, right?" Sears asked.

"Yes, of course I do."

"Well, this young girl mentioned the Enigma machine. What do you think are the chances that a young girl from an isolated fishing community in Newfoundland would have heard about an Enigma machine? Of the 5,000 or more people stationed here, there are probably not a dozen who have ever heard of it."

"Sweet Jesus," said Starling. "Can this be true? Can there really be a U-Boat operating right under our noses? This can't wait. I will need my chief of staff, my chief of operations, the director of intelligence and whoever else you can think of. Go back to headquarters and get them called in. I will be there as soon as I get dressed. Tell them I'll expect them there before I get there. That will give them the sense of urgency I need."

"Wait a minute," he added. "Don't do this on the telephone. I have no idea who may be listening to our communications. Do an alert recall. Get everyone to the command post. We've done this a dozen times in the past six months as part of our exercise procedures. This will be seen as another exercise alert. I'll call the duty officer from here and he will start the process. You go to the command post and wait for me."

Sears left the colonel's quarters and headed back to the base. He was one of the first to arrive in the command post and take up his usual place at the table. The base recall plan was designed to have all unit commanders at the command post within one hour of the alert call. All commanders were required to make a central control agency aware of their location at all times. If an alert was called, a telephone call would be made or a person dispatched to alert the officer of the situation.

The command post administrative staff was making the room ready by the time Sears arrived. Nameplates, pads and pencils, jugs of water, and all other required materials were placed at each station around the table. Chairs for the staff of the various unit commanders were around the walls. The staff was on hand in case their bosses were asked something that needed clarification. Within 50 minutes of the call, everyone was seated in the command centre and Colonel Starling began.

"First of all," he said, "thank you all for getting here under the allotted time. This is not, I repeat this is not, an exercise call. This is a 'no duff' situation. I will let Lieutenant Sears provide you with the reason for this alert call."

Sears stood up and went to the front of the room. There was no need for further introductions because they all knew each other. Sears told the same story he had told Starling earlier. As he provided further details, the more shocked the gathered officers became. He had to answer all of the same questions asked earlier and he provided the same answers. Once finished, he returned to his place at the table.

"Thank you, Lieutenant," Starling said. "Now, I want to know how we are going to deal with this. First, I think we're going to have to assume that we are on our own with this one. I can't trust communicating any of this information to higher headquarters. I don't know if our codes have been broken or not. This is just too important to have compromised. Second, we have made several unsuccessful attempts to get our hands on an Enigma machine. If we are successful in this case, we will not only get the machine, we will have the codes as well. Third, if we are successful, we can reverse the roles. We can continue operations and the German High Command will be none the wiser. We have a defector who is a radio operator. He knows their procedures. That is invaluable.

"I want a plan and I want it quick. I want nothing discussed with your staff unless it is done face to face. Keep staff involvement to the bare minimum. Nothing about this incident is to be discussed over telephone lines or by radio.

"You have two hours and then I want to meet back here. I want a plan that will protect the people in Three Rock Harbour. I want that U-Boat and its crew. And I want the Enigma machine. Lieutenant Sears."

"Yes, Sir," Sears answered.

"I want you back at the hospital. Keep a twenty-four hour watch on the girl and the German who says he's a priest. I want to know everything he does. Bring one of your staff with you and says he's a janitor or a clerk. Just make sure we know where this priest is at all times. Brief Dr. Chaytor and tell him not a word to anybody. You remain at the hospital and I will send a runner to you every two hours so that you can get information to me and we can get information to you. Is that clear?"

"Yes, Sir," Sears answered as he got from the table and left the room.

Sears was back at the hospital half an hour later. He had picked up Sergeant Coombs and briefed him on the way. Chaytor was in his office and he briefed him on what had happened at the command post. Chaytor found Coombs a set of hospital whites and told him to wander around the area. He said if anyone asked him who he was he should say he was working for him on a special project. Coombs knew what he had to do.

In the meantime, the issue was what to do about Mary. Clearly, she had to be protected from Lake and a decision had to be made about her 'surgery.' Chaytor and Sears cooked up a plan and went to see her.

"We're going to have to take out your appendix," Chaytor informed her when they got to her room. "It can wait until morning. The inflammation may go away but because of where you live we can't take a chance. The surgery is scheduled for 7 a.m. Unfortunately, we can't let you have anything to eat or drink until then. A nurse will be coming by shortly to take you to pre-op where you will spend the night." He turned to Lake. "I'll get a nurse to change the sheets and you can spend the night here, Father," he said. "By noon tomorrow, Mary should be able to return to her room. We'll find another room for you then or we'll put a cot in here."

"I'd prefer a cot in here. I did promise her family," said Lake.

"I understand, Father," Chaytor said. "We'll get you a cot but she is going to have to spend the night in pre-op. I trust you understand."

"Yes, of course I do," he said.

"Mary," Chaytor said, as he turned to her, "there is nothing to worry about. We do these kinds of surgeries every day. It will take about an hour and you'll be asleep for a couple of hours after that. You won't feel a thing. After a couple of days in recovery you'll be able to go home and be with your family. Okay?"

"Are you sure I won't feel any pain," she asked.

"Positive," said Chaytor. "After the surgery you'll feel a little uncomfortable and then before you know it, there will be just be a little scar to remind you of the entire ordeal."

Chaytor said that although he would not be doing the surgery, he would be there with Dr. Sears. Sears said a few words of encouragement and they left.

They returned to Chaytor's office to await word from Colonel Starling. Sears knew he would hear from the colonel in a couple of hours. He went looking for Sergeant Coombs and told him that Lake would be spending the night in Mary's room and he should park himself somewhere in that area. Depending upon what orders he received later, it might be necessary to find someone to replace him. Chaytor informed the reception staff that he would be spending the night in his office. He said he was expecting someone in a couple of hours, and he should be brought directly to him.

It was nearly 2:30 a.m. when the messenger arrived from headquarters. Major Ernie Woods, director of intelligence, was accompanied by one of his junior officers. They were dressed in civilian clothes. Sears introduced them to Chaytor.

Woods quickly began briefing them on the plan.

"Dr. Chaytor," he began, "you do not have a security clearance and what we are about to discuss has been assigned a Top Secret security classification. Because of the time constraints and the nature of this operation, we do not have the time to do any background checks on you. We have to trust that you will not discuss this information with anyone other than those persons we designate as needing to know."

"Yes, of course. I understand," Chaytor said.

"Good," said Woods. "Right now, all we have is a young girl telling us that there is German U-Boat in a community on the south coast of the Avalon. Only the two of you have spoken with her and the single piece of information that appears to have convinced us all is that she has mentioned an Enigma machine. Other than that, she could be as crazy as a loon. Do you agree with that statement, Doctor?"

"Yes, partially," Chaytor said. "But the information about the priest and the schoolteacher also make her story pretty convincing."

"Yes, that's true. But before we proceed any further, I need to talk with her. If she convinces me, then our plan will go forward. I have pictures of British subs and German U-boats. If she can't tell the difference, then we're in trouble. I also have pictures of British submariner uniforms as well as German submariner uniforms. I'd like her to be able to point out what these people are wearing."

"That all makes sense," Chaytor said. "Let's go see her."

Mary was in pre-op and asleep. Chaytor shook her awake. She sat up in bed and tried to rub the sleep from her eyes. When she was fully awake, he introduced the people with him.

"Mary, I'm sorry to awaken you this early in the morning," Woods said.

"It's okay," Mary said.

"I trust that you understand that, by our nature, we are not a very trusting bunch of people. I'm an intelligence officer and before I can brief my boss on something, I need to know everything I can about a subject. I'm sure you can understand that."

Mary nodded.

"You also must understand that we think that your story is pretty unbelievable," he continued.

"Yes," she said, "but it's true."

"That's what we're about to find out," Woods said. "Tell me about this U-Boat."

Mary looked at Chaytor and then at Woods. "It's black and about a hundred feet long. It has a big gun on the deck and there's a big lump on the top and that's how they get in and get out. There's a rail or something around that lump thing. There's not very much above the water." She paused for a few seconds. "I don't know what else to say about it."

"That's good," Woods said. "Do you think that you could recognize it if I showed you a picture?"

"Yes, of course I could," she answered.

Woods opened his case, pulled out a file and passed her a picture. She looked at it for a few seconds.

"It's the same shape but the lump thing is not the same," she said.

"It's called a conning tower," Woods advised her.

He then passed her a second picture and got the same response. Then a third picture. She didn't hesitate when she saw it.

"That's it," she said. "That's exactly it except that the one in Three Rock Harbour has a flag painted on the conning tower."

"What kind of a flag?" he asked.

"The Union Jack."

"Okay," he said. "Where does this boat dock when it comes into the harbour?"

"There's a big hole in the cliffs on the side of the harbour. It goes in there and I heard the captain tell my father that's so any planes flying over won't see it."

"When did it arrive? Tell me about that," he said to her.

Mary talked about how they are got up the morning of brother's birthday. She described the man who identified himself as Commander Stewart. She also talked about the sailors setting up a radio room in the church and how she came to meet and fall in love with Karl.

Major Woods then passed her various pictures of submariners. From what she pointed out, the sailors on the U-Boat were wearing the uniforms of British submariners.

It took about an hour for Major Woods to get the information he wanted and at the end he was convinced there was German U-Boat in Three Rock Harbour. He then wanted information about its comings and goings and Mary informed him that there was no schedule to their departures and arrivals, but she did say that one time when they went out, two boats were sunk near Bell Island. Another time when they went out the *Caribou* was sunk.

Woods was surprised she knew about the sinking of the boats. She went on to explain that she had a radio set and she listened to the *Doyle Bulletin* every evening.

Woods began writing furiously when he was given that information. This was unexpected. After he finished writing, he began asking questions about the number of crewmembers, if they came ashore, and other details. Mary was not able to tell him how many people were on board because all she ever saw was the captain, a few crew, and the radio operators. She said there were two radio operators and they stayed in the church, even when the boat went to sea. And there was of course Father Lake and Blair, the schoolteacher.

Woods finished with his questioning and thanked her for the information. Chaytor told her while she wouldn't be having surgery they would be bringing her into the operating room to give the impression that she was having surgery. They said goodnight and went back to Chaytor's office.

"I'll have to advise the chief of surgery what's going on," Chaytor said once they were settled.

"I don't want anyone else aware of what's happening," Woods said.

"I have a girl up in pre-op and I'm going to take her into surgery this morning and not do anything. I have to tell the chief of surgery. There's just no way out of it."

"I'm sorry," Woods said. "I understand. But I want to be there when you talk with him."

"So, do we have a plan?' Sears asked.

"Yes, sort of," Woods said. "But now that we know there is a way to communicate with people there, hopefully without the Germans finding out, we may change it."

"What was or is the plan?" Sears asked.

"There are several plans in the works, but the main problem with all of the plans is knowing where the submarine is at any given time. If we didn't care about the Enigma machine then all we'd have to do is put a couple of destroyers outside the harbour and blow it all to hell when it came out. But we want the Enigma machine and we want the codes. If we flew over the community and could see the boat was in the harbour we could send in a boarding crew and try to overpower them. There would be very little element of surprise. There would be lot of people killed and they would have time to destroy the machine and the codes. So the problem we have is finding just the right time to attack and how to attack."

"I understand the dilemma," Sears said.

"According to Mary, the boat was at sea when she left to come here. The boat had been gone for a few days and also again, according to Mary, she never stayed away much longer than four or five days. If that boat's the one that sunk the *Caribou* then she's probably headed back to port right after and she's either there now or should arrive soon," Woods said.

"We have to know when she is in port, and to make it perfect, our coming has to be a complete surprise so we can board her and get the Enigma and the codes. At the same time, or earlier, we have to get control of the radio to prevent any warnings been sent to the sub or other U-Boats in the area. That's why we don't have a plan. But now that we have a way of getting messages to someone in Three Rock Harbour, I think we can come up with a plan."

Woods and his assistant left a few minutes later to go back to the command post to brief Colonel Starling. On the way, the plan was being formulated.

CHAPTER SEVENTEEN

It was 4 a.m. when Woods returned to the command post. Everyone there had broken off into little groups and was still trying to come up with a plan that would allow them to capture the sub and the coding equipment with a minimal loss of life. Colonel Starling called everyone back into the command post when Woods arrived.

"There is no doubt that there is a U-Boat in Three Rock Harbour," Woods began. "The young girl identified the pictures, the fake British uniforms and her other details leave no doubt in my mind. I have found out they are operating a radio unit in the church and it is manned by two of the crew from the boat. The priest and schoolteacher are German and at any given time there are four of them ashore. The only other person who regularly leaves the boat is the captain. So, in a worst case scenario, there would be five Germans ashore at any one time." He paused to get a drink before continuing.

"Our problem, if you remember, from our first meeting, was trying to determine when the boat was actually in port. We can't send anyone there with a radio because the Germans would pick up our transmissions. We could send someone to hide out there, but the problem remains of getting a message out to us. And we also have the problem of getting information to our person there. As a result of talking with the girl, I think I've found a way to get information there."

Woods had everyone's attention as he continued to speak.

"Mary, the young girl, told me that every night she listens to the *Doyle Bulletin*. I don't know how many of you have ever heard of it or listened to it, but for people outside St. John's it's their only way of getting news and information. People send messages to family members telling them they arrived safely or are getting out of the hospital and on their way home. A whole host of information messages. Using the *Doyle Bulletin* we could get messages to anyone we have in Three Rock Harbour."

"That's great," Captain Els said, "So anyone we send will need a radio."

"What if we already have someone there who has a radio?" Colonel

Starling asked.

A chorus of 'who?' echoed around the room.

"What about the girl?" Woods asked. "How about if Mary is the one we pass the messages to?"

Most agreed perhaps that would be the easiest thing, but they were still faced with the problem of getting information from her. One-way communication would serve no purpose. They had to come up with a way to allow her, if she was the one, to get information out to them. And, the information given to her had to be transmitted in such a way that only the sender and the receiver would understand the message. If Mary were to receive messages, a code would have to be developed and taught her in a couple of days. Because, in a couple of days, she would be going back home.

Sears left the table and went over to his two staff seated against the wall.

"Get working on something right away," he said. "I want it simple and I want her to be able to learn it quickly. It has to be sent on the *Doyle Bulletin* and it's got to fit in with the other messages."

They left the room to get to work and Sears returned to the table.

"We'll come up with something, Sir," he said to Colonel Starling.

"Great," Starling said. "Now that leaves us with coming up with a way for her to communicate with us. What do we have to work with?"

They knew Arns, the merchant, had a radio transmitter in his shop. However, one of the tubes was missing and if it was activated there was a very good chance it would be detected by the Germans. There was also the German-controlled radio in the church. It seemed that unless a radio set was transported to the community and set up with a radio operator, communications were going to be one way only.

"What about this Karl who defected?" Sears said to no one in particular. "He's a radio operator. As far as the Germans are concerned, he's dead. I don't think that he can get into the German radio room, but he shouldn't have any problem getting access to the radio transmitter in the merchant's shop."

"Yes, that's possible," one of the officers conceded, "but you've already said that the Germans have removed tubes from it."

"Yes," another said, "but it shouldn't be too difficult to find out what kind of a set it is and what kind of tubes it uses. You should have no problem determining that, Ken."

"You're absolutely right. I can send a few tubes back with Mary. She can give them to the German and he can operate the set. All we need to know is when the boat is in port. He can send us one-word messages to answer the questions we ask in the *Doyle Bulletin*. The chances of the Germans picking up on that are pretty remote. We can keep the boat in port once we know she's there, we'll just schedule an exercise in that area. We'll send a few destroyers and make a lot of noise and she won't dare leave with all that tonnage around. We'll just say we'll be running back and forth from Argentia. That should keep them bottled up for awhile."

"That sounds like it just might work," Starling said. "You all know what has to be done so let's get at it. I want an operations order by noon today. I also want a way to communicate with Mary via the *Bulletin*. Let's get to it."

Mary was wheeled into the operating room at 7 a.m. Lake was told the surgery went fine and he would be able to see her around lunch time. Mary was put in isolation and the time used to brief her about what was being planned. She said she and Karl would do whatever was necessary. All was needed now was a way to communicate with her. By 10 a.m. Sears' staff had developed a simple code.

At the end of each night's *Bulletin* the announcer passed along the messages about people arriving and leaving St. John's, as well as admissions and discharges from hospital. The plan was that messages to Mary would be concealed using these kinds of messages.

All the messages to her would be sent from people whose surname began with 'M.' They would also be the final message on each broadcast. Messages would consist of a series of short sentences. The first sentence would be a preamble advising her to get ready. The actual message would follow with the initial word in the first sentence being the first code word, and the last word in the second sentence being the second code word. This could repeats until the message was understood. The final line is as is with no code words. So, a typical message would be like this:

*The last message of this evening is from Bill Murphy to his family in Englee. **Is** safe in St. John's. Paid passage for **boat.** **In** with your sister. Tomorrow will leave **port.** **Will keep you advised.***

Unscrambled, the message read: Is boat in port?
The response would be a simple: The family is home or no one is home.
The only thing left to chance would be the use of the radio transmitter. Karl would have to be able to get into Arns' store and use it without being discovered. The answer to all messages would be sent each morning at exactly 3 a.m. Mary would be given a pocket watch to give to Karl so he would be able to tell the time.

At noon, Lake was shown into the recovery room where Mary was in bed. Her stomach was bandaged for effect, and Dr. Chaytor was there with her as was Sears. Lake was told there was no complications with the surgery and Mary would be allowed to return home the following morning. It was suggested a message should be put on the *Bulletin* asking her father to meet her and Lake in Salmonier mid-afternoon. That would allow plenty of time for the taxi to get them there.

Lake appeared to be very pleased with the turn of events and was anxious to get back to Three Rock Harbour. He quickly left to arrange a taxi and ensure a message was broadcast on that evening's *Doyle Bulletin*.

In his absence, the radio tubes were carefully packaged in Mary's bag and she was told how she should walk and act if she had really had her appendix removed.

The next day, Mary and Lake set out on the return trip to Three Rock Harbour.

Bill and Ray were waiting for them on the wharf in Salmonier. Bill ran towards Mary when he saw her and made an attempt to embrace her. She placed one hand on her stomach, and held up the other to ward him off.

"Oh," he said as he got the message. "How are you, sweetheart?"

"I had to have my appendix removed and I'm still a little sore," she lied.

Bill turned to Lake and reached out his hand.

"I don't know how we would have gotten through this without you," he said as they shook hands. "I'll never be able to repay you for what you've done, but let me know how much it cost for everything and I'll find some way to repay you."

"Don't you worry a thing about it," Lake smiled. "What better can I do with my money than to help one of my parishioners?"

"Nevertheless, I will find some way to pay you for all you've done."

"I'm a little tired now, Dad," Mary said, as she interrupted them.

"I'm sorry," Bill said as he quickly turned his attention to her and, with an arm around her shoulder, helped her aboard the boat. Ray stood on the deck and led his sister to the cabin. Minutes later they were underway.

There were a couple of dozen people on the wharf when they arrived. All of Mary's family were there as were a few of her friends. They waved frantically as they watched the boat come in the harbour and as she stepped onto the wharf everyone cheered. Mary saw them, but it was her father's barn up on the hill that got all of her attention. She also looked at the *Sea Shark's* mooring and saw the boat wasn't there. Maybe, she thought, they had left for good and there would be no need for what was planned. Then she remembered that Lake was part of the crew and surely they would not leave without him.

Everyone wanted to hug her but she did pointed to her stomach and held them off. She answered a hundred questions about how she was feeling and a hundred more about St. John's and what it was like. Nobody in the community had ever been to St. John's, few had been as far as Salmonier.

Janet helped Mary up the stairs to her bedroom and insisted she go to bed. Mary tried to protest but to no avail. Her mother wanted her to spend the next couple of days in bed just to be on the safe side. Mary reluctantly agreed, but longed to go see Karl.

By 10 p.m. the lamps were out and those in the house who weren't asleep were not far from it. Mary decided to wait until 10:30 before making her move. It was the longest 30 minutes of her life. Finally, it was 10:30 and she quietly got out of bed and dressed.

The stairs creaked but she tried to be a quiet as possible by not walking in the centre of the steps. If anyone heard her, she would tell them she was going downstairs for a drink of water. There was a full moon and the light was enough for her to find her way around the kitchen. She put on her coat and boots, and then remembered the moose stew Janet had cooked for supper.

There was stew left in the pot on the stove so she decided to bring some to Karl. The stove was still warm and so was the stew. She filled a bowl to nearly overflowing and put a spoon in her pocket. Carefully and quietly she opened the kitchen door and made her way to the barn.

Karl had not been expecting a visit from her, and he was startled when the door to the barn opened below him. He listened as the door opened and closed. He heard footsteps cross the barn to the ladder.

"Karl," Mary called. "Karl, it's me, Mary. Can you hear me?"

Karl threw off the blankets that covered him. "Yes, I hear you," he said excitedly.

"I have some stew for you. Come down and help me with it," she said. "Open the doors so we can see."

Karl had only been eating raw vegetables the last few days. Janet had all of the preserves neatly arranged on shelves in the cellar and he was afraid that if he took just one it would be noticed. He quickly opened the doors and went down the ladder. He took the bowl of stew from Mary and she passed him the spoon. He began shovelling it into his mouth ravenously.

"Well it seems that you missed my mother's stew more than you missed me," Mary grinned.

Karl paused between spoonfuls and tried to speak.

"It's been so long since I had anything to eat that was cooked that..." He stopped talking as he filled his mouth again.

Mary laughed. "I was just joking. Finish the stew."

Karl continued to eat as though it was his last meal. When the bowl was empty he used his finger to wipe the sides of the bowl and then licked his finger.

"You were hungry, weren't you?" Mary said.

"I was nearly starved. I was afraid to touch your mother's preserves but I had made up my mind that if you didn't return by tomorrow I was going to chance it." He put the spoon and bowl on the floor and reached for Mary, who came willingly into his arms. He kissed her and she responded.

"I really missed you," he said, as he broke away.

"I missed you too," she said, as she kissed him again.

"I watched you come up the path to your house this evening," he said, as they stopped kissing. "You looked like you were in pain."

Mary laughed. "I had to make it look like I had surgery," she said. "Let's go up to the loft in case someone comes in."

They climbed the ladder and sat on the blankets. Mary pulled one blanket up over her as Karl sat beside her and did the same.

"Tell me everything. Tell me everything that happened," Karl said.

For the next fifteen minutes, Mary told him about her experiences. She told him the plan about getting access to the radio and the tubes that she had brought back with her. She had written instructions for him from the people in St. John's and she also told him about the plan to get messages by listening to the *Doyle Bulletin*. They would have to get access to the radio transmitter as quickly as possible so they could let St. John's know if the boat was in the harbour. Tomorrow evening, she would give him the tubes and they would have to try and get to the radio transmitter.

Karl listened intently and agreed to cooperate. He would do anything to help her get rid of his former crewmates. However, he expressed great doubt about successfully capturing the submarine. The only person who regularly left the boat was the captain. Even though English was the working language of the boat, the captain didn't want to take any unnecessary chances and let anyone ashore who might inadvertently spoke German. That would spell disaster.

It was nearly midnight when they finished talking and after some intimate kissing and touching, Mary made her way back to her house.

CHAPTER EIGHTEEN

Mary went home to bed, but not before finding out that the boat had left the harbour a day earlier. Tomorrow night, she and Karl would have to break into Arns' store and get the radio transmitter working. The people in St. John's had discussed the idea of sending a plane to have a look but that was quickly rejected because they didn't want the submarine's crew to become suspicious.

Mary got up the next morning around 10 a.m. Her mother was very concerned when she walked into the kitchen, but Mary said the doctors had told her to walk a little each day and she intended on following orders. Staying in bed was the worst thing she could do. Besides, she wanted to go back to school in a couple of days. This was her last year and she wanted to graduate so she could go to St. John's and find a job.

She sat at the kitchen table and had a cup of tea and a slice of toast. Sometime today she would have to get the radio tubes to Karl, as well as the note. Her father had not gone fishing today because the sea was too rough. That meant her mother would not be going down on the wharf to help clean fish. Hopefully sometime today she would go out to visit or to get something, and Mary would be able to get the tubes to Karl.

It was mid-afternoon when her mother announced that she was going to her friend's house to help her with house cleaning. The friend had just had a baby and had not yet regained all her strength.

Mary took the opportunity to put the tubes and pocket watch into a pillowcase and take them to the barn. She made Karl a few sandwiches and stuffed them in too. She looked around to see if anyone was watching when she went into the barn and didn't see anybody. Karl was very glad to see her. He quickly ate the sandwiches as he read the note instructing him what frequency to use and what to say. They decided the best time to break into Arns' shop. Mary would come to the barn at 2 a.m. and from there they would go to the shop.

Mary ate supper with the rest of her family and helped with the dishes afterwards. The Sullivans listened to the *Doyle Bulletin* and Mary knew there would be no messages for her. After the *Bulletin,* everyone went to bed except Mary. She said she wanted to stay up and read a little. She had missed quite a bit of school and wanted to catch up.

Time passed slowly for her, but finally it was time and she dressed and headed for the barn. Karl was on the main level waiting for her and after an embrace they began making their way towards the shop. Mary knew that Arns and his family lived above the shop. Hopefully, she and Karl would be able to get in unnoticed and send their message.

It took them about five minutes to get to the shop. Mary tried the main door and wasn't surprised to find it was locked. She remembered there was a cellar in the shop where Arns stored barrels of salt beef and apples and other items that he didn't have room for in the main area. There were stairs leading up to the main floor from the cellar. They went around the corner of the building and down the couple of steps to the cellar door. Karl twisted the wooden closing button and pulled on the handle. The door opened and he and Mary looked at each other with delight and surprise. It was pitch black inside, and without some kind of light they would never find their way. Mary quickly produced a box of *Eddy* matches and struck one. She had to light several more as they made their way up the stairs to the main floor.

Fortunately, the door at the top of the stairs was unlocked. The rusty hinges squealed as it opened and they stepped through. There was enough light coming in through the windows to allow them to see where they had to go. Mary knew where Arns kept the radio set and led the way towards it.

When Karl saw the radio transmitter, he instantly left her side and walked to the back of the set. "Give me the matches," he said. He lit one and looked into the back of the radio transmitter. He took the pillowcase from Mary, found the tube, and pressed it into the missing spot. He next moved around to the front of the machine to make sure the volume button was turned down. He took the piece of paper from his pocket and, using it as a guide, turned the dial to the correct frequency. According to the note, the people in St. John's would be monitoring the frequency from midnight. It was nearly 2:30 a.m. when Karl flicked on the power switch. Immediately the radio transmitter began to crackle, and the orange glow from the tubes began to light up the shop. Mary quickly removed her coat and threw it over the set to dim the light.

It took a few minutes for the radio transmitter to warm up. They looked at each other several times during that time. Finally, Karl spoke. "It's ready to go," he whispered, as he reached for the microphone and gently wrapped his fingers around the shaft. He took a final look at Mary, put his mouth close to the microphone and squeezed the button. "No one is home," he tapped each letter on the key. "No one is home," he repeated. He immediately turned off the set. He got up, passed Mary her coat, removed the tube, and motioned to Mary that they should leave.

Quietly, they left the shop and walked down the stairs to the cellar. Mary lit the matches to light their way. A few minutes after the message had been sent, they were walking back to the barn. It was cold, and they held hands as they hurried along.

Inside the barn, they stood in the dark and kissed.

"I was so afraid we were going to get caught that I almost wet myself," Mary said.

Karl laughed. "If you had, it would have frozen on the way up here."

"I'm freezing," she said. "I must have gotten a chill."

"Come here, I will keep you warm," Karl said, as he drew her closer.

"I have to get home," she said. "If anyone gets up and discovers me gone they will worry."

"No one is going to find out that you're gone," he said. "Stay a little while longer with me, please."

"Fifteen minutes, and then I have to get home."

"Good," he said. "Let's go up to the loft and cover ourselves in the blankets. We'll be warm up there."

They made their way to the ladder and up to the loft. Being careful not to strike their heads on the roof they managed to make it to where Karl spent most of his time. They fell into the hay and pulled the blankets over them.

Their lips met in the dark and they kissed passionately.

"When are we going to be able to lie in a real bed?" Mary asked, as she touched his face without seeing it.

"It will soon be all over, sweetheart," he said. "Soon the Yanks will come and we'll be free to spend the rest of our lives together."

"I can't wait," she said.

Karl moved his hand up to her front and felt her breasts.

"It feels so good when you do that," Mary said.

Her words excited him and he moved away from her a little and undid the buttons on her blouse. She shivered as her bare breasts were exposed to the cold air. Karl put his hand over one breast and instantly her already hard nipple hardened even more. He moved his head down and took her nipple in his mouth. She leaned back her head and moaned as Karl drew her breast fully into his mouth and sucked it.

"Do the same with this one," she whispered, as she reached for her other breast and cupped it and directed it towards Karl's open mouth. She felt herself getting very wet between her legs. Karl's hand suddenly slipped under her skirt and into her pants and she gave a loud moan as he began to rhythmically massage her. Her body rose to meet his hand and her moans became so loud he had to put his hand over her mouth to silence her.

"Wow, I feel like I've been to the top of a mountain and back," she said, as her body collapsed into the hay and she reached up and kissed Karl on the lips. "Oh Karl, Karl, I love you."

"I love you too," Karl whispered. "Oh Mary, Mary, I want to be inside you."

"I'm afraid."

"I would be careful, Mary. Ohh Mary, let me make love to you."

She put her arms around him and they kissed, a long lingering kiss. "Ohh Mary," Karl moaned as Mary reached over and boldly unbuckled his belt. "Here, let me help you," he said, rising up to slip his pants down to his knees. "Touch me Mary, just touch me."

Mary reached out and put her hand on his erect penis.

"Oh yes Mary, ooh that feels so good." Karl lay back on the hay and moaned as Mary continued to stroke his penis. Occasionally, he moved her hand a little up the shaft, so that at the top of the stroke she was touching his most sensitive area. He moaned with pleasure as Mary held him tight. His moans grew even louder as she leaned over and kissed the top of his penis. "Ooh Mary I love you."

As Mary cuddled closer she could feel his heart beating wildly. His moans became louder and louder until finally he gasped and his body went rigid. Mary held his penis as wetness from it spread over her hand. She continued to hold it as it grew limp.

"Mary, Mary I love you," Karl said, smiling as he leaned over and kissed her softly on the lips.

"I love you too."

They lay quietly in the hay for a long time. They were almost asleep when Mary gave a start and jumped to her feet.

"Karl, it's late and I have to get back."

"I wish you could stay. Oh Mary, I wish you could stay with me." Karl stood up. He pulled up his pants and buckled his belt as Mary quickly buttoned her blouse and fluffed her hair.

"I have to go," Mary said, as she gave him a last kiss goodnight.

Mary was smiling as she walked to her house and climbed the stairs to go to bed. She fell asleep with a smile on her face, thinking how much she loved Karl and what a wonderful life they would have together.

The following day, the U-Boat returned to the harbour. Mary saw it when she was going to school and Karl saw it when he peered out through the loft doors. They knew that tonight they would have to repeat what they had done earlier.

They met after midnight and made their way to Arns' shop. Karl inserted the tube, switched the radio transmitter on, and sent the message.

"Everyone is home safe," he sent and then repeated it.

At 8 p.m. that evening Mary sat on the floor of her house with a pencil and paper waiting for her message.

As far as her family was concerned, she was doing her homework as she listened to the *Doyle Bulletin*. When the time finally arrived for the messages, Mary paid particular attention. Finally, she heard what she was waiting for.

"Tonight's last announcement is from Bill Martin to his wife Elsie," the announcer said.

"Your sister is fine. Got your message. Received package today. Let us know when family leaves again."

Mary scribbled down the entire message and extracted the words she needed: *" Message received. Let us know when family leaves again."*

She concluded from the message that nothing was going to be done until the boat left again.

CHAPTER NINETEEN

With the boat back in the harbour, the team in St. John's had a little breathing room. From their previous discussions with Mary they knew that the submarine normally stayed in port for three or four days after a sortie. They would have that time to develop a plan.

To help them extend the time in port, they had already scheduled a training exercise in the area. The radios buzzed with talk about the exercise, and everyone hoped the Germans were monitoring them and learning that the exercise had been scheduled to begin the next day. That would mean increased ship traffic in the waters around Three Rock Harbour and therefore keep the Germans bottled up in port for an extra few days.

Colonel Starling wanted a plan that captured the boat and the Enigma machine. He especially wanted the machine. He had been a colonel for three years, a year longer than he'd anticipated. By accepting the posting to St. John's, he had concluded he might never get the promotion to brigadier general. He'd had little choice about his posting, but, if he could capture a functioning Enigma machine, complete with codes and a person capable of operating it, he knew his promotion would be a sure thing. Not only would he be assured of his first star, the second and third would be very attainable. He was disappointed about the new orders that had been relayed to him through Lieutenant Colonel Bush. But even though he would no longer be in charge, he would still be involved with the project enough to get partial credit for its success, and none of the blame if it failed.

The meeting had been scheduled for 0900. Everyone was seated in the briefing room when Starling arrived. He took his place at the end of the table. To his immediate right was Major Geoff Atkinson, the Chief Administration and Personnel Officer. He was the officer responsible for all issues dealing with staff at the unit. To his right was Major Tom Harris, Chief of Financial Operations. Next to him was Lieutenant Colonel

Stewart Weatherbee, Unit Construction Engineering Officer. He was responsible for the entire infrastructure of the facility. To his right was Lieutenant Colonel Bob Wakeham, Chief of Transportation. Everything that moved at the unit with wheels was his responsibility.

At the end of the table facing Colonel Starling was Lieutenant Colonel Ken Meeker, Chief of Flying Operations. Everything that moved in the air was his responsibility.

To Meeker's right was Major Bill Coaker, Communications Officer. Next to him, Commander Gerry Whalen, Chief of Naval Operations. Then Lieutenant Colonel Fred Bush, Chief of Land Operations. And finally, Lieutenant Colonel Roger Whitt, Chief of Planning. Seated at chairs away from the table and against the walls were a dozen or so other support officers.

"Okay, Fred, what do you have for me?" Starling began. "I know you guys have been meeting almost non-stop for the past twenty-four hours."

"Well, Sir, as you know, based upon Bill's recommendations, we have not communicated about the issue in any way other than face-to-face. All written documentation is secured at the end of our meetings. As I discussed with you earlier, we sent one of Bill's officers, Captain Wally Gillingham, to headquarters to brief them about what we had uncovered and to seek direction as to how we should proceed. Wally was accompanied back here by a team that will help with this operation. The team is lead by Colonel Bill Cummings. Bill," he motioned to an officer seated against the wall, "you have the floor."

Bill Cummings got up from his chair and walked to a podium at the end of the room. Seated to his left was an enlisted man with an overhead projector in front of him. "Good morning, Colonel, and gentlemen," he said as he adjusted the microphone.

"As Lieutenant Colonel Bush indicated, my name is Bill Cummings and I am the special advisor to the Director of Naval Operations Atlantic, Rear Admiral Quentin Rumbolt. My job is to review plans submitted to the director for his approval and to recommend approval, rejection, or change. For the past year, I have been working exclusively on planning projects designed to capture an intact Enigma machine. I have already met with Colonel Starling and briefed him that I will now be taking over command of this project." He paused for a moment as Colonel Starling nodded his assent.

"Because," Cummings continued, "we cannot communicate with headquarters for fear of our communications being overheard or our code broken, we are on our own. I have the full authority of the director to do whatever is necessary to ensure that we capture this submarine intact and, what's even more important, we capture the Enigma machine intact. No one is indispensable. I will take whatever steps I deem appropriate to make sure this mission is a success. So that you understand completely what I am saying, no loss of life is unacceptable to complete this mission. The capture of an intact Enigma machine could shorten this war insignificantly and result in the saving of hundreds of thousands of Allied lives."

He paused again for effect:

"It would be a very simple procedure if we only wanted to destroy this boat. We could fly over the community and drop a few bombs. That would make all of our lives a lot easier. But as I stated, we want this boat, the crew, and the machine.

"We do have something we overlooked up until our most recent discussions. We have a member of the submarine crew who knows their routine. He knows everything about the operation of the boat and that information is invaluable. We need to know the exact complement and the shift schedule. We need him. So, we are going to extract him this evening. We have a message prepared for the *Doyle Bulletin*. The extraction team is in place. He will be picked up at 2400 hours."

Colonel Cummings continued to brief the others on his plan, but without providing all of the details. Only Colonel Starling and a couple of other senior officers knew the full plan.

Mary listened to the *Doyle Bulletin* and acted as though she were doing her homework. She wrote down the message and read it several times to ensure she was getting it right. There was no doubt however. They would be coming for Karl at midnight and picking him up at Beachy Cove, a place about a quarter mile from Three Rock Harbour.

Immediately after the *Bulletin,* everyone went to bed. Mary made the excuse that she had some things to finish and she would go to bed afterwards.

"Don't stay up too late," her father said, as he left the kitchen and went upstairs.

Mary waited ten minutes to make sure everyone was asleep. She then got dressed and made her way to Karl. He was shocked, but very pleased to see her again. He quickly opened the loft door to let light in.

"Why are you here?" he asked. "Is everything okay?"

"No, it's not okay," she answered. "I just received a message on the

Bulletin that the Americans are coming to take you out by midnight. You don't have very long to get ready."

"What? They are coming to take me out? Why would they want to take me out of here? I don't understand."

"I don't understand either, but that was what the message said. They will pick you up at midnight in Beachy Cove."

Karl stood up and looked at Mary without speaking.

"What is it?" she asked.

"I'm not sure I want to go. I am a German sailor. I don't want to be sent back to Germany and kept in a war camp. I want to stay here with you and your family."

"I don't think they are going to send you back to Germany. You know they want to capture the submarine and they probably need your help to do it."

"I deserted my boat and my crew. I will have to live with that for the rest of my life. But I don't want to be responsible for them all being captured."

Mary approached him. "I don't know what they want. All I know is that we can't let that boat stay here and go out sinking our ships. If they need your help to stop them, then you have to give it. If you love me like you say you do, then you have to help the Americans put a stop to this. You said you want to stay here with me and my family. If you want to be accepted by my family and everyone else in this place, you have to show them that you are one of us."

"Okay," Karl said reluctantly. "Seeing as how you put it that way, then I will have to go. But I don't like it."

He quickly gathered up his few belongings. After closing the loft door, he and Mary went down the ladder and left the barn.

"Where is Beachy Cove anyway?" Karl asked.

"If you go down to the wharf, you'll see a footpath in front of Dad's stage. Follow it that way," Mary pointed. "It's about a quarter of a mile up the shore. The path will take you right down onto the beach. It's where we go to get caplin."

"Caplin?" Karl asked.

"They're little fish that come to the beach to spawn in the spring. It's a big sandy beach and you can't miss it."

"Aren't you coming with me?" he asked.

"No, I can't go with you. If Dad or Mom should get up and see that I'm not down in the kitchen, they might panic and start looking for me.

That might alert the sub crew and we don't want that to happen. You go. I'm sure that the Americans have a plan that will make this all end very soon. Then we can be together."

They held hands as they walked towards the house. They paused outside and embraced.

"I will miss you," Karl said.

"You had better," Mary said, as their lips met. She pushed him away a few seconds later. "Go, you don't want to keep them waiting."

Karl did as he was told. When he saw Mary turn and go into the house, he continued to her father's stage where he found the footpath and began following it up the coast.

The moon was bright enough to allow him to make his way without difficulty. The path followed the cliffs along the coastline, about ten feet from the edge. He guessed that he was being picked up by a destroyer, so he strained to look at the ocean while being careful not to wander too close to the edge of the cliffs.

It was a mild evening with little wind. He could hear the waves crashing into the cliffs below, but he was unable to see anything on the water. Suddenly, he heard a screeching sound in front of him. He stopped dead in his tracks and his heart raced. But it was only a bird that had resting or nesting near the path in front of him.

There were many rocks on the path and it was slow going, trying to manoeuvre around them. About fifteen minutes after he'd left Mary, he noticed the path begin to slope down towards the ocean. He finally reached the bottom and stepped onto the sand. It was loose around the cliffs where the water had not reached and his feet sank into it. He slowly walked towards the beach. The closer he got to the water the more hard-packed the sand became. He looked around to see if he was alone and saw that, with the exception of the gulls, he was the only living soul on the beach.

He stood on the beach for a few minutes, staring out at the ocean and realized that he truly was alone. Maybe Mary had got the message wrong, he thought, as he backed away from the water and headed towards the cliffs behind him.

He found a ledge and sat down. How long would he be expected to wait? Mary said that they were picking him up at midnight. He tried to figure out the time. He guessed it was probably 10:30 when she alerted him. By the time he got dressed, gathered up his few belongings, and left Mary, it was 11 p.m. It took him maybe fifteen minutes to get to the beach so it was probably no later than 11:15 now. He would have at least a forty-five minute wait. Then he remembered that Mary had given him a pocket watch. He tapped his pocket. It wasn't there. It must have fallen out in the hay.

Karl sat watching the waves breaking on the beach. He thought of counting to sixty so that he would know when a minute had passed. He tried it once, but quickly realized that it made the time seem even longer. He paced back and forth in front of the cliff counting each step but soon became bored with that as well. After what he figured was a few minutes, he resigned himself to the fact that he would simply have to tough it out.

As he stared out across the ocean, a speck appeared. He strained to see if it was a boat or just his mind playing tricks on him. He rubbed his eyes to clear them, and squinted as if that would help. It wasn't his imagination. It was a boat. A fishing boat heading in his direction. He had watched many other fishing boats from his loft and this boat looked like the hundreds of others he had seen. But normally they had a light at the top of the mast. There was no light on this boat.

He tried to estimate how far offshore it was. Maybe a mile or more, he guessed. He continued to stare at the boat as it got closer to the shore. Soon, it was close enough for him to see that it was a fishing boat, maybe thirty feet long. He considered walking down the beach and waving, but decided against it. Maybe it was just a fisherman on his way to his trawl. That was quickly discounted because of the time. Karl stayed where he was.

The boat approached the beach and soon it was close enough to hear the engine. The boat slowed. Karl could still hear the engine, but the boat's progress toward the shore slowed and finally stopped. He saw two men appear on the deck and move to the stern. The men pulled a small dory towards the starboard side of the boat. One untied it as the other got in and put the oars in the oarlocks.

Karl watched as the dory was rowed towards the shore. The man in the front jumped out when the dory touched the sand. He pulled it up on the beach as the other held the oars in place. Karl remained near the cliff.

"Karl," the man called out. "Karl."

Karl appeared from the shadow of the cliff and hurried towards them.

"Get in the dory. Quickly," the man said, without any introductions.

Karl did as he was told, stepping over the rower's seat to the one at the stern. The front man pushed the dory off the beach and jumped in. The rower pulled hard on his right oar while pushing on the left as he turned the dory and headed back towards the fishing boat. Karl wondered if he would ever see Beachy Cove again.

They arrived at the fishing boat and the front man pulled the dory around so that it was side on. Another man was on the deck. "Get up," he said to Karl, pointing to the handhold on the side. Karl stepped from the dory and pulled himself up to the deck. A helping hand was extended and he took it.

The man on the deck instructed Karl to follow him towards the cabin. As they approached, a light came on and the boat began to move further offshore.

Although the light in the cabin was very dim, it took a few seconds for Karl's eyes to adjust.

"Good morning," a voice said, as he stepped inside the cabin.

"Good morning," Karl answered, shaking the hand extended to him.

"My name is Bill Cummings," said the man, as Karl sat at a bench beside a very rough table. "Colonel Bill Cummings, United States Air Force. You are, I am told, a German sailor who has defected. Is that correct?"

"I am," Karl answered.

"Good," Colonel Cummings responded. "I also understand that it is your wish to remain in Three Rock Harbour. Is that correct?"

Karl nodded.

"Then, if that is going to become a reality, we need your full cooperation to allow us to achieve our mission of capturing your boat and former crewmates. If you do not cooperate, there is a good chance all of them will be killed. Those who survive will be kept in a prisoner- of-war camp until the end of the war. As we speak, the camp is being built in a little place north of St. John's called Victoria. You will be returned to Germany at the end of the war and your superiors advised of your involvement in this mission. Your fate will certainly not be one of a life of luxury, if you get my meaning?"

"What do you want from me?" Karl asked.

"Let's get some coffee," said Colonel Cummings. "You have to be fully briefed in a few hours."

CHAPTER TWENTY

As the sun rose above the horizon, Colonel Cummings finished briefing Karl. It had been an exhaustive period as Karl explained the operation of the submarine, the crew complement, and all the necessary details Cummings required. At first, he was reluctant to cooperate. But when Cummings explained that the crew of his submarine had sunk a passenger ferry, the *Caribou,* Karl became cooperative. He knew a little about the sinking from Mary, but Cummings had all the details.

As the briefing continued, the fishing boat made its way towards the fishing grounds offshore of Three Rock Harbour. The captain of the boat was Joe Sampson from Salmon Arm, a community further up the shore. Sampson had his trawls set in the same area as the fishermen from Three Rock Harbour. They all knew each other as they fished the same grounds. Joe had been briefed by the Americans earlier and told what he had to do.

As they drew near the fishing grounds, other boats could be seen scattered around the area. Sampson headed the boat in the direction of Bill Sullivan's moorings. As they approached, they could see Bill on deck, pulling in the trawl.

"Bill," Joe called out.

"Morning, Joe," Bill called back. "You're a little late getting here, aren't you?"

Joe laughed. "I've got a little package for you," he said. "Found this feller here floating in the bay a week or so ago. Lucky feller he is because we had engine problems and spent the night out there. One of the crew spotted this feller in the water half drowned. We fished him out, and he's been out like a light since yesterday. Lost his mind, he said, and then remembered that he fell off a government boat in Three Rock Harbour and hit his head. He said that he was supposed to be spending some time with you. Any of that make sense to you?"

Bill turned to see who Joe was talking about. Karl waved. Bill remembered him as the young sailor Mary was sweet on.

"My Jesus, we thought that you were drowned," he said.

"Hello, Mr. Sullivan," Karl said. "No, I'm alive. My boat is supposed to come back to Three Rock Harbour and I was wondering if you wouldn't mind taking me in with you so that I can wait for her."

Bill appeared confused, and then realized that Karl was trying to keep the submarine location secret.

"No sweat," he said. "Come aboard. But you are going to have to work until we get this trawl hauled."

"Fine, Sir," Karl said, as he prepared to jump aboard Bill's boat.

"We thought you were dead. What happened?" Bill asked, after Joe had said his goodbyes.

"I was doing the night watch and there was a quick swell and it threw me overboard. I must have hit my head, but the last thing I remember was waking up. The special suit I was wearing must have kept me alive. Mr. Sampson said my heart was beating so slow when they fished me out of the water that they couldn't tell whether I was alive or dead. I don't think I was in the water very long because there was a very strong tide. I couldn't tell Mr. Sampson about us, so I told him that I was on a coastal boat moored in the harbour. That would explain the uniform."

"You're some lucky, that's all I can say. Get over here and help us with that," Walt said, as they tried to finish hauling the trawl.

By mid-morning, the trawl had been hauled and they began making their way back to Three Rock Harbour. Karl became very nervous. It was easy enough to convince a few local fishermen, but how would his captain react? As they approached the harbour, Karl spotted the familiar conning tower of the submarine.

As they neared the boat, the sailor on watch yelled something below and Commander Stewart appeared on deck.

Bill stopped and waited. "Good morning," he called. "Got something here that you weren't expecting, I'm sure."

Karl looked sheepish as he appeared on deck. Stewart's jaw dropped when he saw him.

"That was my reaction too," Walt said, as the boat moved closer to the submarine.

"I fell overboard, Sir," Karl said. "A fisherman took me to his home and nursed me back to health. When I fell, I must have hit my head, and I lost my memory for a short time. It only returned yesterday. Permission to come aboard, Sir?"

Commander Stewart nodded. Bill brought the boat close enough for

Karl to jump off.

"Thank you, Mr. Sullivan," Karl said, as he pushed the bow of the boat away from the submarine.

As Bill moved away, the captain motioned for Karl to go below and he followed. As they made their way toward the captain's quarters, the crew looked in disbelief at what they thought was a ghost.

Graf was relentless in his questioning of Karl. Karl explained how the suit he was wearing kept him alive and said, without it, the frigid water would have surely resulted in his death. He said Mr. Sampson was offshore with engine problems in his boat and it so happened that the tide carried him right to Sampson. He said he was very lucky.

Captain Graf was concerned that while Karl was unconscious he may have mentioned the submarine or spoken in German. Karl said when he finally came to and realized who he was and where he was, he subtly questioned his caregivers to see if indeed he had said something out of the ordinary. They confirmed there were times when he mumbled things they didn't understand, but said it was all pure gibberish. Once his memory was restored, he said he worked out a plan to be dropped off. The plan included Mr. Sullivan bringing him back to the submarine.

Captain Graf had concerns, but still he was glad to get a crewmember back, especially one who highly trained in the use of the Enigma.

Karl would be put back on shift, but not in the church. He would be given a regular shift in the radio room on the submarine. After being dismissed by the captain, Karl spent the next hour explaining to his crewmates what had happened to him. That evening, Karl was assigned his shift in the radio room. Operators usually worked alone, except when there was Enigma work to be done.

One of the U-Boat's main weaknesses was its communications system. By this time the Allies had developed a direction finding system that allowed them to very quickly locate the source of a radio transmission. Karl knew that his transmissions had to be of very short duration to avoid detection by the Allies. He knew too that knowing what the enemy was saying in one of their transmissions was more important than knowing the source of the transmission.

German commanders had ordered that all U-boats report their locations daily. These transmissions not only gave the Allies the opportunity to locate the boats. If decrypted, the messages could provide actual locations. Messages were sent in Morse code and always encrypted. The main encryption device was known as the Enigma.

Essentially, the Enigma consisted of a keyboard, a scrambler and a lamp panel. The keyboard was used to input the letters, the scrambler scrambled the letters, and the lamp panel illuminated the letters that the scrambler had changed. An operator would begin typing the message into the Enigma. As each letter key was pressed, the scrambled letter appeared on the panel. A second operator recorded the letter on a message pad, recording each letter until the first operator had finished. So, a message typed into the Enigma such as: *Our boat is located at Three Rock Harbour* might be scrambled into *aqev frtjk plkh tuia qwed srty hbvg uuuy mxct*. The scrambled message was sent via Morse code. When it was received, the operator entered the scrambled letters, and the unscrambled letters appeared on the panel where the operator recorded them.

The brain of the Enigma machine was a series of three rotors or wheels that had all 26 letters on them and were positioned on a shaft. The three rotors were capable of being pre-set in 26 different positions, which essentially meant that when the machine was readied for encryption each rotor was set at a particular starting function letter. As each letter was typed the rotors turned, giving a combination of 17,256 possibilities (26x26x26). The starting position of the rotors was knows as the Schlussel key. There was a different code key for each calendar day, and the key was changed each day at 12 p.m. German time. When a U-Boat sailed, the captain was given the keys for the period of time the boat was expected to be at sea. If the boat stayed on an extended patrol, the captain would have to get the keys from another boat, an event that was a regular occurrence.

Each branch of the German military used their own keys to prevent the possibility of compromise. There were four different keys, with the Triton key used exclusively for U-boats. The Germans considered the breaking of the Enigma highly improbable.

The Germans were unaware that Enigma machines had been captured intact by the Allies, along with the keys. Without the keys, the Allies could still break the codes, but it sometimes took many months.

What complicated the Allies' efforts was the development of a four-rotor Enigma in February 1942. This increased the possible combinations to 456,976. The Allies wanted a four-rotor Enigma like the one on *U-69*, complete with 6 months of keys.

With the machine and the keys, and if the capture was not discovered by the Germans, the Allies could decrypt all Enigma traffic from U-boats until the codes expired.

CHAPTER TWENTY-ONE

During the time Karl was away from the submarine, his crew had rendezvoused with a German supply boat and been given supplies and mail. Mail was the most precious of all items the crew received from the supply boats. It was their only contact with home and family.

Karl's family lived in Reichenbach, on the western edge of the Black Forest region of Germany, where the Schutter Valley merged into the upper Rhine River Plains. His father was a farmer who grew corn for his dairy herd and enough vegetables for the family, with some left over to sell locally. The town, with a population of approximately 1,000, was a borough of Lahr, just a few kilometres away. Lahr had a population of 15,000 and was the economic centre of the region.

Karl had two older brothers who were serving in the army, and a younger sister who had stayed at home to help her parents work the family farm. His mother couldn't read or write, so all letters Karl received were from his father, who had been a sergeant in the Great War and was considered a hero in Germany.

There was only one letter awaiting Karl and it was from his father. As soon as he had gotten re-acquainted with his crewmembers, he found a quiet place to read it.

Reichenbach
July 18, 1942
My Dear Karl,

I pray that this letter finds you in good health. I write you with the sad news that your beloved brother Heinz was killed in Belgium on July 9. We received word two days ago and over the objections of your mother, I am writing you with the news. Your mother's health has suffered greatly with this news and we pray daily that you and your brother Wener will be safe. We have not heard from Werner in two months. Fortunately he is not on the front line and so we believe that he is safe.

The herd is healthy and although we have not had very much rain this season the crops are fine. The dry weather means that it will be a good year for wine but yesterday it rained all day and that put new life in the corn. I believe that we will have a good crop with some left over to bring to the market in Lahr.

Your sister has asked me to send you her love and says she is demanding that you return home safely. She has turned into a beautiful young lady and she is engaged to be married to Helmut Issenmann, who was wounded and was sent home. Freda has said that she will not be married until you are back and can attend her wedding.

We were told the last time we delivered mail to Lahr for forwarding to you that letters could not be any longer than one page, and so although we have very much to tell you, I will have to try to tell you everything in one page.

We received two letters from you in May. I have read them to your mother so many times that now she can recite them without me even speaking. Every night before we go to bed she kneels and prays that you and your brother will be safe and that this war will soon be over. It has broken her heart that Heinz will be buried in a foreign country. We pray to God that some day we will get to visit his grave.

We all send you our love and ask that you be careful. We pray for the day that we will once again be together as a family. God bless you and keep you safe.

The letter was signed by his father, mother, and sister. A tear trickled down Karl's cheek as he pressed the letter to his chest and closed his eyes and tried to picture his family and their farm. Oh, how he longed for his mother's hug and for her food. He licked his lips as he thought of her schnitzels and the pear schnapps that followed all of their meals. He could almost taste the ice-cold Riesling wine they drank with their meals and that his father made from their own grapes. He missed the sounds and smells of home.

His father was a very highly decorated soldier in the Great War and was held in very high regard in their village. At Gasthaus Kaufmann, he had a special place with a special chair. This was an honour reserved for very highly respected members of the village.

Karl remembered what it was like before the war. They had a good life and although his father rarely talked about his experiences during the war, there were constant reminders. They had frequent visitors and his father would be invited to special events in Karlsruhe and in Frankfurt. Karl had accompanied his father to an event in Karlsruhe and many, many people came up to speak with his father and applaud his accomplishments.

The more Karl thought about home, the sadder he became. His father was a war hero and Karl was a traitor who could never return home again. He would never see his mother or his father or attend his sister's wedding. His family would be told what he had done and they would live in disgrace.

Karl suddenly thought of Mary. Oh how he loved her, but could he give up his family and his country for her? Could he desert everything and live in a foreign country for the rest of his life? What would happen if Germany won the war? Would his family be persecuted for what he was doing?

He had an attack of conscience like nothing he had ever experienced before. These crewmembers were his friends as well as his comrades. Like him, they were acting under orders. They might not always agree with the orders, but they were sailors and morally bound to follow these orders. He had not considered many of these things when he agreed to cooperate with the Americans.

He thought about home, and the fact that if he did what he was about to do he would never see his family and his beautiful homeland again. He would never again eat in Gasthaus Schultz. He would never again go hunting with his father. He would never hug his mother. "Oh what have I done?" he said out loud.

Karl was scheduled to work the evening shift in the submarine's radio room. Once he was alone there he could relay messages to the Americans without his crew knowing.

During the time he spent on the fishing boat being briefed, Karl was given a tiny codebook. It measured barely two inches square and less than a quarter inch thick. It contained over a thousand words, and each word had another meaning. Karl simply had to find the alternate word for each word in his message, and then send the alternate words. The book had been placed inside his sock and, as expected, he had not been searched so it had not been discovered.

Karl ate lunch in the galley and thought about Mary and his homeland. He was torn between a love of Mary and a longing for his homeland.

He approached the officer of the watch and asked for permission to go on deck. He explained that he was feeling nauseous and wanted to get some fresh air. His request was flatly denied. The captain had given very strict orders that he was not to go on deck for any reason while the boat was in port.

He knew better than to question why the captain had given such an order. But the officer of the watch explained. Karl had fallen overboard once, and the captain was not going to chance it happening again. Also, the boat was very low in the water and there was basically no deck to stand on. There was a lookout at the top of the conning tower and little room for anyone else. Karl resigned himself to the fact that he would not be going on deck and decided he would write his father and take a nap before his shift.

Writing his family was one of the most difficult things Karl ever did. He wanted them to know that he was safe, but knowing that he was about to betray his comrades was very troubling. Surely, he thought, there was a better way. The Americans knew where the sub was. Why didn't they just sail into the harbour and capture it? He knew the answer even before he thought of the question. It was the Enigma machine and the codes. That was what they wanted more than anything else, and without the element of surprise there was a fear that the machine and the codes would be destroyed.

Unfortunately, the radio room did not have a door. Otherwise he could have locked himself in and stayed there until the Americans captured the boat. So they had to develop another plan. One that would deliver the Enigma machine and the codes to the Americans fully intact.

The attack would take place when Karl was working. He would be given the exact time and his first task would be to take the codes and put them in a secure place where they would remain until they could be retrieved by the Americans.

In Germany, Karl had been taught that the moment there was a fear the sub would be captured, his job would be to destroy first, the codes, and second, the machine.

In the radio room there was a bucket with a small bottle of fire accelerant attached and this was where the codes could be destroyed at a moment's notice. Even though the codes had been printed on paper with a kind of ink that dissolved in water, his orders were to burn them instead.

A metal mallet hung on the wall and, as the codes were being burned, he was supposed to beat the Enigma machine to tiny bits.

The plan developed by the Americans was to have Karl find something to throw in the bucket to simulate the codes being burnt. Karl would find some old paper to use for that purpose. There was an old three-rotor machine in the radio room that could be used to show that the four-rotor Enigma machine had been destroyed. The latter would be hid and the parts of the three-rotor machine spread around the room to give the impression that both machines had been destroyed.

Nothing would begin until Karl sent his message indicating that he was safe aboard the boat and working in the radio room. He would send that message shortly after he went on shift. He would have to be alone and the message would last a few seconds. Anyone intercepting it would think it just noise and not pay it any intention, he hoped.

Karl finished his letter to his father, placed it in an envelope, and addressed it. The envelope would not be sealed until after the captain read it. He made his way to the captain's quarters and placed the letter in a box put there for that purpose. As he slid the letter through the slot he wondered if he would ever hear from his father again.

He tried to sleep but memories of home filled his thoughts. He thought about his brother Heinz and the day they had been given permission to shoot a deer. Karl accompanied him into the forest and, with the deer in his sights, Heinz passed the rifle to him. Karl thought his heart would explode as he put the rifle to his shoulder. When he had the top of the front sight barely visible through the groove in the back sight, he pulled the trigger. The force of the explosion drove him back several steps and when the smoke had cleared, the stag lay dying on the ground fifty metres in front of them. The antlers were proudly placed above the door to the barn and his name and the date were carved below. He could see those antlers as clearly as if he were standing beneath them.

He could see the fields of corn that would have been several feet high when his father had written the letter, but by now would have been harvested, with the only evidence that corn was planted there the few inches of stalk above the ground. The only crops remaining in the ground would be root vegetables and some of them would stay there all winter. The grapes would also have been harvested. In the hills surrounding the village, the lanterns would be lit tonight. They would be waiting for the frost to touch the grapes, after which they would be picked and made into ice wine.

He could smell the cattle and hear the noise as his father, mother and sister began the process of milking the cows. How many times had he drank the warm milk from the buckets and wiped his face with the back of his hand?

Karl longed for home. Nothing was as good as his mother's schnitzel and warm potato salad. And he remembered the first time his father offered him a glass of schnapps. It was his twelfth birthday. His father's mother, Karl's Oma, had been alive then. She had died the following year. She was an expert in schnapps, as his father reminded him on several occasions. His mother simply said that she drank too much.

After they had eaten their meal, it was tradition to have schnapps. There were many kinds of schnapps and every farmer had his own still. The fruit was fermented and then distilled. Apples and pears were fermented together to create Obstwasser. Pears alone created Williamsbirne. Plums made Zwetschgenwasser. Cherries made Kirschwasser. Each was generally referred to as Obst, Williams, Zwetschgen and Kirsch. Those were the main fruits used by the Germans to make schnapps. However, other berries such as raspberries, and even grains and seeds were used. Williams was usually drank after a meal. On his twelfth birthday, Karl was given a small glass filled with Williams.

Urged on by his Oma, he put the glass to his lips and drained it. At the time he couldn't remember ever having drank anything so horrible. He didn't swallow, but the schnapps still burned its way to his stomach. Everyone laughed because they had gone through the same process themselves. Karl smiled as he remembered the day, and longed for a glass of Williams.

With fifteen minutes before his shift was due to officially start, Karl arrived in the radio room and relieved Max. Before Max left, there was a quick briefing, that included Max telling Karl that radio men Peter Blom and Paul Klass were now manning the radio in the church. When he was alone, Karl put on the headset, wrote his name into the log indicating that he was on duty, and settled back for his shift.

There was very little to do while on shift. The time was normally spent writing letters home, reading, or doing anything to help pass the time. Messages sent to the boat were very short and normally dealt with the movement of Allied shipping. Other messages gave the location of U-Boats where they could meet to pick up mail or, if they were at sea longer than anticipated, to pick up Enigma codes and fuel. Messages were sent in Morse code and encrypted using the Enigma. The operator on duty would record the message and get another operator to assist while the message was encrypted.

The Americans had given Karl a call sign and a frequency where he could send and receive messages from them. Two hours exactly after Karl had advised that he was on shift, they would reply. If the Americans did not receive an acknowledgement, they would know he was with another operator and the message would be sent one hour later. After an hour or so on shift, Karl sent his first message to the Americans:

on duty on duty on duty.

He waited for the acknowledgement and re-tuned his frequency.

About halfway through his shift his key began clicking and he knew he was about to receive a message. He acknowledged that he was ready to begin receiving and reached for his pencil. The message was in code, which meant he had to be very careful when recording it. It was transmitted much more slowly than messages not sent in code. Karl carefully recorded the message. He noted it had the very highest precedence, which meant that as soon as it was received he would set up the Enigma and find Max.

It took a couple of minutes to record the message. Afterwards, he went to the safe in the radio room and retrieved the pamphlet containing the codes. He found the date and went to the Enigma.

The wheels on the machine were about four inches in diameter and sat in a cradle. He lifted a latch and removed the first one. He looked at the codebook. He then set the letter on the wheel to correspond to the letter of the code by depressing the centre of the wheel and turning the outside. He did this with each of the wheels and then locked them in place. The machine was then plugged in and he performed the five-letter test. As he typed in each of the five letters, he looked at the screen and then at the codebook. If the letter on the screen was the same as the letter in the codebook then he had set the rotors correctly. When all five letters had been typed and it was confirmed he had done everything correctly, he left the radio room and went looking for Max.

Max was in the mess playing cards. He had a big pile of chips on the table in front of him and was upset that he had to leave the game. He promised his anxious crewmates he would return soon.

Karl and Max made their way to the radio room.

"Do you want to type or record?" Max asked.

"I'll type," Karl said.

They took their positions in front of the Enigma machine and Karl began typing the message. As he typed each letter, Max recorded it on a sheet specifically designed for that purpose. As each letter was recorded, Max said it out loud. When the word was determined, he said that out loud too.

For U-69 eyes only graf
Start
Information from French contact that recent return to your boat is collaborating with Americans take necessary action
end.

Max repeated the message. He looked at Karl and then at the message.

"The only person who has recently returned to this boat is you," he said. "I thought that your story was not believable. How could you do this to your friends and your country?"

"It's not what you think," Karl said, as Max looked at him with hatred in his eyes.

"What I think," Max said, " is that you are a traitor. Your father was a hero to the Fatherland. How will he react to this when he finds out?"

Max stood up, ready to bring the message to the captain.

"Wait," Karl said. "Listen to what I have to say. The Americans have promised me that when the war is over they will let me live wherever I want. They will give me money, a house, everything I need to lead a comfortable life. Things I would never get at home. Things they will give you too. No one will die. They know we are here, so we will be captured no matter what you do and spend the rest of the war in a prisoner-of-war camp. When we are sent home, we will be disgraced because we allowed ourselves to be captured. Think about it, Max. A life of everything we ever dreamed about or a life of disgrace."

Max stepped back and stared at Karl.

"You are willing to betray everyone and everything. When the captain gets this message he will call for volunteers for a shooting squad. I will be the first one to volunteer. And when I tell the others about what you were planning to do, they will beg the captain to let them be on the squad."

Max moved towards the exit. Karl was standing, blocking it.

"I can't let you tell the captain," he said.

"You can't stop me," Max said, as he shoved the message in his pocket and grabbed Karl's shoulders to push him away from the exit.

Karl reacted by pushing Max towards the back of the room.

Max held his position as he reached for the knife all submariners carried in a pocket halfway down the side of their trousers. He swiped the knife at Karl, who then pulled his knife out and tried to fend Max off. They circled the tiny room, making jabs at each other.

"This is crazy," Karl said. "Why are you doing this, Max? Let's sit down and talk. We don't have to fight like animals. Please."

Max backed off and stood upright.

Karl breathed a sigh of relief.

Max was finally coming to his senses.

Karl moved to sit down.

As he did, Max drove his knife into Karl's stomach.

Instinctively, Karl thrust up with his knife, catching Max in the throat.

Max fell to the floor as blood spilled from his severed jugular vein.

As Max fell, he pulled his knife out of Karl's stomach.

The front of Max's shirt quickly became soaked with his blood.

Karl realized that he, like Max, would be dead in a few minutes. He would never see his Mary again. He had resigned himself to never again seeing his family, but now he knew would never again see Mary again.

When Captain Graf read the message, he would know someone had hid Karl and would immediately assume it was Mary.

Karl fell to his knees, determined to find the message in Max's pants pocket.

Max was dead. His eyes twitched, but he was dead. Karl reached into Max's pocket and pulled out the message. He prayed he would live long enough to destroy it.

But there was also the message he had written. Another operator would decode it. The message was still on the table. Karl reached for it.

The book containing the codes was not on the table. He looked around and saw it under the desk. He reached out for it. He needed the bucket too. The bucket that was to be used to destroy the codes in the event the boat was captured.

But he could not destroy the codes. The Americans wanted them.

Karl tore out today's code and the ones for the next two days and threw them into the bucket. A small vial containing a fire accelerant was attached to the side of the bucket.

Before he had a chance to do anything else, there was a sudden noise.

A bang on the wall was followed by a shout.

"Is everything okay in there?" someone called, but didn't come in.

The curtain covering the entrance to the radio room was drawn, and everyone aboard knew they were not to enter when the curtain was drawn.

"Yes, everything is fine here," Karl managed. "I tipped over my chair."

Karl unscrewed the cap on the vial and threw its contents on top of the papers in the bucket. He took a match from the pack next to the bucket, scraped the match against the rough surface of the bucket, and dropped it in too. As the match touched the liquid and everything became engulfed in flames, Karl collapsed. He fell face forward towards the bucket.

CHAPTER TWENTY-TWO

Shortly after the fire was lit, smoke began to seep out from under the radio room door. Helmut Mann was walking by when he smelled smoke and then saw it. He grabbed a fire extinguisher, pulled down on the fire alarm besides it, and instantly an almost ear piercing squeal was heard in every part of the boat.

A fire aboard a submarine, even one tied up in port, can result in its destruction in a matter of minutes. Fire drills were practiced aboard more often than any other boat activity. Helmut knew what he had to do.

Sliding back the ceiling to floor curtain, he was enveloped by a cloud of smoke. He coughed but kept moving forward. The fire alarm he'd pulled had triggered emergency lights to come on, making the radio room several times brighter than it usually was. As he moved into the room, he could see the source of the smoke. Helmut directed the fire extinguisher at the smoke. As he did, he heard shouting behind him. He continued to stream the chemicals at the bucket. The flames were quickly extinguished. The smoke began to clear as the fans sucked it out.

The officer of the watch, Becker, touched his shoulder.

"My God," Becker said, as he surveyed the awful scene in front of them.

Max was slumped against the wall. There was a huge gash beneath his chin, and the blood that had spurted from it soaked the front of his shirt. Karl had fallen headfirst into the bucket. His head was covered in foam. Becker could only imagine its condition.

"Go outside and secure the area. Keep everyone out of here except the captain," he ordered.

The words were barely out of his mouth when Graf appeared. "What happened?" he asked.

"Two dead," said Becker. "Looks like one stabbed and the other... I don't know what happened to him."

"Looks like they had a fight. But why the fire?" Graf asked.

"That's the bucket they're supposed to use to destroy the codes if we're ever boarded. I don't understand why they would be using it now," Becker said.

Graf looked around and found the codebook. He picked it up and thumbed through it.

"They weren't trying to burn this," he said. "Is there any record of problems between the two of them?"

"I'm assuming that the person in the bucket is Karl," Becker replied. "If there were problems between him and Max, I was not made aware of anything."

"I have two crew dead," Captain Graf said. "Two of my radio men. I want to know what happened here. Get a team in here. Get me some answers."

Within the hour, all of the crew had been interviewed. But none could recall any incidents between Karl and Max that would cause them to want to kill each other.

After that avenue was investigated without any success, the possibility that a third sailor had been involved was discussed. There were only three sailors on board who did not have an alibi at the time of death. One was the captain. The other two were asleep in their bunks. The clothing of the sleeping sailors was checked because there was no way anyone could have killed Max without getting blood all over them. No blood was found. By midnight, when Becker reported to the captain, he had to admit he was no further ahead at determining what had happened in the radio room.

Graf was understandably furious. He had two dead sailors on the boat, and no idea who had killed them or why they were dead. There simply was no reason for it to have happened. If they had killed each other, there had to be a reason. If a third sailor was involved, the questions remained of who and why. There were lots of questions and no answers.

"I don't know, Sir, why this happened," the frustrated watch officer responded.

"Okay, clean up the place and get the bodies ready for burial," Graf ordered.

Becker had turned to leave when he suddenly stopped in his tracks.

"What are we going to do with the bodies, Captain?" he asked.

Graf was about to respond when he realized the problem. In the heat of the boat the bodies would become smelly very quickly. If the bodies were dropped over the side, the strong undertow would bring them ashore no matter how much weight was buried with them.

"We will have to bury them ashore," he finally said. "I will discuss it with Bill Sullivan tomorrow."

Next morning, Captain Graf rowed the small rowboat to the wharf and tied it up. It was low tide and he had to climb up several rungs to get to the top of the wharf. It was Sunday and the wharf was deserted. He walked up the footpath to the Sullivan's house. Bill saw him coming and met him at the door.

"Good morning, Captain Stewart," Bill said, as he greeted him with an outstretched hand.

"If I've told you once, I've told you a hundred times, it's Tony," he said, as he took Bill's hand and was motioned to come inside.

The Sullivan family was sitting around the kitchen table having breakfast. They smiled in Stewart's direction when he walked in.

"I didn't mean to interrupt your breakfast," he apologized.

"You're not interrupting anything, Captain," Janet said. "Sit down and have something with us."

"Thank you, no," he answered. "I've just finished breakfast on the boat, but thank you very much." He turned to Bill. "I wonder if I could discuss something with you outside. It's not something to talk about over breakfast."

"Sure," Bill answered, as he walked to the door and held it open.

"Good morning," Stewart said to the family, as he tipped his hat, smiled, and stepped outside.

The men stood on the veranda, looking out over the bay.

"We had an accident on the boat last evening," the captain said.

"Nothing too serious, I hope," Bill said.

"Yes, unfortunately it was. Two of my sailors were killed. It was a freak accident that happened in the engine room," he lied. "Two of my sailors were in there and they shouldn't have been. I won't bore you with the details, but I'm now faced with the dilemma of having to bury them. As a result of what happened in the engine room, we won't be able to go to sea for a few days. We'll have to bury them ashore."

"My God, that's too bad," Bill said. "Were they any of the sailors that we met?"

"I think you may remember Karl. He was one of the young men who worked out of the church and was becoming friends with your daughter. I had to put a stop to it for obvious reasons and I think you understood those reasons."

"Yes, I certainly did and I thank you for doing that," Bill said. "That young man certainly has had a run of bad luck. When we thought he was dead he suddenly appeared and now, here we go again. Your decision certainly wasn't very popular with Mary at the time but she hasn't mentioned him since."

Stewart just nodded.

"So, as to the burial, I don't think that will be a problem. I'll get the graves dug and speak with Reverend Lake. We can do it tomorrow afternoon. I'll have Harry Purdy make a couple of coffins. We'll all be in from fishing and if we do it at 2 p.m. then it won't interfere with anything."

"Oh, there's no need with that," Stewart said. "We'll just have the boat crew attend."

"No, I won't hear of that. Everyone here will want to be there. That's part of our nature. I'm sure that you will have a special service that you will discuss with the reverend and people will want to attend to see it. This will be a military type of funeral I assume, so it will be different, right?"

"Yes, of course. We will have an honour guard. Okay, then," the captain relented.

"Now that that's out of the way, are you sure that you won't join us for at least a cup of tea?" Bill asked.

"I'm sure. We have a lot to do before tomorrow, but tell your missus I appreciate the offer and perhaps some other time."

"Okay," Bill said, as they shook hands and the captain made his way down the path to his boat.

"What was that all about?" Janet asked, as Bill returned to the kitchen.

"They had an accident on the boat," Bill said. "It happened in the engine room. Two of his sailors got killed. Damaged the engines and now they can't go to sea. He wants to bury them up in the graveyard and I said it would be okay."

"My God, that's terrible. Those poor young men," said Janet.

"Did he say who they were?" Mary asked, as she drained the last of her tea.

Bill went over and sat beside her. "One of them was the young feller you were sweet on. I think his name was Karl."

All the colour drained from Mary's face. She dropped her cup and it fell to the floor, shattering into little pieces.

"What is it?" her mother asked. "Mary, what's wrong?"

Mary sat staring straight ahead. Her mother came over and gently touched her face. Janet lifted Mary's head and looked into her eyes. "What is it, Mary? What's wrong, my dear?"

Mary continued to stare straight ahead without speaking.

"What happened to her?" Janet asked, as she looked at Bill.

"I told her that one of the sailors who had been killed was the young feller she was sweet on," Bill said. "I didn't think she would take it this hard."

"Mary, Mary," Janet said, as she turned her attention back to her daughter.

Mary looked at her mother and then turned to her father.

"Dad, I need to talk to you," she whispered.

"Sure honey," Bill answered, "what is it?"

"Not here," she said. She got up from the table and walked to the porch where her coat was hanging on a hook. She put her coat on and passed her father his. "Put this on and come with me, please," she asked.

With her father beside her, Mary walked silently up the footpath to the hay barn behind the house.

"Why are we going here?" her father asked, but Mary simply held up her hand.

Mary pulled open the door and went inside. Her father followed. Once inside, she turned to him.

"Dad, I am going to tell you a story now that you are going to have a great deal of difficulty believing, but I want you to know that every single word is the truth. I should have told you sooner but I was afraid for you and for everyone in Three Rock Harbour."

"What are you talking about, child?"

"Please don't interrupt me when I begin," she said. "This is very difficult."

Her father nodded his assent.

"You remember Karl when he was working at the church. Well, we started talking and we would sit sometimes and he really is, or was," she corrected herself, "nice and I liked him a lot. One night there was a dance and the captain saw us together and sent him back to the boat and ordered him to stay there. We used to send messages to each other in cans that we would throw in the water. Finally, Karl couldn't stay on the boat any longer so he made believe that he fell over and drowned. But instead of drowning he came ashore and he stayed up in the loft."

"What?" Bill shouted.

"Please, Daddy," Mary whispered.

"Our plan was that when the boat left, he would stay and no one would suspect anything. But Daddy, I was listening to the *Bulletin* one night, the night after the *Caribou* was sunk, and I was really mad at the Germans for what they did. I was telling Karl how much I hated the Germans. And that's when he told me something, Daddy. You are going to be shocked when you hear it."

"What is it, Mary," he asked.

"They're Germans, Daddy. The submarine is a U-Boat and the captain and the crew are all Germans. Reverend Lake and Mr. Blair, that's not their real names, are also German. They are telling everyone that they're British but they're not. They hide here and go out and sink our boats."

Bill looked at his daughter and his jaw dropped. He moved towards her, put his hands on her shoulders and looked into her eyes.

"Mary, my darling," he said, "you must be still suffering from your operation." He smiled weakly, trying to say something comforting to her.

Mary pulled away. "There was no operation, Daddy. I made believe that I was sick so I could go to St. John's and speak to someone about all of this. I never had an operation."

She opened her coat and pulled up her sweater. She patted her stomach, which she had been falsely complaining was tender. "Look, Daddy, there is no scar. I never had an operation. I met with Dr. Chaytor, and Lieutenant Sears and the other people and I told them my story and they believed me. Daddy, you have to believe me. They are all Germans. They are not British sailors."

Bill looked at his daughter's smooth white stomach. Mary pulled up more of her sweater and pushed down her pants to show that there was no scar. "I'm telling you the truth," she said.

Bill backed up and sat down on an old wood-horse. He stared at his daughter with a look of disbelief.

"I can't believe that you kept all of this from me. I can't believe that you hid away one of them in my loft and you didn't tell me. You went all the way to St. John's and still didn't tell me," his voice trembled as he spoke.

"I didn't want anything to happen to anybody," she said. "When I told the people in St. John's what was going on, they said they would send me messages on the *Bulletin*. We would reply by breaking into the shop and sending them messages on Arns' radio transmitter. A day or so ago, they sent me a message saying they wanted to meet with Karl. So he left and then returned to the boat. I don't know what he told the captain, but he must have believed him. At least that's what I thought. But now I know that something has gone wrong. The captain must have found out what was happening and they killed him." She buried her face in her hands. "I think I loved him, Daddy," she sobbed.

Bill moved towards his daughter and took her in his arms.

"This is the most incredible story I have ever heard," he said. "They're Germans and we have been helping them kill our own people. My God, what is going to happen to all of us? As soon as they mentioned money, that was all we thought about. What's going to become of us?"

Mary broke her father's embrace. "We have to do something," she said. "I don't know what the Yanks were planning, but I do know that they said they were going to have an exercise out in the bay and that would keep the Germans here until they came up with a plan. They must have a plan and Karl was probably a big part of it. But they don't know that he's dead. And we don't have any way of telling them."

"What I don't understand," Bill said, "is that after you convinced the Americans that they were all Germans, why they just didn't sail into the harbour and blow them out of the water. It would be like shooting turrs with a muzzle loader."

"There's a machine on the boat called an Enigma. It's used for sending messages in code. The Americans want it more than anything, and that's why they had to have a plan that allowed them to capture it before it was destroyed."

"This is the most incredible story I have ever heard," Bill admitted. "What are we going to do?" he asked, not expecting an answer.

"The Germans obviously found out that Karl was going to help the Americans. That's why they killed him," Mary said, trying to make sense of the situation. "What did Karl tell them before he died? That's the big question. If he told them about what I did, then God only knows what they will do. But I think that Karl loved me as much as I loved him, so I don't think he would tell them about me. Regardless, we have to assume that the Germans know the Americans are aware they are here."

"No," Bill interrupted her. "We can't assume that. The captain, Tony, or whoever he is, agreed to have the funeral tomorrow. If he believed that the Americans knew what you said, wouldn't it make more sense for them to try and sneak out of here tonight?"

"You might be right, Daddy. Maybe Karl never told them anything. Maybe they caught him sending a message to the Americans and they killed him. I just don't know."

"Is there anyone else in Three Rock Harbour who knows about this?"

"No, it's just me."

"Okay," Bill said after a few minutes of silence. "The Americans must have a plan that involves Karl. But Karl is dead now so that plan is useless. But they don't know that Karl is dead so whatever the plan was, they might try and go ahead with it anyway. Karl operated the radio on the boat so he must have been talking to them. When he doesn't respond, what will they do?"

Mary didn't have an answer. She looked at her father.

"You're a fisherman, I'm a student, and we're trying to figure out a plan that the Americans would use to capture a German U-Boat. If this wasn't so serious it would be laughable."

Bill stood up and paced the hay-covered floor. Another few minutes passed in silence.

"But," Mary said, breaking the silence, "what if we came up with our own plan? What if we came up with a plan to capture the submarine?"

Her father stopped his pacing and looked at her. Suddenly a huge smile appeared on his face.

"Mary, my daughter," he said, "you have to be out of your mind. You're suggesting that we come up with a plan to capture a German U-Boat. We're just going to get in my boat, go over to theirs, point an oar at them and say, stick 'em up. Is that what you're suggesting?"

"No, that's not what I'm suggesting. I don't know what I'm suggesting, but we just can't wait and do nothing. When this is all over and if any of us are alive, everyone in Newfoundland will judge us by what we did. We might get forgiven for believing the Germans when they first came. But now that we know who they are, we have to do something."

"Yes, I agree we have to do something. But what? We're fishermen, Mary. We're not sailors or soldiers. All that will happen is that we'll end up getting ourselves killed. As soon as we try something, the Germans will turn that big gun they have on the top of the boat in our direction and we won't have anywhere to hide. They will butcher every man, woman and child in Three Rock Harbour. They don't need us. Especially not now, if they believe that the Americans know about them."

Mary felt the same frustration as her father.

"When the Americans find out that Karl is not answering, they will know something is wrong and they will attack. No one can condemn us. We have no weapons, no skill, no idea how to attack a boat and capture it. It would be suicide. The only memory the people Newfoundland will have of Three Rock Harbour will be the tombstones in the graveyard where we will all be buried," Bill said.

Mary opened her eyes a little wider in reaction to her father's last comment. "Maybe that's it," she said. "Maybe that's how we do it."

"Do what?" Bill asked.

"You told the captain he could have the burial tomorrow afternoon. They will have a service at the church and at the graveyard. I would bet they want it to look good so they will send all but a few sailors to the church for the service. That will leave maybe one or two on the boat. We have to have a plan to capture them in church. And, at the same time we need a plan to capture the boat when it is at its weakest time."

"So, who is going to do all of this capturing?" Bill asked. "I'm going to get my muzzle loader and hold an entire boat crew hostage, while you row out to the boat and charm those remaining into turning over the boat to you."

"Be serious," Mary said. "It's a suggestion. It's all we have right now. I'm not saying that we have to do it by ourselves. The other fishermen can help us."

"And how do we tell them about our plan? We can't call a town meeting. We can't go to every house in Three Rock Harbour. The Germans watch our every move. If they saw us going door to door they would suspect something was going on."

"Tomorrow morning all the fishermen are going to go out fishing," Mary said. "No one will be there but people from Three Rock Harbour. That's when we get everyone together and explain what's happening. We have to be the first boat out of the harbour tomorrow morning. Then as the other boats come out, we tell them what's going on and we get all the boats to meet by our trap berth. All the fishermen have guns. We might not be able to do it by ourselves, but together we can."

Bill looked at his daughter proudly. "I don't know Mary. I suppose it's worth a try. But we still don't have a real plan."

"We have a lot more than when we came in here a little while ago," Mary said. "The more we talk about this the better our plan will be. I think we should go get a few of the others. The Germans won't suspect anything if a half dozen or so fishermen get together here in the barn. Someone else might have a better idea. I can go get them. Who should I get?"

CHAPTER TWENTY-THREE

Bill's boat was the first to leave the harbour on Monday morning. His sons Ray and John were with him. Mary wanted to go but her father said that the Germans knew girls never went out in the boats, and if they saw her they might suspect something was up. Besides, after meeting with the other fishermen yesterday, she had lots to do.

The fishermen who had met with Mary and her father in the barn waited outside the harbour, out of sight of the U-Boat. They directed the other fishermen to a meeting place. The surprised fishermen slowed when they saw the others and then reluctantly agreed to go to the meeting place. The sun was barely up when all of the boats were bobbing up and down near Bill's trap berth.

It took Bill five minutes to tell the others about the U-Boat and Mary and Karl's involvement. Looks of shock were obvious on everyone's face as they strained to catch every word. It took him another five minutes to tell them the plan they had developed the previous day. That's when all hell broke loose.

Many felt the plan was too dangerous. None of them were trained soldiers and they were naturally concerned for their safety. One man asked if they would still be getting the money that had been promised to them, and that resulted in threats of his boat being sunk.

Bill tried to explain that their plan was the best thing they could come up with. If anyone had a better one, then he was ready and willing to listen.

A couple of the fishermen thought they should just wait and do nothing. Bill explained that the Germans might know that Mary knew who they really were and she might have told everyone else. If that was the case then after the burial service God only knows what they might do.

Another fisherman suggested that they try and contact the Americans and tell them what was going on. Bill said they had no way of contacting them. But when it was pointed out that the American destroyers were travelling between Argentia and St. John's and maybe someone could intercept one, Bill and then the others thought it was a good idea. The only thing was it looked like the weather was about to change and to send someone out in an impending windstorm would be suicide.

In the meantime, Bill suggested that the best chance they had to control their own destiny was during the funeral service. That was when the Germans would be the most vulnerable. Despite the risks involved, they would have to at least try. He said everyone would have to take part in the plan if it was to be successful. There could be no abstentions. He said they had always managed their community with a majority rule and this was going to be no exception. He asked that everyone express their opinion. After everyone had their say, he called for a show of hands as to whether or not they should proceed with their plan. A few raised their hands immediately. Slowly, the rest raised their hands. After every hand went up, Bill explained in greater detail what they would do.

Once all the fishermen had been briefed, they left to tend to their fishing gear. As it was, they would be later than usual getting back into the harbour. That meant later than usual cleaning up their fish. The service was scheduled for 2 p.m. so they hoped they wouldn't have a record haul this morning. They didn't have to worry. An hour later there was a raging windstorm and they had to head for the safety of the harbour.

CHAPTER TWENTY-FOUR

"We haven't heard from the German radio man since his transmission last evening," the young corporal said in response to a question from Major Coaker.

"Goddamn it," Colonel Cummings said, as Coaker turned to him and shook his head. "He told us there were set times for sending and receiving messages so he could go there at any time and talk to us. He said the radio room on the boat wasn't manned all the time. He knew how important today was. I'm not sure we can risk this attack unless we're sure that he can get control of the Enigma. And we have no way of communicating with him?"

"No, yes, sir, we can communicate with him but he has to initiate it. We respond to his messages and we know he has his equipment tuned to our frequency. We could send him something, but we have no idea whether or not he receives it unless he responds," Coaker said.

"So, what in the fuck do we do now? I want that goddamn machine. It could shorten the war considerably if we can get it along with the sub crew. We could communicate with other U-Boats and eventually rendezvous with one. Jesus Christ, I hate not knowing what's going on. Anyone have any suggestions, because right now I'm open to just about anything?"

"Sir," Commander Whalen spoke. "We have the submarine bottled up so it's not going anywhere. We have no reason to suspect the Germans know we're on to them. I suggest we just sit tight a while and wait for our man to contact us."

"Maybe we need to go have a look," Lieutenant Colonel Bush said.

"What do you mean?" Cummings asked.

"We should be prepared in case we don't hear from him. We could put together a small landing force. We could put them ashore this evening and they could have a look around to see what is going on. We could actually get them to talk to the girl, what's her name?"

"Mary," one of the others answered.

"Yes, Mary, that's right," he finished.

"I'm not sure I understand what this landing force would accomplish," Cummings said. "You're suggesting we send some people to look around. What would they be looking for?"

"They could see if the submarine is still where we think it is. They could check and see if everything is status quo. In other words, do the Germans suspect anything," he said.

"Perhaps that might give us more information than we currently have. But I don't know how we can make contact with the girl."

"We could get a message to her via the *Bulletin,*" Bush said. "Maybe she knows what's going on with Karl. We could ask her to meet the landing force at the same location we picked up the German."

"Yes, yes, I think that would work," Cummings said. "Get the message ready to send and as soon as our men make contact with the girl, I want to know exactly what she knows. Regardless what she tells us, I want a plan in place for tomorrow. Is that clear?"

A chorus of 'Yes, Sirs was heard as the colonel left the room.

CHAPTER TWENTY-FIVE

The first of the fishing boats began to arrive back in the harbour around 8:30 a.m. and the last at 9 a.m. Instead of going to their homes to have a meal before clearing away the fish, the men carried out the parts of the plan they had been briefed on earlier that morning. Once that was done, they returned to their boats and began the process of cleaning their fish. Their wives wondered what was going on, but they assumed it had something to do with the funeral that afternoon.

Mary hadn't slept a wink the previous night. All morning she waited for her father to return and confirm that the others accepted what they had discussed. Together they had met with Paul Arns and briefed him. He was the only person in the community capable of operating a radio transmitter. When the time was right, he would broadcast a message to the Americans. At least that was the plan. But when Paul explained that any message he sent could be picked up by the Germans that plan was scrapped. They would just have to do what they had to do and wait for the Americans to come.

Shortly after Bill arrived back in the harbour, he took the dory and rowed towards the submarine. One of the sailors on the deck saw him approaching and immediately went looking for the captain. Graf came on deck as the deckhand reached down and stopped the bow of Bill's dory from striking the submarine. In recent weeks, Bill had been allowed to approach the U-Boat.

"Hello, Bill," Graf called out. "What can I do for you this morning?"

"Hello, Tony," Bill said, trying to sound cordial. "We were wondering how many of your crew would be attending the funeral this afternoon. The women will be preparing some grub for after the service, and they want to make sure that they have enough."

"There will only be a few of us attending. Maybe six or eight."

"I know that a funeral is hardly the right time to socialize, Tony. But people here have only met a few of your crew. As you said that you'll be leaving before Christmas, we thought this might be the only time we get a chance to get together before you leave."

"I don't know about that, Bill."

"It's only going to be for a couple of hours and everyone would really like to meet the rest of your crew. It's not as if you were at sea. I'm sure your crew would enjoy having a taste of our hospitality."

The sailor who had been holding the dory looked at his captain.

Graf paused for a few seconds before answering. He didn't want to leave his boat unmanned, but he was in port and his crew could use a little time ashore.

"Okay," he said. I'll leave two of my crew aboard and the rest will attend the service. Like you said, it will be an opportunity for all of us to get together before we leave. There will be 41 of us attending the service."

Bill tried not to show his relief.

"That's great. The women will be very pleased as will everyone else. I'll have a boat sent out shortly to transport the bodies to the church. We'll have another couple of boats sent out to transport your men to the service."

"Fine, Bill. We look forward to it," the captain smiled.

The deckhand pushed the bow of the dory away from the boat, and Bill headed towards the wharf. Some fishermen were on the wharf when Bill arrived.

"All except two of them will be attending the service," was all he said to them.

The message was circulated to the others. Within a few minutes of Bill climbing up on the wharf, all the fishermen knew what they had to do. Their wives and children would be told what they had to do over lunch.

After lunch, Bill took his boat over to the submarine and the two bodies were loaded aboard. Reverend Lake and two sailors accompanied Bill back to the wharf. They would stay with the bodies until after the service.

Mary watched as the bodies were taken from the submarine and loaded onto her father's boat. First one, and then the other. She wondered which one of them was Karl. Although she had only known him for a short while, she had made up her mind he was the man she wanted to spend the rest of her life with. That was something that would never be now. A tear trickled down her cheek as she closed her eyes and thought about Karl's joyous smile.

The bodies were lifted from the boat to the wharf. Harry was there with two wooden caskets in his horse-drawn wagon. Each of the bodies was placed in a casket. With the two sailors walking alongside the car, Harry and Reverend Lake rode up the hill towards the church.

The previous evening, all of the women had been busy preparing food. As soon as lunch was over they began transporting it to the church basement. Following the graveyard service, they would gather there to eat. The sailors watched the activity on shore from the submarine as they looked forward to a meal ashore.

With all of the activity, Bill and the others hoped that the portion of the plan now being executed would go unnoticed.

Women and children moved towards the church. As they approached and were out of sight of the submarine, they began moving inland. They carried extra food and clothing. The elderly were carefully put aboard wagons and the others walked behind. While this was happening, lookouts ensured that Lake, Blair and the two sailors watching the bodies were kept busy.

The evacuation of the town would be in two phases. The elderly and the very young would go in the first phase. When the service began, the others would begin to leave.

Out of sight of everyone, they would make their way inland to the hunting shacks. They would stay there until they received word that it was safe to return. A couple of armed men would accompany them, and do whatever was necessary to cover up their tracks. No fires could be lit in the cabins until after dark. And only dry wood could be used in order to prevent smoke from being seen.

At 1:30 Bill and another fisherman moved their boats towards the submarine. As they approached, the sailors began to appear. Bill watched carefully as they got into the boats. It appeared as if only four of them were armed. They carried rifles and Bill assumed they would be used for a salute of some kind at the funeral service. They were bolt-action 303 calibre rifles. Bill figured there would be a maximum of twenty rounds of ammunition between the two of them. He realized that could pose a serious problem.

Despite the solemn occasion, the sailors were surprisingly jovial. Time off the boat and the promise of a good meal put them in a good mood. Many of them, Bill guessed, did not know the circumstances surrounding the deaths of their shipmates. Bill figured he knew why Karl had been killed. But he couldn't guess as to why a second sailor was dead.

A few minutes after leaving the boat, they were on the wharf. For most of the sailors it was the first time they had been ashore in Three Rock Harbour. As they stepped up on the wharf, they fell into formation. As the last person fell into place, a short, bearded sailor yelled something and they became as rigid as boards. After another couple of orders, they made their way, in step, up the hill towards the church. The captain and a couple of others followed.

At the church, the procession halted. The sailors were dismissed and told they could smoke before they went in if they wished. With five minutes to spare, everyone went into the church. The rifles were stacked in a tepee shape on the step outside. Bill saw this as an opportunity to remove the threat from them.

Reverend Lake was at the front of the church, standing in front of the pulpit. The two coffins were on tables in front of him, draped in sailcloth. The captain had explained to Bill that they didn't have any flags on board, and it had been his decision to cover the coffins with sailcloth, the same as if it was a burial at sea.

The sailors sat as a group at the front of the church in seating reserved for them. The captain, Blair, and two other officers sat in the pew in front of the sailors. Behind them, were approximately fifty members of the community, the majority of them men.

Bill had explained to Reverend Lake earlier that many men would be leaving near the end of the service in order to help the women get the basement ready to host the reception. He said a couple of the men would take some food over to the two sailors on the submarine.

The plan was that when the men passed the sailors their food they would overpower them and take control of the boat. Bill had omitted that little detail when speaking with Father Lake.

Lake began the service in the traditional manner. The two altar boys taking part in the service were a concern to Bill and the others. But, without telling the boys what was happening, one of the men had instructions to get them down to the wharf the moment the sailors left the church to go the cemetery.

As the end of the service drew near, the fishermen and their families quietly left the church. Bill had told Captain Graf he felt it would be best if the sailors said goodbye to their shipmates privately. He said too he thought it would be best if just the sailors went to the graveyard. Tony thanked Bill for his consideration. At the end of the church service, the sailors filed out of the church. With the pallbearers carrying the two caskets, they made their way to the graveyard at the rear of the church.

Bill and the others had very little time to spare. Fortunately, things had gone very well when food was brought to the two guards on the U-Boat. The fishermen were a welcome sight to the sailors but that quickly changed when they produced a gun and ordered the sailors to lay down their rifles. The sailors were brought below, their uniforms removed, and the two people standing guard now were fishermen. If the captain or anyone else were to look out at the U-Boat while they were on their way to the cemetery they would assume that everything was okay.

Almost everyone left in the community was in the stages down by the wharf.

As soon as the sailors disappeared around the back of the church everything came to life.

The fishermen didn't want to start their engines so oars were used to move people out to the U-Boat. All the boats in the harbour were taken out. The goal was to make sure that the Germans had no way of getting out to the submarine. Within minutes, all the boats were on their way and a few minutes later they reached the U-Boat.

The service in the cemetery was brief. If anyone was waiting for the rifles to sound in salute they would have had to wait a long time. Bill had removed all of the bullets from their magazines while the rifles were stacked outside the church.

It didn't take long for Captain Graf to realize something was wrong. When the rifles wouldn't fire, and his men told him that the bullets had been removed, he came running around to the front of the church. What he saw left no doubt that the jig was up.

CHAPTER TWENTY-SIX

Captain Graf looked out into the bay and couldn't believe what he was seeing. Fishing boats surrounded his submarine. Any boats not around the boat were on their way towards it. The boats were filled with people, and those not in the boats were on top of the submarine. As he stared in disbelief, other sailors came around to the front of the church. It was obvious to everyone that the people of Three Rock Harbour had finally realized who they really were and taken control of their submarine.

Captain Graf signalled for Weber and Becker to join him. The three of them moved away from the others.

"It looks like they know who we are," Graf said.

"There's no doubt about that," Weber answered.

"I wonder how they found out," Becker asked.

"That's not the issue facing us now," Graf said. "The issue is how we're going to get our boat back. Any suggestions?"

They looked at each other with blank stares.

Weber spoke. "We don't have any weapons, and even if we did we don't have a boat. I have to commend them though. It looks like they have taken care of every detail. Everyone is where we used to be, and we're here with no way to get out there."

"There has to be a way," Becker said. "We just can't sit here and do nothing.

"That's right," Graf said. "We have to do something. There has to be a boat or a weapon of some kind. They're a bunch of ignorant fishermen. They must have overlooked something. Get the crew together and tell them to search every house, barn and stage in this place. We need something to use as a weapon and something to use to get out to the boat."

Weber and Becker returned to the men. They briefed them and the sailors left in pairs to begin the search. Graf left the group and walked down the hill to the wharf. He stood at the end and looked out at his boat a few hundred feet away.

As he stood there staring out at the boat, a couple of fishermen noticed him and called out to Bill, who was inside the submarine. Bill appeared shortly after being called. He looked over in Graf's direction.

"Well, Bill," Graf called out, "it looks like we have a bit of a situation here."

Bill smiled. "Yes, Captain, it does look like we have a bit of situation here."

"What do we have to do to resolve this?" Graf asked.

Suddenly Mary appeared on the deck.

"You murdered Karl and you sank the *Caribou*, you filthy Germans," she shouted.

"Yes, we sank your boat you call the *Caribou*," Graf shouted back, "but it was a mistake. We thought that she was an ore carrier. It was a tragic error. We would never knowingly sink a passenger boat. As to Karl, we did not murder him. We don't know the circumstances surrounding his death. All we know is that we found him and another sailor dead in the radio room."

Mary was going to respond, but Bill stepped in front of her and indicated she should remain quiet. He turned back towards Graf.

"We know you're Germans and have been lying to us ever since you came here. You used our place to come and go and to murder civilians. The solution to this is that you will all be captured and put in prison for the rest of the war."

The other fishermen mumbled their support for what Bill had said.

"You know I can't let that happen," Graf shouted back. "We will have to do whatever we can to get my boat back, and a lot of you could lose your lives with this silly endeavour."

Bill smiled. "I believe that we have the upper hand here, Captain. As soon as this weather clears we will be sending a boat out to alert the Yanks. If you resist when they arrive it will be your crew who will suffer the loss of life."

"Is there no other way that we can resolve this?" Graf asked.

"No, I don't think so," Bill asked.

"We have a lot of money aboard the boat. We could give it to you and then we would be on our way and no one would be any the wiser."

"I believe that if you check you will see that you don't have anything aboard the boat. We have what is aboard the boat, and that includes the money."

Bill turned to his daughter.

"Go below and find the money. Make sure it's somewhere safe. He promised us that he would buy our fish before he left and I don't think he is going to do it willingly now."

Mary went down into the submarine.

"Let's be reasonable, Bill," Graf said. "This isn't your war. Why do you want to endanger your lives for this? There is nothing to be gained with all of this."

Bill turned without responding. There was nothing else to be said. Graf remained at the end of the wharf staring at his boat. He felt completely helpless. That helplessness quickly changed to a hatred for Bill and all of those who had taken his boat.

Graf finally left the wharf and found Weber.

"There is no reasoning with him. And he's right. He does have the upper hand. Unless we can find a boat and some weapons we are helpless. How is the search going?"

"Nothing yet. But I have noticed something, Sir."

"What is it?"

"I only see men out there. Where are the women and children?"

"You're right. I never noticed that. Where are the women and children?" Graf repeated. "If they're not out there with the men then they must be here somewhere. If we can find them we can use them as bargaining chips. Get a few men to scout around. They wouldn't keep them here. They must have sent them inland."

"Right away," Weber answered.

Meanwhile, back on the boat, Mary and Bill began searching for the money. The two German sailors had been taken below and chained. Mary approached them.

"Where would the captain keep the money?" she asked. The sailors looked at each other and then at her. They answered in German.

"I know you speak English, but if that's the way you want to act then you'll stay where you are until this is over," she said, walking away from them.

"The Enigma machine must be in the radio room," she said, as her father joined her. "We have to make sure no damage comes to it. Our prisoners won't tell me anything, so we'll have to search for the money the captain was talking about."

"We talked about sending a message to the Yanks to come and take this over. Where's Arns?"

"He's in the radio room."

Arns was examining the equipment in the radio room.

"Can you operate any of this?" Bill asked.

"Yes, I can operate the radio," he answered.

"What about sending a message?" Mary asked.

"It's like I said before. I can send a message but everyone who has a radio will hear it. If there's another German U-Boat in the region that's closer then the Yanks, then they will be the first to get here. We can't fight off a U-Boat. They won't stop to negotiate. They will torpedo us and we won't even know what hit us. I don't think we can take the chance. They can't do a thing where they are."

Bill looked at his daughter.

"He's right," Mary said. "We should wait. I bet that the money is in the captain's cabin," she continued, changing the subject. "Let's see if we can find it."

"Okay, but you don't need me," Bill said. "I want to stay up on deck to keep an eye on everything. You look for it."

Mary left the radio room and went looking for the captain's cabin. His name was on a plate beside the door. Mary tried to open the door. It was locked. She looked around and saw an axe hanging on the wall. She wondered why an axe was hanging on the wall, not knowing it was there to be used for exactly the purpose she intended to use it. She removed the axe from the hook and moved towards the door. Lifting the axe above her head she swung it down at the door handle, which bent but didn't break. She swung at it a second time and the handle fell to the floor. She pushed on the door but it still wouldn't open. She jabbed the axe where the handle used to be. The door was metal and all she succeeded in doing was making a small dent in it.

She moved to the side of the door and swung the axe in a sideways motion. The door flew open, and parts of the latch went flying across the cabin. Mary laid the axe against the outside wall before walking into the cabin.

To her left was a neatly made bunk. To her right was a desk with an attached lamp and basket filled with papers. There was a shelf over the desk with a lip to prevent anything from falling off. A picture of a young woman Mary guessed was Graf's wife was on the shelf.

There were two drawers on either side of the desk. She sat in the chair and pulled open the drawer on the lower right. There were several files on the bottom. On top of the files was a small rectangular shaped can. She took it out and put it on the desk. She slid a lever but the cover didn't lift.

It was locked.

There was a centre drawer and she pulled it towards her. There were several pencils and other writing materials in it. She rummaged through the things, looking for a key. She found a tiny key that looked like it was the one she needed. She fed it through the lock on the can and tried to turn it. It worked, and this time when she slid the lever it moved and the cover lifted. Mary gasped when she saw what was inside.

The can was filled with money. She stared at the bills. Newfoundland money in all different denominations, with an elastic band around each bundle, as well as bundles of British pounds and Canadian dollars. Mary guessed there must be at least a thousand dollars, with similar amounts in the other currencies. It was more than enough to pay the fishermen and their families what they had been promised by the Germans. Mary closed the can and locked it. She put the key in her pocket and put the can under the blanket at the end of the captain's bed.

Back on shore, the German sailors went from door to door. Everyone knew what they were looking for, but they had taken care to ensure that all the guns had been brought with them. Nearly everyone in the harbour owned a gun. There were a few old war rifles, a few shotguns, and a couple of muzzleloaders. The shotguns had been given to the men who went with the women and children. The rest of the guns were with those now on or around the U-Boat.

It was getting close to 4 p.m. and in an hour or so it would be dark. The wind continued to howl and there was a very heavy sea on. Food and drink had been brought to the submarine and the couple of women who had accompanied the men were down in the boat's galley preparing supper. The smells coming up through the open conning tower made everyone's mouth water. A voice was suddenly heard, calling out from across the harbour. Captain Graf was at the end of the wharf again.

"Bill," he called out. "Bill Sullivan."

"Bill," a couple of men called out to Bill, who was below. "He's looking for you."

Bill appeared a few seconds later. "Yeah," he called. "This is Bill. What do you want?"

"This has got to stop, Bill," Graf called back. "Give us our boat back and we'll leave and you won't see us again. You can keep the money and our weapons. We won't be able to harm you if you have our weapons."

"What about the Enigma machine?" Mary asked, as he stood beside our father.

There was a pause. "I don't know what you're talking about," the captain called back.

Mary laughed hard enough for him to hear.

"You sure do know what we're talking about. Will you let us keep the Enigma machine and all the codes?" she repeated.

Again there was a pause.

"Bill, you have to come to your senses. This is only going to end in the death of a lot of innocent people. You can stop all of this."

"Is this what you called me for?" Bill asked.

"Obviously, reasoning with you is not an option," Graf said. "You either give me back my boat or we'll burn every building in this place to the ground. Your house will be the first. Am I making myself clear?"

Mary squeezed her father's arm. This was something they had not considered. They all looked at each other. Everything they owned, other than their boats, was ashore. They began to talk to each other and the comments were all the same.

'This is not our fight, let them have the bloody boat, we'll never survive the winter without our houses. Where will we go?"

"Let's not lose it here," Bill said. "We can't give in to him. They would kill us just as quick as they'd look at us. We can't turn back now."

"I'm waiting for an answer, Bill," Graf called out again.

"You and your crew should wait until the Yanks arrive," Bill called. "Then the war will be over for you. If you start burning houses you can bet that you might not get to a prison. Remember that we're the ones with the guns."

"It looks like I've hit a nerve," Graf said in a mocking voice. "I take it from your response that it's a no, is it?"

Bill didn't answer. Graf turned his back and shouted something. Suddenly flames began to light up the shore.

"Jesus Christ," someone said. "They've set your house on fire."

"Dad," Mary shouted. "Everything we own. Oh my God. Look what those animals are doing. We have to stop them."

Bill looked ashore.

"Stop! Stop!" he called out. He reached for the painter on the little rowboat. A couple of fisherman moved towards him. "You can't go ashore, Bill," one said. "They'll kill you," another said.

"I can't stand here and watch everything I own go up in smoke," Bill shouted. "You son of a bitch," he called out. "You stinking son of a bitch. I'll see you dead if it's the last thing I see before I close my eyes."

183

"I gave you a chance and you didn't take it," Graf called back. It was getting difficult to hear him over the cracking of the fire as it licked its way up over the whitewashed clapboard of the Sullivan's house.

"I'll kill you if it's the last thing I do," Bill yelled.

"There are many more houses here to burn," Graf called back. He tried to say something else, but the noise of the fire drowned him out.

"I'll kill him. I swear to God, I'll kill him," Bill said, as the men continued to hold him as he ranted and raved.

"Let me go," Bill said, pushing them away. "It's too late now. We couldn't save my house even if I wanted to. Everything I ever worked for was in that house. My God, it will kill Janet when she finds out."

The others gathered around and considered their fate. They knew it was just a matter of time before their homes went up in smoke. They began grumbling. Maybe they should have left things the way they were. Look at the mess they were in now. As they talked, the flames gradually enveloped the entire Sullivan house. The German sailors kept back from the fire and several could be seen laughing and carrying on as the house rapidly turned into cinders.

Bill wondered if it had been a mistake. But his wondering quickly turned to hatred and a desire for revenge began to churn up his insides.

CHAPTER TWENTY-SEVEN

Sergeant Tom Burns and Corporal Joe Slaney rowed ashore in their inflatable boat landing at 9 p.m. They had three hours to find out what was going on. They would be picked up at midnight. They landed in the same cove the Germans had used earlier. The rubber bottom of the dinghy made a soft grinding sound as it ran a few feet up onto the sandy beach. The men jumped into the few inches of water and then quickly pulled the dinghy up over the beach until it was below the cliff and out of sight of anyone who might be looking down from above them.

They moved noiselessly up the footpath to the top of the bank. As they reached the summit they could see a glow in the direction of Three Rock Harbour and wondered what it might be.

Both men were in their 20s and strong and agile. They stopped every few minutes to look around. They were dressed in black skin-tight clothing with their faces covered with black cam stick paint. Each man wore a toque pulled down over his head. They carried knapsacks with their uniforms in them on their backs.

"What do you think is causing the light," Burns whispered, as he and Slaney came together several hundred feet from the beach.

"It looks like a fire," Slaney answered. "When we were on the boat coming in I thought it looked like it was a big bonfire."

"It could be one of those Newfie traditions," Burns laughed.

They continued to move up the path towards the community. The closer they got, the more often they paused to look around. There was a full moon and they were approaching the community from a downhill position. They had expected to see the lights of kerosene lamps from the windows of the houses. But there were lights in only a few houses.

"Maybe they're in the church for some kind of social," Burns whispered, as they came together again. "That's why there are only lights in a few of the houses. The rest of them are at the social."

As they got closer they spied the U-Boat in the harbour.

"I see it," Slaney said. "And hey look, there are lots of lights on it."

Burns nodded. "I wonder what all those boats are doing around it. It looks like half the boats in the harbour are out there. Perhaps they're celebrating Oktoberfest with the Germans," he laughed.

They continued to edge closer to the community. As they did, they saw that a house had burned down and all that remained was a pile of smouldering embers. The heavy winds were blowing sparks all over the place. It was fortunate no other houses were close.

They got close enough so that they could hear voices. It was too dark to make out very much. And they still couldn't figure out why so many of the houses were dark. They looked up at the church and there were no lights on there now, so their idea that perhaps there was some kind of a community get together was not the answer.

"Halt, don't move," a voice shouted from behind them.

Tom moved his hand to the holstered gun on his side.

"Touch it and it will be the last thing you touch," another voice said. "On your stomachs with your hands in front of you. Now!"

Both men fell to their knees and then on to their stomachs. They stretched their hands in front of them. As they did someone reached to their sides and removed their weapons.

"Now, get on your feet," the second voice shouted. "Fold your hands behind your heads and walk in the direction of the burnt house."

The men did as they were told. It was only a few hundred steps to the ruins of the house. When they arrived, they were ordered to stop.

"Get the captain," one man shouted to a couple of others who were standing by the barn door smoking. One of them ran off in search of the captain while the second moved towards the prisoners.

The captain arrived a few minutes later. "What do we have here?" he asked.

"It looks like a couple of Yanks out for an evening on the town, Sir," one of the guards said. "But it's not going to end as they had planned."

Burns and Slaney were ordered to sit on the ground not far from the ruins. The two guards quickly briefed the captain about their capture. Weber joined the captain a minute or so later. Graf took one of the handguns from a guard and Weber took the other.

"You two go up to the church and get a lamp lit. We'll follow with the prisoners."

The guards raced up the hill, following Graf's orders.

"Get up and follow them," Graf said to the prisoners, waving the pistol at them.

By the time they arrived at the church, several lamps had been lit and the light spilled out through the main door. Becker stood by the door and directed the prisoners to the front of the church.

"Return to your duties," Weber said to the guards as the prisoners were seated in the front pew. Graf moved so that he was in front of them.

"So, tell me Yanks, what brings you to our little community this evening?"

They didn't answer.

Graf looked at Weber and then at the prisoners.

"It appears that I may have to be a little more convincing. I'm going to ask you again and I expect an answer. If I don't get an answer then my questioning techniques might make you a little uncomfortable."

"My name is Sergeant Tom Burns. United States Army Special Forces. Number 100476543."

"My name is Corporal Joe Slaney. United States Army Special Forces. Number 101673455."

Graf looked at Weber and then at the prisoners. In a split second, he raised and fired the pistol at Sergeant Burns, hitting him in the foot.

As the weapon fired, Burns reacted by pulling his foot off the floor. The bullet tore through his boot and foot, exiting out through the sole. Burns howled with pain as he recoiled backward. He lifted his foot high in the air and looked at the hole in the top of his boot. He couldn't see the gaping hole in the sole and the bits of blood, flesh and bone that the bullet had drawn with it as it tore through his foot.

"The next one will be higher," Graf said, as he trained the pistol on Burns's genitals.

"Now tell me what you're doing here."

Weber pointed a pistol at Slaney.

"We were ordered here to see what the situation was and to report back to our superiors," Slaney blurted out.

"How were you to give your report?" he asked.

"We are being picked up at midnight. Then we will radio St. John's with our report."

"That's better. That's a lot better," Graf smiled. "See, how easy it is if you cooperate. If your sergeant had cooperated in the beginning, he wouldn't be able to see through his foot now. How much were you told about what's happening here?"

"We were told that there's a U-Boat here and that there are a couple of people who knew about it."

"Well it appears that your intelligence was wrong," Graf smirked. "It appears as if every goddamn fisherman and his spawn know about it." He pointed in the direction of his boat and then paused for a few seconds. "You said you were being picked up. How are you being picked up?"

Slaney looked to Burns for support. Burns looked down at the floor.

"He's not going to help you," Graf said to Slaney. "But I'm not forgetting about you, Sergeant Burns, I believe that's what you said your name was. How about you take a turn? How are you being picked up?"

Burns lifted his head, looked at Slaney, and then at Graf.

"Go fuck yourself, you Nazi Kraut," he said, from between clenched teeth.

Graf smiled. He looked at Becker and then at Burns.

"It seems that Sergeant Burns doesn't want to cooperate and I can tell from his answer that he doesn't like me very much. I don't understand why you don't like me, Sergeant Burns, when you don't even know me. But that's the way you Yanks are. Well, no one else will ever be bothered by you not liking them." Graf lifted the pistol and pointed it at Burns. Burns looked directly at him and smiled. As he did, Graf pulled the trigger.

Smoke from the spent cartridge wafted its way to the ceiling of the church, not unlike the ceremonial incense that had been burned there on many previous occasions. Graf held the pistol in front of him as Burns's head jerked backward and a geyser of blood, hair, brains and spent bullet flew from the fist sized hole at the back of his head and splattered over the backs and seats of the pews.

Almost as quickly as Burns's head was jerked backwards, it came forward and carried his lifeless body to the floor in front of Graf's feet. Graf didn't move, just stood there with the pistol held in the same frozen position.

"That's what we do with people who don't cooperate," he said, as he lowered the pistol and looked at Slaney. "Now, we were talking about being picked up."

"We rowed ashore in a dinghy. The destroyer will be picking us up at midnight. We just row straight out in the bay and a motor escort will meet us and bring us to the ship," Slaney said, with obvious fear in his voice.

"Good, that's what I'm looking for. Where is the dinghy now?"

"It's on the beach up the shore from here, where we landed."

"So, you have no way of communicating with your superiors until you are brought aboard the ship. Is that right?"

"Yes, that's right," Slaney said.

Graf moved away from him and motioned for Weber to join him. They walked to the side of the church where Slaney could not hear them.

"I don't think there is anything else he can tell us," Graf said.

"I agree, and it leaves no doubt that the Yanks know about us. When they don't hear from these two they will come in. So," Weber continued, looking at his watch, "that gives us just a few hours to get our boat and to get out of here."

"Yes, but how do we get our boat? We have two pistols, no boat, and no way I know of overpowering them and taking back the boat."

Graf paused for a few seconds to reflect.

"How could I have been so goddamn stupid? To leave my boat and to have her captured like this? If only we had weapons and a boat. At least we would have a fighting chance."

Graf looked at Slaney. Graf held the pistol in his hand and then thought to check to see how many bullets he had left. He removed the magazine from the handle and pushed down on the bullets. "There must be eight remaining," he said to Weber. "How about you?"

Weber checked his pistol. "It's full," he answered.

"Well, at least we have two weapons," Graf said.

"What about the dinghy?" Becker suddenly remembered. "Couldn't we use it?"

Graf stared at him. "You're a fucking genius," he said. "A fucking genius," he repeated. He smiled from ear to ear. "We have a boat," he said, smiling as he walked towards Slaney. "Where exactly is that dinghy?"

"It's a ten or fifteen minute walk north of here up the coast," he answered. "We pulled it up the shore and put it below the cliffs."

"Thank you. Thank you very much," Graf said. "Say hello to Sergeant Burns for me," Graf smiled as he lifted the pistol and, without warning, recoated the pews behind him with bone, blood, and brains.

"Let's get their uniforms out of their knapsacks," Graf said. "We don't have much time."

CHAPTER TWENTY-EIGHT

Bill watched as the fire destroyed his home. Mary tried to console her father, but nothing she said could help. Other than his fishing boat and what was in the barn, everything they owned was gone. A lifetime of work and it was all gone in a few minutes.

"We can't let them do any more damage," one of the fishermen said, as they stood silently on the deck of the U-Boat and watched the fire.

"What do you think we should do?" Bill asked.

He didn't have an answer, nor did any of the others. Bill questioned himself as to whether he had taken the right action or not, but it was too late now to change what was done. As the fire began to die down, so did the wind and the decision was made to send someone across to Salmonier to alert the Americans. There was still a big sea on, but at half-speed and being careful they should be able to get to the other side safely.

It was nearly 10 p.m. when Guy Bursey departed. His brother accompanied him, and they were confident they would be okay. Shortly after they left, a noise echoed throughout the community that got everyone's attention. It sounded like a gunshot. Everyone looked to see where it had come from. Bill was especially concerned because he thought the only weapons the Germans had were the rifles he'd removed the bullets from. The shot didn't sound like a rifle, though. It was more like a pistol shot. Maybe, he thought, the captain had been carrying a sidearm. But he couldn't remember seeing one.

Ten minutes later, a second shot rang out. This time, there was no doubt as to where it came from. It came from the church. As all eyes fell on the church, they could see that someone was there because lamps were lit.

Their next thoughts went to their families. Surely none of them had been captured. It was at least an hour's walk to where they had hidden and the men guarding them had weapons. So the question remained as to where the weapons had come from to fire the rounds. And, equally as mysterious, why were the shots being fired?

Another twenty minutes passed and there were no other shots fired. It was getting late and they had to make arrangements to bed down for the night. Several of the fishing boats had wheelhouses and were each able to provide sleeping accommodations for a couple of people. Fishermen decided to stay with their boats, while the others climbed into the U-Boat.

Bill wanted guards posted, even though there was no way for the Germans to get at them. There was still the possibility that they could build a raft or find something that would float them out to the boat. It was decided they would have two men stand two-hour watches. Bill said he couldn't sleep and, while he wouldn't take a shift, he would remain awake and alert to anything unexpected. By midnight, everyone was bedded down and the first two men were on watch. Bill was outside with them, pacing up and down the length of the boat. He couldn't get the destruction of his house out of his mind.

Gradually, all of the lamps in the community were extinguished, except for the ones in the church. The hatred Bill felt for Graf was dominating his thoughts and nothing would satisfy him except seeing the man dead for what he had done. Bill made up his mind to wait a little while and go ashore. He would find Graf and get his revenge.

As Bill stood there plotting his revenge, he saw someone come up on deck. It was Mary.

"What are you doing up?" Bill asked.

"Dad," she whispered, so that the others wouldn't hear, "I have been down below doing a little digging around. The Enigma machine is down there and, God forbid something should happen, but we have to make sure that it's safe. I don't think that it's safe here."

"What are you thinking?" he asked.

"We have to hide it somewhere and that somewhere has to be off this boat. We have to get it ashore."

"Where?" Bill asked.

"We could take one of the dories, head out in the bay and up to the herring gulch. It would only take us half an hour round trip and we'd be back, with the machine safely hid. The Germans wouldn't see us because they would have to go out there on the head," she said, pointing. "It's still high tide so there's no way they could get out there."

"Is that machine as important as you think it is?" he asked.

"Yes, Dad, it is. If the Americans had this machine they could understand every message that the Germans are sending."

"Okay," Bill said. "How big is it? Can we move it ourselves?"

"Yes, we can," Mary said, pleased that her father understood the urgency of saving the machine. "I have it wrapped in oilcloth and I can bring it up here by myself. You get the boat ready."

Bill had been a little disappointed when his firstborn was a girl, but right now he was never prouder of his daughter.

"Go get it," he said.

CHAPTER TWENTY-NINE

Becker left the church and returned with a couple of sailors. Lake and Blair were with them. They were unaware of what had happened and were briefed quickly.

"Get their bodies out of here," Weber said to the sailors.

"I have a plan that may get us out of this mess after all." Graf said, as he turned to Becker. "Take a couple of men with you and go up along the coast. There's a cove, and up against the cliffs on the beach there is supposed to be a dinghy. Check it out for me and get back here as soon as you can. Leave a sailor there to guard the dinghy. And time how long it takes to get up there."

Becker left immediately. Graf looked at his watch. It was 10:45. He had less than an hour to get everything together.

Becker took the Americans' uniforms out of their knapsacks.

"So, Captain, what are you planning to do with these uniforms?"

"We needed weapons and now we have them," Graf said, as he held up the pistol. "Now we need a boat and if my plan works we will have that too."

"We can't do much with a dinghy," Becker said.

"The dinghy is only an end to a means," Graf said, smiling. "The dinghy is going to bring us to the boat we want. The Yanks aren't going to send their destroyer into the cove to pick up their men. They are going to send in a motor launch. There will be maybe two or three men on the launch, and there will be two of us in the dinghy. There's a very good chance that a different crew will be used for pickup. They won't suspect that it's our men in the dinghy. And even if they do, it will be too late. Our men will take control of the launch before they realize what hit them."

Weber smiled. "It could work, Captain. In fact, I think it will work."

"I know it will work. As soon as our men have control of the launch they will come ashore and pick up a few more sailors. We will then approach our submarine from the sea. The fishermen will think that help has come for them. They won't suspect a thing. Before they realize it, we'll have our boat back and we'll take our chances at sea."

"Who is going to wear the uniforms?" Weber asked.

"There are two considerations. First, the uniforms have to fit and second, we have to use our best people for the job."

"Heinz is the best we have at hand-to-hand combat. I think that he could fit into one of these uniforms. Helmut is a close second at hand-to-hand combat, but there is no way he could come close to getting one of them uniforms on. I'll say it will have to be Werner. He's a good man. I believe that he and Heinz can certainly overpower the two or three men who are on board the motor launch and take control."

"Good," Graf said. "Get them here right away. We don't have any time to waste. I need to brief them."

Weber ordered the sailors who had removed the bodies to go search for Heinz and Werner. He said he wanted them there within ten minutes.

"Is this our only option?" Lake asked.

"I can't think of anything else," Graf answered. "We burned down Sullivan's house and that didn't get them to change their minds. We could burn down every building here, but I don't think they would give up and come ashore. This is it. If Werner and Heinz can't get control of the motor launch, then we might as well sit down and wait for the Yanks to come and pick us up. As soon as they realize that the motor launch didn't return to the destroyer, the Yanks are going to know something is wrong. I'd say we have until daybreak to get control of the submarine and get out of here."

As Graf finished speaking, Becker came into the church.

"The dinghy is there, Captain. Exactly where you said it would be. High and dry under the cliff."

"Good," Graf said. "Now all we need is Werner and Heinz. See what's holding them up."

Graf was holding both pistols. He removed the magazines to double check the ammunition. There was enough to get the job done. He would have to give both weapons to Werner and Heinz to ensure they could overpower the crew from the motor launch. As he was putting the magazines back in the pistols, the two men arrived. Weber brought them directly to the captain.

"Put those uniforms on," Graf ordered, pointing to the uniforms draped across the pulpit. "I'll give you your orders as you do it."

The men obeyed without question.

"You two are our only chance to get out of here. There's a dinghy up along the coast a short distance. You have to use it to paddle out in the bay where you will be met by a motor launch from a Yank destroyer."

"There's a flashlight in the dinghy," Becker interrupted him. "I would say it's to signal them."

"Yes," Graf said. "It is going to be dark and there's a good chance the Yanks will have a different crew coming to pick the men up than dropped them off."

"What men?" Werner asked.

"Don't worry about that," Graf said. "All you have to remember is that the motor launch is back to pick you two up. Keep your heads down when you approach just in case it's the same crew that dropped the men off. When you get the chance you have to overpower the men in the launch and take control of their boat. If you can do it without firing a shot it will be perfect. We may need every one of the bullets in these two guns." He held the pistols up. "These are the only weapons we have. At least, the only weapons we have with ammunition," he corrected himself, after remembering about the rifles. "We need that boat if we're to get our submarine back. When you get control, bring it back to the beach where we will have more of the crew waiting to help you get control of our submarine. Are there any questions?"

"No, Sir," they both answered.

"Good," Graf said. "Just make sure you do this as quietly as you can and check the bodies for weapons before you dispose of them. Now, go with Lieutenant Becker who will take you to the dinghy."

The sailors left with Becker. Graf turned to Weber.

"Our lives depend upon those two men. With the hope that they will succeed, we are going to need a boarding party. I need our best six men to go with you and Werner and Heinz. Choose them and meet me at the beach."

Weber left to select his boarding party and Graf left for the beach.

CHAPTER THIRTY

By 12:45 a.m. the wind had died down and the sea was calm.

"Now would be a good time to leave," Mary said to her father. They had been waiting on the deck for the right time.

"Yes," he said. "Get the Enigma machine and we'll put it in the dory. It doesn't look like there's much activity on shore now. I'd guess the Germans are planning to do something in the morning. Hopefully, Guy will be back with help by then and all this will be over."

Mary picked up the Enigma machine that had been wrapped in the oilcloth and moved to the dory. The fishermen standing guard had been leaning against the conning tower and they reacted to her movement.

"Keep watch," Bill said to them. "Me and Mary have a little work to do. We won't be gone too long. Be alert," he warned them.

Bill stepped into the dory and Mary passed him the machine wrapped in oilcloth. He put it in the bottom of the dory. As he stood up, Mary passed him a second package.

"What's this?" he asked.

"Those are other parts for the machine," she said.

Bill put the second package next to the first one.

As Mary pushed the dory away from the submarine with her hand, she looked at the packages and saw a rifle beside them.

"What's that?" she said. pointing.

"I don't want to be without a gun," her father said.

Bill dipped the right oar into the water and pulled hard. A couple of strokes and he was turned and heading for the drop off. It took only a few minutes to reach it but the tide was still high and waves were crashing into the tiny opening making a landing impossible.

"It will be like that until morning," Bill said. "We're going to have to find somewhere else."

He turned the dory around and headed for the community.

"We can't go in there," Mary said.

"We have to," Bill said. "It's the only place we'll be able to land. We'll go over by Junior Sutton's place. No one will see us there."

Bill dipped and pulled on the oars noiselessly. Ten minutes after leaving the U-Boat, they were beside Sutton's wharf. Bill lifted the oars and the dory drifted into the wharf. He and Mary looked around and then cautiously Mary stepped out of the boat. Bill passed her the two packages. He joined her with the rifle in his hand. He dropped the painter rope over the post to secure the boat. Mary took the larger package while her father carried the smaller one and the rifle. They crept up the wharf.

Every few steps they paused and listened. Other than the sound of the waves crashing into the rocks, they heard nothing else. They reached the end of the wharf and made their way up the footpath to Sutton's house.

"Where are we going to hide this stuff?" Bill asked.

Mary looked around. There were some low bushes next to the outhouse.

"Over there," she whispered, as she pointed.

They hid the packages in the bushes.

"They will be safe here until we need them," Mary said.

"Right," Bill said. "Now, let's get back to the others."

They crept silently back to the dory. As they did, they heard a sound like an engine.

CHAPTER THIRTY-ONE

When Graf arrived at the beach, his men had the dinghy moved up closer to the water. At exactly midnight, Werner and Heinz pushed it off the beach and jumped in. They had to be careful not to swamp it as the waves tried to force them back to shore. With Heinz in the front and Werner in the back, they made their way out into the bay.

They had their pistols in the pockets of their wind pants, and Heinz had the flashlight beside him on the floor of the dinghy. They paddled in unison and without speaking. When they were about a mile offshore, Werner spoke.

"How about turning on the light now and waving it about a little."

Heinz stopped paddling and reached for the light. He turned it on and waved it a few times out in front of him. He waited, repeated the action, and did it again. There was no response so they continued to paddle.

"Listen," Werner said a few minutes later.

Heinz stopped and listened.

"It's a boat," he said, reaching for the light and waving it in front of him.

This time, he got a response. A light flashed off in the distance.

"It's them," Werner said, as he reached to touch his pistol.

They stopped paddling and waited. Every fifteen seconds or so the light would flash from the motor launch and Heinz responded.

After a few minutes, they could make out the outline of the boat on the horizon. Heinz flashed the light again. The boat slowly approached them and they could see there were two men in it. One was holding the tiller, while the other was in the front acting as a lookout. When they were about a hundred feet away, the man in front shouted.

"Did you have a nice vacation, boys?"

"Sure did," Heinz answered, trying to muffle his voice.

The boat slowly approached them and was soon broadside.

"Hop aboard," the man holding the tiller said. Heinz threw the painter to the lead man and he held onto it as the two Germans hopped aboard. When they were safely on board, the lead man passed the painter back to the man in the stern to secure it. For a second or so, the two Americans were in the stern and the two Germans in the front. This was their chance.

"Stay there," Heinz shouted, as he pointed his pistol.

Werner was also pointing his pistol.

The lead man reached for something.

"Careful," Werner said, "or this could be the last thing you'll reach for."

"Who are you?"

"We're not who you expected us to be," Werner said.

"We need your boat," Heinz said.

"What do you mean, you need our boat?" the tiller man asked.

"Over the side alive or with a bullet in you," Heinz said.

"You can't do that to us. We'd freeze to death before we got fifty feet. At least give us the dinghy," the man pleaded.

"I won't say it a second time," Heinz shouted, as he pointed his pistol menacingly. "I'll count to three and if you hear the three it will be the second last sound you'll hear. Move," he shouted. "One."

The tiller man went over the side.

"Two," said Heinz, as the second man joined the first in the water.

Werner moved to the stern and grabbed the tiller. He slowly moved the throttle forward and steered for the beach.

"We forgot to see if they had any weapons," Heinz said, as they got underway.

Werner didn't answer.

On the way out they had kept an eye out for submerged rocks. They tried to follow the same route on the way in. Within a few minutes of taking control of the motor launch they could see the beach. Heinz signalled with the flashlight, and his comrades quickly began to appear on the beach. A few minutes later they were all loaded aboard the motor launch and on their way to the U-Boat.

CHAPTER THIRTY-TWO

"It's a boat," Mary said when she heard the engine. "It's a motorboat. Could Guy have gotten help so quickly?"

"He must have," Bill whispered.

They got in the dory and pushed it offshore. After a few strokes, Bill had pulled it away from the shore.

"We had better wait and see who it is," Mary said.

Bill dug the two oars into the water to slow the dory. He turned it sideways so they could look at the U-Boat. They saw a boat slowly heading towards the it. They could make out at least a half dozen people in the motorboat.

"It looks like the Yanks," Bill said, "but I don't see Guy."

They continued to watch as the motorboat got closer to the U-Boat.

The fishermen standing guard heard the boat and reacted. They hoisted their rifles to the port position and moved to greet the visitors.

"Ahoy there," a voice called out from the motor launch. "Permission to come aboard?"

The two fishermen looked at each other. Then the taller one spoke.

"Come on aboard," he said. "We've been expecting you."

The motor launch approached and the sailor in the front threw the painter to one of the fishermen. He caught it with one hand, and leaned his rifle against the conning tower while he secured the boat.

The sailor jumped onto the deck with his hand extended. The fisherman took it and then he spotted Lake.

"Mr. Lake," he said. "What are you doing with the Yanks?"

Werner reacted by pulling out his pistol.

"I'll take that rifle," he said to the fisherman. Heinz pulled his pistol and trained it on the other fishermen.

Mary and Bill could not believe what they were seeing.

"Jesus Christ," Bill said. "We're done for. I don't where they got the boat, but we're done for now."

He pulled on the oars and headed back to the shore.

"What are you going to do, Dad?" Mary asked.

Bill didn't speak as he pulled on the oars with all his strength. A minute or so later they were back at the wharf. Bill jumped out.

"Dad, what are you going to do?" Mary asked.

"You tie up the boat and hide," he said, as he ran up the wharf with his rifle in his hand.

Bill crept up the side of the hill and moved towards the main wharf. He could hear voices shouting as he approached. Within minutes of the motor launch arriving at the U-Boat, the community had come alive. There were at least a dozen lanterns on the wharf.

Bill strained to see. It was still quite dark around the wharf and no one was looking in his direction. They were all looking out at the U-Boat, so he could move without much fear of being noticed. He got to the edge of the wharf and bent down low so he couldn't be seen. He was looking for Graf. He finally spotted him coming down the path. He was with Becker and both were smiling. Bill waited until they were just about to reach him and then he jumped out with his rifle at the ready.

"That's far enough," he said.

They stopped and turned. Their smiles quickly disappeared.

"Bill," Graf spoke, "it's been awhile."

"Don't give me that shit," Bill said. "You burned everything we own."

"You took my boat, Bill. I had to do something to get your attention."

"Well, you got my attention and right now I've got yours. The two of you are going to come with me, and if you make a move, I'll blow a hole in you as big as where you have that boat of yours moored."

"You'll never get away with this. There are too many of us. You could only shoot one of us before the other is on you," Graf said.

"As long as I get you I will be satisfied," Bill said. "I'm not worried about the one with you. It's not him I want. It's you. This is what we're going to do. You can have your boat and everything else. I just want my people sent back to me safe and sound. When everyone is ashore I'll let you go back to your boat and you can go to hell after that as far as I'm concerned."

"We have no intention of hurting you or anyone else in this community, Bill. I just want my boat."

"Good, then we agree. Give the order," Bill said.

Graf turned to Becker. "Make it so," he ordered. "Prepare to get everyone aboard and get ready to get underway."

"When you send my people ashore, send them with their guns," Bill said. "I don't want your people coming back and butchering us."

Graf nodded and Becker left.

"There was no need for this," Graf said after Becker left.

"Move back here out of the light," Bill ordered. "I don't want one of your Kraut friends taking a pot-shot at me."

"I gave you my word, Bill. You don't have to worry."

"Your word! Your word! The word of a butcher who sank a passenger ferry with over two hundred people on board. The word of a man who came to this place and lied to all of us and built up our hopes. Don't you talk to me about your word."

"I'm a sailor, Bill. I'm under orders. I was just following those orders."

"Don't you use orders as an excuse. You burned down my home. We have nothing now. It's winter. We'll have to leave Three Rock Harbour and I have no idea where we'll go. Everything we owned was here. All I have now is my boat and my barn."

"We're at war, Bill. We're enemies."

"We're not enemies. We didn't even know each other before you came here. How could we be enemies? Someone told you that I was your enemy. I'm just a poor fisherman, Tony, or whatever the hell your name is, but I'm a hell of a lot smarter then you are. I'm not so stupid that someone can tell me who my enemies are. You were my friend until you sank the *Caribou* and burned down my house. You made yourself my enemy."

"My name is Ulrich. Ulrich Graf. My friends call me Uli."

"I won't be calling you Uli," Bill laughed. "If I thought I'd get away with it, without harming my friends, I'd be calling you dead."

Suddenly Bill heard a noise behind him. He jumped to one side so he could keep the rifle on Graf and challenge whoever was approaching.

"Mary," Bill said, with an obvious sound of relief and anger in his voice, "I thought I told you to hide."

"You did, Dad, but I was hiding where I could see you." She turned to Graf. "Why did you kill Karl?"

"I didn't kill Karl," he answered. "We don't know what happened to him. We found him and another sailor dead. It looked as if the two of them had killed each other."

"I don't want you here," Bill said to Mary. "This could get very messy and I don't want you getting hurt. I want you to get as far from here as you can until this is over. Now go and don't come back until this is over."

Mary tried to protest, but her father pointed and she headed off into the darkness and towards the point.

"She's a lovely girl," Graf said, "I wouldn't want to see anything happen to her."

Bill moved the rifle closer to Graf.

"If any harm comes to her, the last thing you will ever see is the fire from the end of this barrel."

"I have no…"

Bill held up his hand.

"Don't speak. You don't have anything to say that I want to hear. Move over there," he pointed, "so I can see if my people are coming ashore."

Bill could see the fishermen starting to come ashore. The motor launch approached, ready to bring its first load of sailors back to the U-Boat.

"How is it proceeding?" Graf asked.

"They're moving now," Bill said.

"Good. Now, I've kept my word. How about if you keep yours? Let me join my crew and we'll be gone before you know it."

"When all my people are ashore then you can go. Not before."

Bill continued to watch as the fishermen came ashore and the sailors went back to their submarine. It took three trips in the motor launch to get all the sailors out. When the third trip was underway, Bill indicated to Graf that he should move towards the wharf. Graf did as he was told and slowly they moved from where they were hiding.

They stopped at a stage on the end of the wharf.

"Everyone move off the wharf and go to your homes," Bill shouted. The people from the village did as they were told. When the last of them had left, Bill motioned Graf to move forward. Bill remained hidden behind the stage.

"Go up to the end and wait for your boat," Bill ordered. "Then take that thing and get out of here. I don't know why I don't just shoot you for what you did to my house."

Graf opened his mouth to say something.

"Don't say anything or I may change my mind," Bill said.

Graf turned and moved up the wharf. The motor launch moved towards him. At the same time, the lines were being cast off the U-Boat and the water began to churn around it. Graf walked up the wharf without turning. When the launch arrived he jumped in. Within a minute, it was at the U-Boat. Graf stepped onto the deck and turned and waved at Bill. A few seconds later, he disappeared down into the conning tower. The launch was cast off and the U-

Boat moved from its mooring into the centre of the harbour. Bill breathed a sigh of relief as the boat got underway. As he did, Mary joined him.

"I don't know what I have to do to get you to obey me," he said, as he smiled and put his arm around her shoulder. Mary just smiled.

They watched as the submarine turned and headed out the harbour and out of their lives forever. Suddenly it stopped. Bill held his rifle in the port position.

"What now?" he said.

They watched as the U-Boat stopped its forward position and the conning tower hatch opened. Graf appeared. He had a bullhorn in his right hand. He put it to his mouth.

"You have taken something from us and I want it returned," Graf shouted.

Bill looked at Mary.

"They know that we've taken the Enigma machine," she said.

Bill and Mary remained hidden behind the stage.

Graf lifted the horn again.

"You will return our equipment to us or we will destroy this place. You have one minute and we will commence firing," he shouted.

"Everyone take cover," Bill yelled from his hiding place.

The word spread quickly and as the people began to move, Graf knew that they were not going to cooperate. Several sailors appeared on deck with rifles and another moved to the deck gun.

"Get behind the rocks," Bill said to Mary. They moved from behind the stage to the rocks just below where their house used to be. They waited for the worse.

From their position, they could make out one sailor behind the deck gun, waiting for an order from the captain. They didn't have long to wait as Graf looked at him and nodded.

The big gun came to life and in the darkness they could see the fire shooting out of the barrel and hear shouts as bullets tore into the sides of the houses in Three Rock Harbour.

"Douse the lamps," Bill shouted, as the big gun continued to fire.

Then, as directed by Captain Graf, the gun was trained on a huge tank that held the diesel fuel the fisherman used for their boats. It only took a few shots and it exploded, lighting up the entire community.

"He's going to burn the entire place," Mary said. "Maybe we should give the machine to him."

"No, he's not getting it. He will burn the place down anyway. But maybe we can stall him."

Before Bill had finished speaking, another voice was heard. They looked in its direction and were shocked to see the lights of what appeared to be a small destroyer at the mouth of the harbour.

"This is the *USS Callahan*. Lay down your weapons and prepare to be boarded," the voice ordered.

"Guy made it," Bill said, beaming. "He has brought the Yanks."

Graf turned. He quickly realized that if he had left a few minutes earlier, he might have submerged and avoided the Americans. But now it was too late. He was trapped. His only hope was to get a torpedo launched and blast his way out of the harbour. He silently gave the order.

The Americans anticipated what he'd been planning.

"Turn your bow to the starboard," Graf was ordered. "You have ten seconds to begin turning or we will sink you."

Captain Graf looked at his crew.

"Fire when ready," he said, knowing it would take minutes.

The U-Boat never turned. And true to its promise, a huge ball of fire appeared from the deck of the destroyer. A second later, it smashed into the side of the U-Boat. It was aimed perfectly and a tremendous explosion followed. Those sailors standing on the deck, including Captain Graf, were blown to bits. Parts of the U-Boat and human remains flew high in the air and began raining down onto the surface of the harbour.

When heads were lifted and everyone looked out to where the U-Boat used to be, all that could be seen was a hull with its top completely blown off. Smoke and fire still spewed from the submarine's belly, but there was doubt that no one had survived.

Slowly, as the sun came up over the horizon, the people from Three Rock Harbour began to crawl out from behind their hiding places and the full appreciation of the destruction of the U-Boat was realized.

"Send someone to bring back the women and children," Bill said to Mary. "I think this nightmare is finally over."

Mary ran to do her father's bidding.

Bill watched as a heavily armed motor launch came into the harbour and approached the smoking remains of the U-Boat. He walked up the wharf to greet the Americans when they came ashore.

EPILOGUE

As Bill made his way up the wharf, Mary was close behind him. They saw Guy stop beside the American boat and the captain and a couple of others get in. The boat approached the wharf. They arrived just as Bill and Mary got to the end.

"You're a sight for sore eyes," Bill greeted them. "Good job, Guy."

"I'm Lt. Commander Roger Warren," the officer said, as he stepped up to the wharf. "This is Colonel Cummings. You must be Mr. Sullivan."

"Yes bye, that's me," Bill responded. "And this is my daughter, Mary," he said proudly.

"I'm very pleased to meet you both. And Mary, it's especially good to meet you. We've certainly got a lot to thank you for."

Mary smiled.

"We're going to be here for a few days cleaning up," Cummings said, as he surveyed the smoking U-Boat. "It's too bad that we didn't capture the submarine, but I couldn't give them the chance to launch the torpedoes. We really wanted them alive and the boat in one piece. We were particularly interested in one piece of equipment that she was carrying."

Bill went to speak, but Mary reached and touched his arm.

"I assume that you are talking about the Enigma machine," Mary said matter of factly.

Cummings looked at the people who had accompanied him.

"What do you know about the Enigma machine?" he asked, obviously surprised.

"I know a lot more about it than you think," she smiled.

Mary became the chief negotiator with the Americans after her news.

"We were promised that all of our fish would be bought at twice the going rate," she told Cummings.

He agreed to buy all of the fish. But, because the Americans had no use for it, it would be kept until the spring where the fishermen could sell it again. So, in fact, they got three times the normal price for their fish.

"We want our home rebuilt, our furniture and our clothes replaced," said Mary.

Cummings promised to send all of the building materials, a construction crew, new furniture and new clothes for all the Sullivans.

When Mary's demands had been agreed to, she retrieved the Enigma machine and turned it over. The Americans were like children with a new toy. Thinking as all military officers do, they knew that this would mean a promotion for all of them.

When everyone was happy and celebrating, Mary dropped another bombshell.

"There is just one more thing," she said. "I have several months of the Enigma codes too."

A sudden hush came over the group assembled in her father's stage.

"You have the daily codes?" one officer asked.

"Yes, I do," Mary responded. "I think there are about three months worth of daily codes."

The American officers looked at each other with disbelief.

If they could keep the destruction of the U-Boat a secret, the Germans wouldn't know the codes had been compromised and the Americans could then monitor all U-Boat communications. The codes were worth more than the machine itself. It was a coup.

"Where are the codes?" one officer asked breathlessly.

"They're in a very safe place," Mary answered.

"I assume that there's a price attached to them," the same officer said.

"Yes, there is," Mary said. "We know that you are going to have to put people here to make sure that word doesn't get out about what happened. That will be especially important when I give you the codes. If the Germans suspect that the codes have been compromised they will change them. So nothing will really change. You will be taking the place of the Germans."

The officers looked at each other and nodded.

"With all of that in mind. and in order to ensure our cooperation, you will provide us with a teacher and a priest immediately. In the spring, you will build us a new church because our present church is in a sad state of repair. You will build us a new school for the same reason."

Cummings and the other officers looked at each other and nodded.

"Finally," Mary said, "we feel somewhat responsible for the sinking of the *Caribou*. The German submarine left from here and returned here after sinking the ferry."

"I don't think you should hold yourselves responsible for that," Cummings said.

"Be that as it may," Mary answered, "we still feel responsible. So, I would like to be assured that the surviving family members of all the people who died on the *Caribou* are cared for. You will provide widows' allowances for the widows, make sure that any children whose parents was lost are cared for, and do whatever else is necessary to give them the same standard of living they had before the sinking."

Again, the Americans looked at each other and nodded in agreement.

"That last request is the most important, so I trust you will keep your word on that one," said Mary.

"We will," Cummings promised.

Mary smiled before going to her hiding place. She made sure no one was watching as she removed the envelope containing the codes from the pile. Only one item remained there. The captain's cash can.

Mary returned to the Americans and passed Cummings the envelope.

He tore it open and looked at it excitedly. The Americans couldn't believe what they were seeing. They looked at the codes, at Mary, and at the codes again.

"Remember," Mary said, "you said you would keep your word."

"You need not worry about that," Cummings said.

"Let's leave now," Mary said to her father.

The ice stayed away and as a result the destroyer was able to get close enough to Three Rock Harbour with all of the building materials necessary to rebuild the Sullivan house. The family stayed at the Pepperell base in St. John's until their home was built. When it was finished, they were brought back to Three Rock Harbour.

The first place Mary went when she arrived was to Karl's grave.

The name Karl was written on a simple white cross. Max was written on the white cross next to it. Mary was startled. She hadn't known the other radio man was buried besides Karl.

Until then, Mary had never seen Karl's grave. She knelt by the cross and wept as she said her final goodbyes to the young man she had loved.

Just before going home, she went to her hiding place. Kneeling down in the grass, she reached in and pulled out Captain Graf's tin can. Holding it tightly to her chest, she walked to her family's new house. Inside the house were all those she loved most in the world. Her father Bill. Her mother Janet. And her brothers: Ray, John, Bob and Shoot.

Shoot was waiting outside on the step when she arrived. He held the front door open for her.

"Welcome home, Mary," he said, laughing.

"Thank you, Shoot," she said, as she kissed his forehead. "Come on inside. I have something special to show everyone."

S.S. Caribou - names of the 137 persons who lost their lives October 14, 1942 near Port aux Basques, Newfoundland as a result of enemy submarine action.

Crew Members

Captain Benjamin Taverner, Israel Barrett, Llewellyn Carter, Elias Coffin, James Hubert Coffin, Howard Cutler, Richard Feltham, Miss Bride Fitzpatrick, Charles Ford, Maxwell French, George Gale, Jerome Gale, Clarence Hann, Harry Hann (Chief Steward), William Hogan, Charles Humphries, Victor Lomond, Thomas Moyst, Charley Pearcey, James Pike, James L. Prosper, Joseph Richards, William Samms, Israel Sheaves, John Skeard, Albert Strickland, Garfield Strickland, Harold Taverner, Stanley Taverner, Arthur Thomas, George Thomas

Army Personnel

C. R. Abelson, Pte. CDO, C. G. Cochrane, L/Sgt. RCA, T. A. Currie, Cpl. PEI H., P. Diamond, Pte, PEI H., E. S. Francis, Cpl. PEI H., L. A. MacIntyre, L/Bdr. RCA, J. C. B. McDonald, Sgt. PEI H., H. R. Mills, Pte, Land W., L. M. Sheppard, Cpl. PEI H., A. A. Sullivan, Sgt. PEI H., H. M. Tough, L/Sgt. Alg. Regt.

Royal Navy and Royal Canadian Navy Personnel

E. Barrett, L/Sea. RN, Eli Maxwell Bishop, Sea. RN, C. Creston, Oiler REA, William A. Glasgow, RCNVR, A. Marshall, PO Cook RCN, G. N. May, SPO. RCNR, J. R. Masson, RCNVR, A. Nash, Sea. RN., W. C. Poole, AB. RN, E. R. Quinlan, Sea. RN, G. W. Randall, Shpt. RCNVR, N. Rowe, Sea. RN, R. J. Skinner, AB. RCNR, R. Smith, Sea. RN, J. Tapper, AB. RCNR, W. J. Vey, Sea. RN, E. Warren, Sea. RN, R. White, AB. RN, Miss A. W. Wilkie, NSRCN, J. W. H. Windsor, Sea. RN

Royal Air Force and Royal Canadian Air Force Personnel

J. H. Barrett, RCAF P. O., R. Chatson, RCAF AC1, F. G. Coulson, RCAF AC1, T. H. Cummings, RCAF AC2, H. H. Elkin, RCAF Cpl., D. C. Glover, RCAF AC2, W. P. Howse, RCAF Cpl., A. W. Jones, RCAF LAC, L. E. Legge, RAF P. O., C. M. McCaroon, RCAF LAC, D. L. Mitchell, RCAF LAC, M. N. Oiring, RCAF LAC, G. W. Parker, RCAF AC2, E. A. Thistle, RCAF AC2, L. William Truesdale, RCAF AC2, E. G. Walker, RCAF LAC, R. Watson, RCAF AC2, W. B. Wilson, RCAF AC2

U. S. Personnel

J. C. Abernathy, Major USA, E. T. Bothsa, Sea. 1st Class USN, J. M. Burns, CMM. USN, J. C. Elzer, Sea. 2nd Class USNR, E. Hand, 1st Lieut. USA, R. M. Penfield, C3rd. USA, E. G. Shultz, MM1C. USN, J. Waldman, PTR. USA

Civilians

Mrs. Ada Allan, Caroline Allan, Constance Allan, Claus Bang, Baby Girl Bernard, Mrs. Harriet Bernard, Charles Berry, Mrs. Pearl Beswick, Robert Butler, Albert Coombs, Preston Cowley, Harold Chislett, William Carteret Freeham, Louise Gagne, Mrs. Katherine Gardner, William H. Garth, Myrtle Gilbert, Hugh B. Gillis (superintendent of mines for Cape Breton's Dominion Steel and Coal Corporation)., Gerald Hammond, Wilfred Hathaway, Mrs. Maggie Hedd, Miss Myrtle Kettle, Edgar Martin, Harold McCarthy, Kevin McCarthy, George Penham, George Pike, Mrs. Elizabeth Randell, John Ronan, Margaret Rose, William Byrne, John Sheppard, Mrs. Blanche Short, Basil Skinner, Mrs. Kathleen Skinner, Nancy Skinner, Mrs. Gertie Strickland, Holly Strickland, Myrtle Strickland, Nora Strickland, Donald Tapper, Mrs. Hazel Tapper, John W. Tapper, Lillian Tapper, Catherine Walsh, Patrick Walsh, Mrs. Helen Wightman, Margaret Wilkinson, Mary Young.

Other titles by the author

A Broken Arrow

The Man Inside

Opinion Pole

Prince of the Slipper Fits

Sheila Na Geira, The Pirate Princess

Honour Thy Mother

Honour Thy Daughter

Honour Thy Son

Grieving Hearts Talking: The Matthew R. Churchill Story

Honour Thy Father

Cougar Flight 491: The Tragedy of March 12, 2009